# THE HOUSE WITH
# THE BLUE DOOR

## AN AMOS LEE MAPPIN MYSTERY

# THE HOUSE WITH THE BLUE DOOR

AN AMOS LEE MAPPIN MYSTERY

## HULBERT FOOTNER

**COACHWHIP PUBLICATIONS**

Greenville, Ohio

# CONTENTS

# CHAPTER ONE

Mr. Amos Lee Mappin picked up the telephone in his study and heard the voice of his servant Jermyn saying: "It's Mrs. Cassells, sir." Jermyn's voice was expressionless, yet it was clear that he didn't approve of Mrs. Cassells.

Mr. Mappin sighed; Sandra Cassells was always in such a gale and just then he wanted to work quietly. It must be important, or at least she thought it was; he had never heard of her calling anybody up in the morning. Anyhow, Mrs. Nicholas Cassells was not a woman you could put off with impunity, and he said: "Connect her, Jermyn."

The next instant Sandra was pouring herself over the wire. "Lee, darling, now you mustn't refuse me! This is no ordinary request, but very, very special. I'm not asking you to do me a favor either; you'll be doing a favor to yourself. I'm so excited!"

Lee said mildly: "But what is it, darling?"

"I want you to come to dinner tonight; seven-thirty as usual."

"But Sandra, my love, tonight's the testimonial dinner to Albert Caldwell and I accepted a week ago."

"Oh, that's a huge affair; there'll be a thousand people there and you'll never be missed. Send word you're sick. They have nine hours to fill your place."

"What's the special occasion at your house?"

"It's not a party, Lee; just two men and a woman that you must meet. They don't know anybody that you or I know, so no one will know you came."

"Who are they, Sandra?"

"Extraordinary people, my dear! It was only by the greatest luck that I heard of them. They are just your kind, Lee; nobody else could draw them out. Unless you come there's no object in having them."

"What do you mean, my kind of people?"

"I'm not going to tell you any more; I want it to be a surprise."

"How can I draw them out if I don't know who or what they are?"

"You'll find out when you get here . . . And Lee," she added slyly, "I have a couple of brace of canvasback from Richards!"

Lee's mouth watered. "Canvasback! Scandalous! The season closed two months ago!"

"Well, that's not my fault. They're shot now, and somebody's got to eat them. *Canvasback à la Tour d'Argent* as only Emilion can prepare them!"

Lee knew when he was licked. "Very well, darling. I feel like a louse at breaking my date with the Caldwell Committee, but I'll be there."

"Thanks, darling. Don't be late; there's so much to talk about!"

Lee hung up, wondering what new enthusiasm was stinging Sandra now. She got them about once a week. After nearly forty years of conventional society, she had wearied of it, and was ever on the hunt for new sensations. Since her husband's death six months before, she had become more unrestrained than ever—not that Nick Cassells had hampered her much, but of course, now that he was gone, she was far richer. Lee idly figured that the income from the two estates must amount to something better than a million a year; naturally the government took most of it; even so, Sandra had enough left to gratify every whim.

There had been a Swami—but all rich and idle women have a Swami in their entourage at one time or another, and Sandra had soon dropped him as not sufficiently original for her. Her only other excursion into mysticism (that Lee knew about) was by way of the gentleman from Nebraska who called himself Elijah II. He was said to have a chariot ready for his translation to heaven. But his personal habits proved to be unpleasant, and he was dropped quicker than the Swami. Sandra was always looking for "characters" through whom she could attain to "broader sympathies." Among them Lee had met a bus driver, a brew master, and a coal passer. There had also been a fascinating ringmaster who had got into Sandra for some thousands of dollars for a circus which he did not own. He was in jail. Sandra was not much interested in her own sex; "so stereotyped," she said with a shrug.

Lee consoled himself with the thought that, anyhow, the food at Sandra's would be vastly better than a lukewarm banquet at the Vandermeer. Since Sandra had got more and more into the habit of dumping her problems in Lee's lap, Lee had seen to it that after the collapse of France she engaged Emilion St. Cyr, lately chef in the household of M. le Duc de Rochechouart. Emilion was one of the five best cooks in the world. Sandra, who ate no more than a bird, was incapable of appreciating his art, but Lee did, and thus he made sure that at least part of the unjustifiable Cassells income was spent in a good cause. Sandra's new protégés would undoubtedly be as tiresome as the others, but *canvasback à la Tour d'Argent*—Ah! Sandra herself never bored Lee. A simple, kindhearted soul under all the fluff, she baffled him by her very openness. It was always amusing to speculate on what a woman with a completely uninhibited tongue would say next.

Sandra, for pretended motives of economy, had given up her town apartment and Lee was forced to motor up to Westchester County. He saved half an hour of tedious driving through traffic by taking the subway to the end of the line and meeting his chauffeur there. "Brookwood" was almost surrounded by the city now, but it was hard to realize it, once you were inside the gates, so skillful was the planting. Only on the stillest nights was it possible to hear the clang of a distant trolley car or the strains of a wide-open radio. In addition to the huge formal garden, which cost a fortune to keep up and was of no earthly use to anybody, there was a paddock for horses, a small running track and a pasture field with a cow in it. Lee's brain reeled as he tried to compute the value of all this in city lots—and the taxes. Sandra said she was going to die there and the hell with the taxes.

Of the grandiose palaces built at the turn of the century, this was one of the last to be used as a private dwelling. It looked to be about a tenth of a mile long, an endless pile of crass yellow brick with gray stone trimmings, supposed to be in the Italian style and all broken out in loggias, terraces, balustrades and Palladian windows. Inside there was a mighty red-carpeted corridor stretching from end to end, as wide and high as a cathedral with rooms opening off on each side. Needless to say, it was crowded with the richest of furnishings from every quarter of the globe. It achieved magnificence, but Lee doubted if there was a single first-class work of art anywhere between cellar and garret.

Sandra received him in one of the smaller reception rooms. The other guests had arrived and over her shoulder Lee saw with surprise and pleasure that they were young and extremely ornamental. Sandra's previous protégés had been pretty stuffy-looking. Sandra herself, a slender woman, dressed by an artist in clinging black lace with sparing touches of jet, looked handsomer than Lee had ever seen her. Her complexion was as soft as a baby's; her graying hair, arranged in a fashion of her own to suggest the ancient Greek, emphasized the freshness of her skin. She did not look young, either, but ageless. Diamonds all over her, as usual; diamonds at her ears, her throat, her breast; diamonds halfway to her elbows.

Lee kissed her hand, murmuring: "You are lovely!" with a kind of wonder that was perfectly genuine, because he knew that Sandra was actually nearly ten years older than his own fat, bald little self. She was several times a grandmother, but she didn't like to have it referred to.

"I just had my face lifted," she murmured happily.

Lee thought: What, again!

She read the thought. "Ah, but this man knows his business!" She lifted the hair at her temples. "Look! you can scarcely see the scars. And my throat, see! Not a wrinkle! . . . Come and meet my guests!"

"A word about them first so I'll know what to say."

"No! No! I want you to gather for yourself what they are! You wouldn't guess in a thousand years!"

First Lee went to speak to Mrs. Delaplaine, Agnes, a fading, depressed woman whom Sandra, according to her humor, referred to as my dearest friend, my chief of staff, my companion—or that tiresome female! Lee sincerely pitied Agnes and hoped that Sandra paid her a thumping big salary, which she probably did not.

He was then led to the three young people, whose names proved to be Mr. and Mrs. Ammon and Mr. Farren. Ammon was a tall, dark fellow, thirty-five, Lee guessed, a magnificent physical specimen. He had a bold nose, a predatory mouth, and a hard, bright gaze; the figure of a young guardsman. His young wife was an ash blonde, tall too, and of that delicate, fragile type of beauty that makes a man of any age feel protective. They made a striking pair. The other man, Farren, was younger and less imposing than his tall friend. He also was handsome, as blond as the other was dark, but he had a haggard look, and whereas Ammon was as smooth and hard as glass, there was a hint of reckless pain in the younger man's blue eyes that surprised Lee. Farren smiled agreeably, unconscious that his eyes were giving him away. All in all, the three made Lee feel wary. Something queer here. He suspected that Sandra was due to be sold again.

But it was fascinating to watch the three and to speculate on what they were. Every line of the girl's delicate beauty suggested breeding, but that was an accident; for it presently transpired that she had been born in Tenth Avenue on San Juan Hill. Nor was either of the men wellborn, though both had acquired a certain veneer on the way up, especially Ammon. He bore himself as coolly as if he had been familiar with this grand house since childhood. As for the girl, it was impossible to tell what was going through her head; with a faint, fixed smile, she let the others do the talking. Farren was ill at ease and furtive. What was their line? Not business; not the stage; not journalism. Lee had to confess himself baffled.

They were already on a familiar footing with their hostess; that was Sandra's way. Ammon was "Sieg," his wife "Letty," and Farren quite naturally "Blondy." Sandra, as pleased with them as a little girl with a family of new dolls, discussed them as candidly as if they had had no more feelings than dolls.

"Isn't she lovely, Lee? Turn around, darling, and let Mr. Mappin see your behind. What a line from shoulder to hip and from hip to ankle! Perfect! And do you know, Lee, with that exquisite figure she did not have anything fit to put on! I took her down to Hattie's myself this morning and outfitted her. What a pleasure! That dress is an original model and Hattie charged me double for it, but I'll get square with her. We quarreled about that dress, but Hattie was right! Hattie was right! You'd think that indefinite beige would make the girl look sallow, she's so pale anyhow; but nothing of the kind! It brings out the alabaster quality of her skin!"

Sandra turned to the young men. "Of course, after that, we had to buy the boys some clothes. We all went to Brooks's. Fancy! neither of the boys ever had any really good clothes! With such figures! They didn't have to have clothes made. Everything fitted like a glove! Turn around, Sieg. Isn't that a wonderful back, Lee? It was made for a tail coat. And Blondy, too. He isn't so big, but he's just as well made. Only a few men look well in evening clothes."

"And I am not one of them!" murmured Lee.

After cocktails they were led into another small room which contained a round table set for six. "The dining room is so vast," said Sandra, "I thought it would be cozier to eat here."

Lee was glad to see that the handsome, shapely young footmen who used to throng the house had been replaced by maids. It made him uneasy to see able-bodied youngsters waiting on the table. The only man in evidence was old Dunstan, the butler, overseeing all from his post at the buffet. Lee perceived with a smile that the famous gold service had been brought out for the occasion. This was just like Sandra. Since her young guests had never before eaten in such luxurious surroundings, she wanted to let them have the full run for their money. Lee saw Sieg Ammon regarding the gold plates with a glistening eye, and wondered if the young man contemplated slipping one in his pocket. Probably not. There was a masterful look about Sieg, which suggested that he was playing for bigger stakes than a gold plate.

Sandra placed Sieg on one side of her, Letty on the other—"So I can talk to you both," she said. Lee was seated opposite Sandra with Mrs. Delaplaine on one side of him, Blondy on the other. In this situation he could study the faces of the husband and wife, which suited him very well. He would have liked also to search for the explanation of the savage recklessness in Blondy's eyes, but that was not so easy, for Blondy was presenting a shoulder to him. The conversation was brisk and meaningless. Sandra and Sieg supplied most of it. Mrs. Delaplaine occasionally babbled in Lee's ear, but it was not necessary to listen to her. An occasional nod and smile in her direction kept her going happily.

Sieg had himself so well in hand there was not much to be learned from his smooth and comely face. He was bent on making Sandra talk and that, God knows, is not difficult, thought Lee. She was telling Sieg the story of her experience with the ringmaster of the circus and Sieg applauded with laughter. Meanwhile the pale, beautiful Letty was listening with her unchanging, faint smile. At a moment when she thought she was unobserved, Lee saw the girl's downcast eyes creep upward to Sieg's face and hang there with a lost look, the look of a woman who has submerged her whole being in a man. The startled Lee, stealing a sidelong look at young Blondy, saw from the direction of his glance that his eyes were fixed on Letty's face. It provided a key to his savage pain. Hm! In love with his pal's wife! thought Lee; and she is mad about her husband! An interesting situation—with explosive possibilities.

When the conversation became general, it appeared from a remark of Sieg's that he was familiar with Lee Mappin's writings. "You have read one of my books?" said Lee.

"I have read all of them, Mr. Mappin." Sieg rattled off the titles.

"I feel flattered," said Lee. "How did you happen to run across them?"

"In the prison library," said Sieg nonchalantly.

Lee's mind stood still for a moment. His first thought was: This is exactly what Sandra *would* do!

Sandra was saying sweetly, "Sieg has lately been released from Sing Sing." Sandra was shortsighted. She put up her lorgnette in order to enjoy the expression on Lee's face.

Lee wasn't giving her any change. "How interesting!" he said, smiling back. "But I shouldn't think my little studies of murder would be exactly suitable for a prison library."

"Oh, yes," said Sieg. "They were popular with the Gees, young and old. You had to put in your bid in advance to get one. They're moral books because the crook always gets it in the neck."

"Well," murmured Lee, "it's only the ones that get caught that I can study." He began to enjoy himself. It was a piquant situation and the responsibility for anything that might happen was not his. As long as everybody was being frank about it, Lee thought he might venture to ask Sieg what he had been sent up for and he did.

A spasm of rage broke up the young man's smooth mask for a second. "We were framed," he said shortly; "Blondy and me."

"Blondy too?"

"Sure! Blondy's been my side kick, going on ten years now."

"Was it your first experience?"

Sieg carelessly shook his head. "No, I did a stretch at San Quentin in '32 and another at Joliet three years later."

"Tell us about it."

Sieg glanced at Sandra. Her lips were parted with excitement, her vague blue eyes almost ecstatic. Sieg could see well enough that it was the prison stripes which constituted his attraction for her. "Tell Lee," she urged. "Tell him the whole story."

Sieg shrugged with his attractive nonchalance and started in: "I lit out from home when I was fifteen. That's twenty years ago. I just bummed round the country, my great aim being to live without working. I made out pretty well, too, and managed to keep out of stir, except for a couple of short terms for vagrancy and so on in the county jails. And if the weather was cold and I happened to be broke, that was really a convenience. But out in Frisco in '32 I got stuck on a girl—it's always the same story, isn't it? I suppose I wanted to give her a flashy present or something. I forget. Anyhow, I undertook to burgle a men's furnishings store. Clumsy work. Served me right when I was caught. As a first offender I got an indeterminate sentence in San Quentin. It was there I met Blondy and we've been together ever since."

Lee glanced at Blondy. "You must have been a mere boy in '32."

"Sixteen," said Blondy shortly.

"What were you in for?"

Blondy scowled. He didn't enjoy telling his reminiscences. "I cut a man," he growled. "I had good cause, too."

"What were the circumstances?"

Blondy obstinately shook his head. "It's not a pretty story."

Sieg went on: "Well, when Blondy and me got out of San Quentin, we drifted East. We had our ups and downs—eh, Blondy? We made up our minds to cut out the rough stuff, see? Nothing to it. Unless we could get good clothes and acquire some class, we were sunk. Well, that wasn't too easy for a couple of young gees just out of stir. Maybe you know the kind of twelve dollar suits they give you when they let you out."

"I know them," said Lee.

"Well, in Chicago," Sieg continued, "a dame I had known before staked us to a good suit apiece, and undertook to put some polish on our manners."

"What did you do for her?" asked Lee.

Sieg gave him a grin of understanding. "She was a business woman, see? And we rustled business for her."

"I understand. Go ahead."

"This dame had class, see? And she knew class. She started in to teach Blondy and me. We took to it like ducks to water. She taught us how to talk, how to eat, how to wear clothes. And as fast as we improved, she advanced us in her business. At last, when we were perfect gentlemen, she put us into a racket that paid us well for more than a year."

"What was that?"

"We worked the hotels, see? Only the best hotels. All dyked out in tails, white tie, top hat and so on. The solid, out-of-town businessman was our mark, see? The lonely man with the evening on his hands. You'd be surprised to learn how many of them there are. Well, I sit down in the lobby near him, see? And every now and then I look at my watch. Obviously waiting for a girl. And he is looking at me out of the corners of his eyes, kind of wistful; a swell young guy in top hat and tails, waiting for a girl, it is just what he would like to be. And so it's a cinch to get into talk with him, and when she doesn't come he sympathizes with me, and I say, 'The hell with her; let's go and get a drink.' So I take him around town and show him a good time. I know all the best places in Chicago. It was a swell racket while it lasted. Blondy never got caught at it. But when I came to New York, he came with me. In New York . . .'"

Lee interrupted him. "But there wasn't anything crooked about that racket. How come you landed in Joliet?"

Sieg made believe not to hear that question, and Lee said to himself: blackmail probably.

"By the time we got to New York," Sieg continued, "Blondy and me were just about as smooth as they come. For class we could match up with anything the big town could show. Such being the case, there was no lack of call for our services; we worked at this and that, and fluffed around and enjoyed ourselves until we met up with Sam Bartol. You know him?"

"He was the proprietor of El Mirador across the river."

"That's right. The classiest outfit in or around New York. You had to have class to work there. At first we were engaged just to be gentlemen playing roulette for moderate stakes upstairs. That was so we could watch the croupiers for Sam. It's against the rules to play money across on the tables, but the customers will do it, and the croupiers watch their chance to prig what they can. Well, Sam liked our work so much that he promoted us to be his cashiers up in the gambling room. We sold the customers chips when they went in and redeemed them when they came out.

"Well, Sam Bartol was making so damned much money it made Blondy and me sore. And us two just on a salary. Well, it was a cinch to get square with Sam. I got a guy I knew to make me some celluloid chips exactly like those used in the place, and every night we used to cash a few of our own. The amount of chips in the house was always short because the customers always carried away some in their pockets, meaning to play them next time they came. But we got careless, I suppose. We put too many chips in circulation and Sam got onto us. One night we were seized and searched *as we went in* and they found the chips on us. So we were thrown out on our ear."

"Did Bartol prosecute you?" asked Lee.

"A gambler can't prosecute anybody," said Sieg. "He's outside the law. No! it was a dirty frameup! Blondy and I were drinking with a guy on West Fifty-second Street. Neither of us ever saw the guy before. Suddenly he accused us of having robbed him. By a strange coincidence there were a couple of dicks in the place; we were seized and searched and the guy's wallet was found on me, and his watch in Blondy's pocket. A barefaced frameup! As if guys like Blondy and me would come down to picking a guy's pockets! But with our records we stood no chance. The New York police and the District Attorney and all, they were glad to oblige a big shot like Sam Bartol. We were framed and sent up with a brace of years a piece. I used to pace my cell planning ways to get square with Sam Bartol. But somebody took the job off my hands. You may remember the case."

"I remember it," said Lee.

"Sam was found lying on the floor of his place across the river, shot through the heart. The police have never solved the case. God knows Sam had enemies enough to choose from."

"How long have you and Letty been married?" asked Lee.

"Three weeks," said Sieg. "Letty was waiting for me. She was one of the hostesses over at Sam Bartol's and I fell for her. I don't know why." They exchanged a smile full of meaning across the table; Blondy lowered his eyes.

"What are your plans now?" asked Lee.

"We're going straight," said Sieg quickly. "That is, I am." He glanced at his partner. "Blondy must hew to his own line."

"You know how I feel about it," growled Blondy.

"Letty and I are going straight," said Sieg, looking at his wife. She colored to the eyes with pleasure. "Crime doesn't pay. In this state, with three convictions behind me, if I was taken again I'd get life. It isn't worth it. Besides, I've got responsibilities now. I'm a married man."

"Anything particular in view?" asked Lee.

Sieg shook his head. He wasn't troubled by the prospect. "We'll get along. All I have is a talent for making myself agreeable."

"I can see that," said Lee dryly.

"I have plans," put in Sandra.

The canvasback was served. Emilion had done it justice, and Lee left them to their talk of prison life for the time being.

"What a. dreadful young man!" whispered Mrs. Delaplaine. "He seems to be proud of going to prison!"

"Well, it has earned him a dress suit and a good meal," said Lee. "The canvasback is perfection! From Sing Sing to Brookwood is a long step. From a tin plate to solid gold! Would make a good title for a melodrama."

"What will Sandra pick up next?" whimpered Mrs. Delaplaine.

When they had finished eating, Sandra said: "Would you like to walk through the house? Most people are curious to see it."

"Sure!" said Sieg quickly. "This is better than a movie set. This is the real thing."

So they started in procession through the endless vast rooms; drawing room, music room, library, ballroom, conservatory; slender, lace-clad Sandra and tall Sieg in advance, Blondy and Letty following, Lee and Mrs. Delaplaine solidly bringing up the rear.

"It's a silly background, isn't it?" said Sandra, "all for one lonely little woman like me? Fifty-two rooms, they say, but I haven't been in half of them. If I was a sensible woman I'd sell it and move into a comfortable little house, but I never shall. I'm accustomed to it and I'm not going to change."

"Lovely! . . . Wonderful! . . . Gorgeous!" murmured her young guests.

Lee noticed that Blondy and Letty never exchanged a word during the progress. The young man's eyes dwelt hungrily on the girl's beautiful profile. His look was softened now.

Back in the little reception room where they had first met, Lee found himself beside Letty. "Are you enjoying yourself?" he asked.

"Oh, yes!" she said in a tone of conventional politeness. "Mrs. Cassells is so kind!" she added with a tremor of genuine feeling, "It frightens me a little."

"Why should it?" asked Lee.

"It's too good to be true!"

The young people took their leave while it was still early. Sandra had ordered a car to carry them back to town. Letty met the others in the great hall, carrying her wrap over her arm. The wrap was an exquisite garment of brown, uncurled ostrich, evidently a gift from Sandra. Sieg took it from his wife. As he was about to drop it around her shoulders, he bent his head and kissed her neck. Letty's lips parted, her eyes darkened strangely; an inner rapture made her face luminous. The others were looking at her; she had forgotten them.

In a minute they had gone. Sandra stood looking at the door through which they had disappeared, with a scrap of a lace handkerchief clenched in her hand. "Did you see him kiss her?" she said.

Her obvious emotion irritated Lee. "Just a conventional gesture," he said.

Sandra shook her head impatiently. "I wasn't thinking about him, but about her . . . the way she took it with rapture . . . rapture! How I envy her!"

"I was sorry for her," said Lee. "Happiness with a man like that must be pretty precarious!"

"Yes, indeed! Yes, indeed!" agreed Agnes virtuously. "A jailbird!"

Sandra turned on her. "What the hell do you know about rapture?"

Agnes shriveled.

To Lee, Sandra went on: "What's happiness for a woman? A little husband, a little baby, a little house, and every day the same as the day before? That's not happiness but slow suffocation." She raised her clenched hand. "But to go all out for a man . . . *all out!* What else would matter then? The woman who has never known that hasn't lived!"

Lee took a pinch of snuff and, snapping the box shut, returned it to his vest pocket. Useless to argue with an emotional woman.

As Sandra made no move to return to the room where they had been sitting, he saw that he was expected to leave also. He didn't want to go just yet. "Shouldn't you and I talk things over?" he suggested.

Sandra, still abstracted, shook her head. "Not tonight. I'm tired."

"You said you had certain plans for these young people," he persisted.

"All in the air," she said with a wave of the hand. "I promise not to commit myself to anything until I have consulted with you."

"Very well, my dear. Good night."

# CHAPTER TWO

AT FIVE O'CLOCK Sandra, in one of the effulgent Cassells limousines, picked up Lee Mappin at his office on lower Madison Avenue. Lee, as an author, didn't really require an office, but he said it helped to promote habits of industry. Sandra had asked him if he could give her an hour of his time without specifying what for. As they drove away he said:

"I assume that this has something to do with Messrs. Ammon and Farren."

"More or less," said Sandra, toying with a bracelet.

"Where have you got them domiciled?"

"Sieg and Letty are at the Madison."

"And Blondy?"

Sandra shrugged impatiently. "Oh, Blondy's got a job driving a lumber truck."

"Bravo Blondy!"

Sandra frowned. "Really, Lee, it's very hard to understand you sometimes. Why is it a merit in Blondy to insist on being rough and common when I offer him a chance to better himself?"

Lee took a generous pinch of snuff and ignored the question. "Well, what about Sieg and Letty?" he asked.

"It's apparent that you don't like them," she said huffily.

"Not for you, darling."

"Why not for me?"

"They're dangerous."

"Ah," breathed Sandra. "If they only were! I adore danger!"

"I'm not speaking of romantic danger, darling, but a very vulgar danger, such as having your throat cut and your diamonds stolen."

"My diamonds are insured," she said calmly. "If anybody demanded them, I should turn them over and collect the insurance next day."

"If the robber didn't know how reasonable you are, he might shoot you first and take the diamonds afterward."

"Don't be silly, Lee. I know these young people are no paragons of virtue. They're human and passionate. They live close to the earth. That's why they interest me. As long as I give them everything they want, they're not going to turn on me. They look on me as a kind of princess. Indeed, that's the trouble. They won't let me be real pals with them."

Lee took another pinch of snuff.

"You just took snuff," she said irritably. "In a minute you'll be sneezing your head off! It's just a silly affectation, anyhow. You think you're registering superiority that way, but it doesn't fool anybody!"

"My darling," said Lee, "I'm sure you didn't ask me to go driving just for the purpose of scolding me."

"Why don't you like Sieg Ammon!" she demanded.

"Too slick, too smooth for my taste."

"That's only the small change he pays his way with. Under his slick exterior there is a real man, believe me. There is fire, savagery."

"Oh, for God's sake, don't sentimentalize over him!" Lee broke out. "That is more than I can stand!"

"I assure you that I feel anything but sentimental toward Sieg," she said stiffly.

"I don't know whether you do or not. It is possible for a woman to get just as sentimental over savagery and crime as over sweetness and light!"

"And if you think that I am in danger of getting involved with him," she went on, "that is nonsense, too. He and Letty are completely wrapped up in each other."

"What has developed about the girl?"

"Nothing. I don't get anywhere with her. She won't let herself go with me. Not that I blame her especially. I suppose she feels she has to guard her secret from the world. She saves every bit of herself for *him*. They are living in a private paradise."

"I hope it doesn't prove to be a fool's paradise for her."

"Oh, you're impossible today, Lee!"

Lee, noticing that they were still heading downtown, asked where they were bound for. Sandra mentioned a number on Henry Street.

"Henry Street?" said Lee. "Isn't that rather a tough neighborhood?"

"Not tough," said Sandra, "but plain."

Lee touched one of her gleaming bracelets. "Just the same," he said, "this is hardly suitable for Henry Street."

"Don't be absurd," said Sandra. "I would feel undressed if I didn't wear *any* jewels."

"What is our business in Henry Street?" asked Lee resignedly.

"I want you to look at a house I am thinking of buying."

"How can you use a house in Henry Street?"

"My attorney tells me it is a very good investment," said Sandra in a dignified tone that assured Lee she was equivocating. "Property is depressed there at present and is sure to rise."

"I see," he said.

The part of Henry Street that they turned into was lined as far as one could see with rows of modest, old-fashioned brick buildings which had been single-family dwellings long ago. There were even a few skinny trees struggling for existence among the paving stones.

"The Henry Street Settlement plants them," said Sandra. "The Settlement has improved the neighborhood wonderfully."

They drew up before a house that was overflowing with carpenters, plasterers and painters. "I thought I was to be consulted before you took any definite step," said Lee mildly.

Sandra shrugged elaborately. "That would only have meant hours of futile argument, darling. It was simpler to present you with an accomplished fact."

"Quite," said Lee. "Are you going to live here?"

"Certainly not. I shall just be an occasional guest."

"I see. But why should I be brought into it now?"

"Oh, if you don't wish to help me, Martin can drive you right uptown and come back for me."

"Not at all," said Lee resignedly. "Lead on!"

They got out of the car and, picking their way up the steps, entered the littered hall. Lee perceived at a glance that the old house had been charming and would be so again. The rooms were spacious and well-proportioned; the woodwork and mantels of good early nineteenth-century design. A graceful stairway wound up to the second floor.

"Some house," said Lee. "Twelve rooms or more."

"Fourteen," said Sandra proudly.

"Isn't that a lot of space for our lovebirds to flutter around in? Wouldn't an apartment have been more suitable?"

"You don't understand my plans. Sieg and Letty are only a part of it. I am establishing a sort of—what shall I call it?—a sort of hostel. Yes, that's the word, a hostel. Sieg and Letty will run it for me."

"What kind of hostel?" asked Lee grimly.

"For released prisoners," said Sandra brightly.

"Merciful Heaven!" murmured Lee.

"Isn't it a swell idea?" said Sandra with her big blue eyes shining. "One of the worst social problems is what to do with released prisoners. Of course, one house like this is only a drop in the bucket. But it's a beginning, a beginning! It will provide a few men with a decent home until they can adjust themselves. Now you see why I had to have a house in a plain neighborhood. An apartment would never do."

"A swell idea," groaned Lee, "but, my dear friend, you're going to get into trouble—just what kind of trouble I can't foresee; many kinds, I fear!"

"You're just an old croaker!" said Sandra. "My enthusiasm will solve all problems."

"I don't suppose anything I could say to you now would make any difference."

"Not a bit! Everything is settled. But you don't have to be in it if you don't want to."

"Sure, I want to," said Lee. "I wouldn't miss it for anything. But I must drop one word of warning. I will stand by you until the end, darling, but I cannot guarantee to get you out of whatever trouble you are going to get into. The possibilities are staggering!"

"Oh, you're just talking," she said calmly. "Men have to talk!"

They were mounting the stairs. "Sieg and Letty's suite will be in the front," said Sandra. "There's a nice big room, an alcove that they can use for a dressing room or a private sitting room, and a bathroom."

"Sing Sing was never like this!" murmured Lee.

"There are two more large bedrooms on this floor," Sandra went on, "each with a bath; upstairs four smaller rooms and two baths. Do you think five baths will be sufficient?"

"Ample," said Lee dryly.

"It's important that the house should have the atmosphere of a good home. There is a nice bedroom and bath in the basement for a couple of servants."

"Servants, too?"

"Oh, do be sensible!" said Sandra impatiently. "Can you see Letty in the kitchen, or Sieg sweeping the halls?"

"Frankly, darling, I cannot," said Lee.

"There is one thing that troubles me a good deal," she went on. "You could help me with it if you would."

"What is that, dear one?"

"I suspect that Blondy is in love with Letty."

"I am certain of it."

"Then they should not all live together under the same roof. I shall depend on you to get Blondy a job out of town—a good, long way out of town."

"I will see to it."

"If you get him a job, I'll give him an automobile to salve his feelings. I don't suppose he's ever had a car of his own."

"Not unless he stole it."

"A car will help him to forget Letty."

As they returned to the main floor, they met Sieg Ammon coming in from the street with two girls; one was Letty, the other a tall, dazzling brunette in a silver fox jacket and a fantastic hat. She had annexed Sieg and Letty was following them, a little paler than usual and tight-lipped. Sieg introduced his friend as Miss Queenie Deane.

"She's a singer," he said to Sandra. "Perhaps you've heard her in one of the night clubs."

"Haven't had the pleasure," said Sandra dryly.

Queenie took her in from top to toe with eyes as bright and hard as jet buttons. "*The* Mrs. Cassells?" she asked.

"As far as I know," said Sandra, looking bored.

"Sieg and I are old pals," Queenie said in a loud voice, looking fondly in the young man's face. "We put on a dancing act in Chicago four years ago. I haven't danced since." She laughed excessively. "My God! you could have knocked me down with a feather when I heard he was married! I never thought of Sieg in connection with *marriage!*"

"Really!" said Sandra.

Sandra took possession of Sieg and they moved toward the rear of the house, the two girls following. They did not look at each other but their mutual hatred was so apparent that it was like a baleful lightning playing back and forth between them. Lee, behind them, picked his way between ends of lumber.

"I want you to see the tree in the back yard," Sandra was saying. "Fancy, a real tree in this part of town! We can sit under it on warm evenings!"

Lee smiled to himself at the picture this called up; Sandra laden with diamonds, sitting in a back yard on Henry Street.

A large, pleasant room occupied the rear extension with a row of windows looking to the south. "I'm going to have this room paneled in pine," Sandra said, "and call it the taproom."

"And will you furnish the drinks?" asked Lee.

"I hadn't thought of that yet. I suppose so."

"I wouldn't."

Sieg spoke up. "Mr. Mappin is right, Mrs. Cassells. It would be better to let everybody do their drinking outside."

"Oh, very well," said Sandra shrugging. "Then we'll call it the game room and not have a bar."

"But you'll put in a good floor for dancing," suggested Queenie. "Oh, Sieg, wouldn't this be a lovely room for dancing?" Whenever she addressed him, voice and glance were frankly seductive; Sieg lapped it up grinning, and the other women bristled. Queenie must be pretty dense, Lee thought, or else very sure of herself. She was dense, he decided, when he presently heard her saying to Sandra:

"Oh, Mrs. Cassells, I hope you're going to let me come here and live! Of course, I haven't served time, but I could make myself *so* useful. I could sing to the boys every night."

"That would be lovely, I'm sure," said Sandra in a voice as musical as breaking icicles. "Write me a little letter of application, won't you? There are only six bedrooms available, you know, and I already have a pile of applications so high. I'm taking them up one by one."

Even Queenie understood that she had been snubbed. "Oh, well, I don't suppose you want girls in the house," she said, laughing too loudly.

"That depends," said Sandra.

To revenge herself, Queenie went to Sieg and, slipping her hand under his arm, looked up at him fondly. She was letting the other women see what they had been to each other. Sieg pressed her hand against his ribs and returned her glance. Letty bit her lip.

"Well, ta-ta, Handsome," said Queenie. "I have a dinner date and I must go and array myself . . . Good-by, Mr. Mappin. It's been a pleasure to meet you. I'm showing at Le Coq Noir; do drop in some night . . . 'By Letty. You and I must have a heart-to-heart talk one of these days . . . Mrs. Cassells, your house is going to be perfectly lovely. I *do* hope you'll accept me as an inmate. Good-by, all."

She sailed out, leaving a strong smell of French perfume behind her. Sieg went with her.

"For God's sake, open a window!" said Sandra.

Letty threw up a sash and stood with her back to the others looking down into the yard. Sandra was watching the figure of Queenie disappearing through the hall. She couldn't see much at the distance.

"That woman is an unmitigated you-know-what," she said to Lee. "Word of four letters."

"It has five, darling," said Lee.

"Well, I never could spell. She ought to be put to torture. Lord! how I would enjoy stretching her on the rack . . . slowly."

When Sieg returned, the atmosphere was decidedly chilly, but he did not immediately notice it. He was exuding self-satisfaction. "Everything is going well," he said, rubbing his hands together. "The workmen have promised to be out of the house in a week."

"Where did you run into *her?*" asked Sandra coldly.

Letty answered for him from the window. "She came to our hotel."

"Why did you bring her here?" asked Sandra.

Sieg began to look uneasy. "She wanted to see the house. I didn't think there would be any harm in it."

"No harm in it, certainly," said Sandra. "But why do you permit her to act as if she owned you?"

Sieg laughed uncomfortably. "How can a man side-step that sort of thing?"

"Are you asking me?"

Sieg, perceiving that he was in very wrong, quickly changed his tactics. Going to Letty and flinging an arm around her, he drew her close. "Letty, darling, did you mind?" he asked. "I'm damned sorry! You see, Queenie carries on like that with every man. She's a man-eater. Nobody takes her seriously, and that's why it never occurred to me that you would mind."

Letty, unable to resist him, lifted her beseeching face to be kissed. Sandra, however, was far from being placated. She moved around the room, affecting to examine the carpenter work, pushing out her painted lips and frowning. Lee saw a glance of intelligence pass between Sieg and Letty. Sieg, dropping the girl, went quickly to Sandra.

"I'm so sorry, Mrs. Cassells," he said cajolingly. "Queenie's a bad egg and I should have known better than to bring her here. I thought she might interest you as a character. I wouldn't offend you for the world! I owe everything to you!" He lowered his voice and Lee could not hear the rest. There was honey on his tongue, while his hard eyes commanded Sandra. She melted. Laying a gloved hand on his arm, she said:

"Say no more about it, Sieg. What bills have you got for me to pay?"

Lee thought crossly: How easy it is to bring women to heel when you're six feet tall and have all your hair!

Sieg said to Sandra: "First, there's a man waiting to see you. He's out at the door."

"Who is he?"

"His name is Sam Souter. They call him Jimpson, I don't know why. He's just down from the Big House. Seems the word about our place here has already traveled from cell to cell by grapevine and Sam wants a berth here."

"What was he in for?" asked Sandra.

"Shooting a man over a game of cards."

Sandra's eyes widened. "Did the man die?" she asked breathlessly.

"No, he got better . . . Sam thinks he's got a claim on me," he went on, "because Blondy and me bummed across the continent with him seven years ago. He likes to say he taught us all we know."

"Well, why not take him?" said Sandra, "an old friend of yours . . ."

"No!" said Sieg. "You want men here that you can help. Jimpson is an old died-in-the-wool con; been in half the prisons in the country. You couldn't change him. He came from a good home long ago; they're the worst sort. Besides, he's hard to get along with. He'd make trouble in the house."

Lee was a little surprised at Sieg's good sense.

"Then send him away," said Sandra.

"It would come better from you," said Sieg. "He thinks he has a claim on me."

"Very well, bring him in."

Sieg grinned. "Don't let him know that I'm against having him or I may wake up some morning with a knife between my ribs. That's the kind Jimpson is."

Sandra shivered. Nevertheless she looked eagerly for the appearance of Jimpson.

Sieg went to fetch him. When he was brought in, Lee saw a man in his late forties who was already considerably decayed. He was neatly dressed and he still had an indefinable air of breeding and education, but Lee thought he had never seen a more unpleasant specimen. His expression was both mean and base; he looked equally ready to be humble and abusive. Lee was nearest the door and Sieg paused to introduce Souter. The man started at the sound of Lee's name, and his lip lifted in a sneer.

"The detective?" he said.

"Not exactly a detective," said Lee good-humoredly. "I study crime and write books about it."

"Yeah, I've read some of your books," said Souter.

Sandra graciously offered him her hand. Souter took it with an extraordinary expression. He hated her for her diamonds, her elegant clothes, her assured air, but he fawned on her. Sandra said:

"Always glad to meet a friend of Sieg's."

"Yes, Sieg and I have been pals for many a year," Souter said with a horrible smile. "I helped bring him up."

"Sieg tells me that you'd like to come and stay here until you get on your feet. I wish I could say yes at once, but we only have a few rooms and already the applications are piling up. If you'll leave your address, we'll keep in touch with you."

Souter, perfectly aware that he was being let down easily, sneered. "Sieg knows where to find me any time."

"In the meantime, how are you fixed?" asked Sandra frankly. Lee always admired the way Sandra could give alms without shaming the recipient.

"Well, they give you ten dollars when they let you out," said Souter.

Sandra folded a bill small and pressed it into his hand. "Let me add a little to it until you get a job."

Souter tried to mold his features into an expression of gratitude. "Thank you kindly, ma'am." As he looked around the room,
his ugly face really softened for a moment. "You certainly are
going to have things nice here. I'd like to live nice." Then he
sneered. "Much too nice for the likes of me, I reckon."

"Not at all!" said Sandra quickly. "Everybody is entitled to a
decent living."

Souter's lip lifted. "Yeah? Try and get it!" he muttered under
his breath as he went out.

Sandra shivered. "Brrh! what a horrible man!" she murmured.
"He seems to poison the air! How could you ever have associated
with such a creature, Sieg."

"It's prison life that has done it to him," said Sieg carelessly.
"Years ago he wasn't so bad."

IT WAS A MILD NIGHT in early spring and Lee, after the opera and a
little supper in the Iridium Room, decided to walk home in order
to clear his brain for sleep. Walking east in Fifty-fifth Street, he
was faced with the sign of Le Coq Noir and, following an impulse
of curiosity, he turned in. The wide, low room was crowded to the
doors and foggy with tobacco smoke. He found a place at the end
of the bar where he could obtain an oblique view of the dancing
floor, and ordered a highball.

After a troupe of clown harmonica players had finished their
act, Queenie Deane swam out on the floor wearing a costume con-
sisting mostly of a black taffeta skirt and that was split up to the
hip on one side. A handsome, long-legged wench, thought Lee, for
those who like them that way. She sang three songs which were
more than suggestive. She had no voice but plenty of bounce and
brass and an infinite suggestiveness. A popular performer at two
in the morning.

When the furious clapping and the cries of approval died down,
Lee followed Queenie with his eyes as she made her way toward a
little table against the wall. At that moment some intervening figures moved, and Lee saw that Sieg Ammon was occupying the table.
Lee was hardly surprised. Queenie leaned across the table and

planted a kiss on Sieg's lips, then slid into the place beside him. Other men in the neighborhood looked envious.

Lee swallowed his drink and left the place. How sweet was the air of the street! He walked along debating whether or not to tell Sandra what he had seen, and decided that he would not. Women being what they were, Sandra would jump to the conclusion that he had been following and spying upon Sieg. And anyway, she would not blame Sieg but only the woman.

# CHAPTER THREE

BLONDY FARREN, neatly dressed and barbered, stood in front of Lee in the latter's office with his hat in his hands. Working in the open air during the past weeks had brought a wholesome color into Blondy's cheeks; Lee was oddly drawn to the good-looking young man with the firm, shapely mouth and the steady blue eyes with their look of pain borne without flinching. He wanted to win Blondy's confidence, but that promised to be difficult. Blondy answered all questions promptly and briefly and shut his mouth.

"Sit down," said Lee.

Blondy sat bolt upright on a chair with his hat dangling between his knees.

"Where have you been living?" asked Lee.

"Room on East Fifth Street."

"They told me that you had a job driving a lumber truck."

"Part-time job," said Blondy. "Best I could get without a recommendation. Twelve a week."

"You can't do much on that, can you?"

"I get by," said Blondy shortly.

"I reckon you've had a pretty thin time."

"A man has to take things as they come."

"Mrs. Cassells wanted to make things easier for you," suggested Lee.

"I know. She's real kind. But I had too much of that in the past."

"Too much of what?"

"Soft living."

"Now that the Henry Street house is going, you could eat there. They'd be glad to have you."

"I've been there a couple of times. Best not to go too often."

"I have a friend who is an executive in the Ohio Steel Mills near Cleveland. I wrote to him to see if I could get you something better."

"They would never hire me," said Blondy grimly.

"You're wrong!" said Lee. "I told my friend the circumstances and he has a job for you. It's foreman of a small yard gang. The pay works out about forty a week."

This broke down Blondy's defenses. "Cleveland?" he said with a stricken glance.

"Don't you want to go to Cleveland?"

The young man quickly recovered himself. "Sure! Cleveland's an all right town. I'd be glad of it." His voice changed. "Why do you want to send me out of town?" he asked.

"Don't you think it would be a good thing?"

Blondy thought it over and nodded. "You're right," he said, pressing his lips into a thin line. This was as close as he got to being confidential. "When does it start?" asked Blondy.

"As soon as you like."

"I'm ready."

"There's another thing," said Lee. "Mrs. Cassells wants you to have a car."

Blondy shook his head. "I don't need it . . . Much obliged just the same."

"You do need it. The mills are twelve miles out of town. . . . Why not take it?" Lee urged kindly. "It would help make life pleasant for you. Mrs. Cassells can afford it."

Blondy considered the offer. He was tempted. "I never had a car of my own," he murmured. Then he seemed to make up his mind. "If Mrs. Cassells wants to make the down payment, I can take care of the monthly payments myself on forty a week, easy. I'd rather have it that way."

Lee liked this young fellow more and more. "Very good," he said. "We'll fix it like that. What kind of a car do you want?"

"I leave that to Mrs. Cassells."

"All cars are the same to her. You might as well have what you want. I am authorized to buy it for you."

A gleam appeared in Blondy's eye. "Do you think she'd stand for a convertible?" he asked diffidently. "They cost more. Boy! I like driving with the top down!"

"Surely!" said Lee. "We'll go look at them as soon as I sign my letters."

"Write a letter to the man in Cleveland for me to take," said Blondy, "and if there's a car in stock I'll light out this afternoon."

"Don't you want to say good-by to your friends?"

He shook his head. "I'd be obliged if you'd thank Mrs. Cassells for me. I'm tongue-tied with a lady. . . . I'll write to her after I get there."

"Okay," said Lee. "And, Blondy, I want you to know I'm your friend, too. If you ever get in a jam let me hear from you. Lord! I was young once. I know how things are. Don't forget that, Blondy."

Blondy hung his head so low Lee could not see into his face. Kindness, it seemed, was the one thing that broke him down. "Thanks a lot, Mr. Mappin," he mumbled. "Certainly is white of you!"

"Don't mention it," said Lee. "Sit down in the outer office while I dictate the letter for you to take."

SPICK AND SPAN in its dress of white paint and pastel wallpaper, the house on Henry Street had been open for a week. The ancient front door and the window frames had been painted a sprightly blue. Sandra and Letty had indulged in an orgy of spending; kitchenware, dining-room furniture, chairs and tables for the game room, sets of furniture for nine bedrooms; rugs for all the floors and curtains for the windows. To Letty it was like a dream to be able to buy everything you wanted at the time you wanted it.

"Everything must be plain, unpretentious, and of the best quality," Sandra had pronounced. "Quality is important for the psychological effect."

It had been easier to furnish the house than to fill it with boarders. All the applicants turned out to have unpleasant predilections, such as whisky, cocaine, kleptomania. After a week they had found two only: Hattie Oliver, better known to the police as Handbag Hattie, and Joe Spencer, an old-time forger who, after thirty years in prison, looked at a new world in trembling amazement. Hattie had overcome Sandra's objections to having women in the house because she was so small, gentle, and anxious to please. Long ago she had cut a dash in the Tenderloin, but of late years it had been hard going, and her pleasant room on the second floor and three square meals a day seemed like heaven.

For nearly half a century Hattie had worked the department stores. Whenever a woman laid down her handbag to examine some goods, Hattie carelessly dropped her jacket over it and worked with lightning fingers under cover of the jacket. In a few seconds she would pick up the jacket and walk on humming a little tune. There were more than forty endorsements on her card in the record room at Police Headquarters. Opposite the last one was written: "Hattie is growing old now, and her fingers have lost their cunning."

Nobody knew Joe's other name. He was called Spencer because he wrote such a beautiful flowing hand. He wore a little white beard carefully trimmed to a point, and was extremely neat; one might almost say elegant, in his dress. He sat at a front window all day watching the traffic in Henry Street. He was afraid to go out. He was as timid as a hare and strongly addicted to hard candy.

Sandra was dissatisfied with her first guests. "I didn't set out to open an old peoples' home," she complained. "Hattie and Joe are played out. They can't do any more harm. I want to get hold of them while they're worth saving; hot-blooded, passionate, dangerous to society."

Lee took a pinch of snuff.

They had taken in for house servants an old safe cracker called Soup Kennedy and his wife, Mary, who had served time for one thing or another. They were a slow, heavy old pair, eternally grumbling and very inefficient servants, particularly Mary, who could not roast a joint without spoiling it. Lee groaned in spirit at the thought of the meals he would be expected to eat in that house. The worst of it was, you couldn't fire them like ordinary hired servants because they had no other place to go.

The dining room was under the extension in the basement. To-night Sieg occupied the head of the table flanked by Sandra and Lee, then Joe Spencer and Hattie, sitting opposite each other and quiet, Letty at the foot. The heavy-footed Mary waited on the table and joined freely in the conversation. Sandra would not allow Sieg to correct her. "I want this to be a true democracy," she said. As a psychologist, Lee was intrigued by the oddly assorted household. With Sandra present, everybody was on his best behavior; they chose their words with care and Hattie curled her little finger elegantly whenever she lifted her cup. Lee guessed that it was freer and easier on other nights.

Anecdotes of prison life constituted Hattie's and Joe's main stock of conversation. "When I was in Dannemora," said Joe, "I was in the next cell to Dan Wicksteel, the famous murderer. He was a lifer. As nice a man as you would want to meet. He taught me the Morse code, and when we couldn't sleep we'd talk together half the night by tapping on a pipe. He told me the whole story of his life. It was a caution. He had killed five men, but all in a fair fight or self-defense, you understand."

Hattie put in: "When they took Ruth Snyder to the death house she walked right by my cell. I saw her four, five times, just as close as I am to you. Beautiful blonde, my eye! that was all newspaper talk. Her face was all streaky like, her eyes were red and her hair was coming in brown at the roots. A man who would do murder for her sake must have been loco!"

Letty, who had a kind heart, treated Joe and Hattie like elderly children, and heaped their plates with the sweets they loved.

At the other end of the table, Sieg Ammon, dark, ruddy and handsome, devoted himself to Sandra. Lee thought: Whatever there is in him that gets the women, I can't see it. Certainly it isn't his brains. And his eyes have no more expression than black glass. Perhaps that's it. The attraction of a hidden personality.

"Have you had any new applications?" asked Sandra.

"Plenty," said Sieg, "but nothing I would consider. Bums mostly, poisoned with smoke. When a man gets to drinking that stuff, there's nothing for him but the hospital and the morgue . . . Do you remember Jimpson Souter?"

"Remember him!" said Sandra with a shiver. "I wish I could forget that horrible man!"

"He dogs my footsteps," said Sieg with a laugh. "He knows we haven't got a houseful and he's sore. Blames me for keeping him out. Threatens to sing to the D.A. about my past life if I don't give him a room."

Sandra's eyes widened. "What does he know about you?"

"You can search me! Long ago when we were camping in the jungles, I supposed I used to brag about my crimes. I posed as a bad man then. But that's not evidence. He doesn't know anything that he could use against me."

"Are you giving him money enough to live on?"

"No. We would never get rid of him then. Let him alone and he'll soon get into trouble with the police again."

"He's a dangerous man," murmured Sandra. "I shall never have any peace until he is safe in prison."

"Why doesn't Blondy come and live here?" asked Letty in her quiet way.

Sieg grinned. "Do you like to have him around?"

"Yes," she said. "Blondy's on the square. You can depend on him."

"Well, I'm sorry, but Blondy's got a job out in Cleveland."

Letty shrugged indifferently.

"I got a letter from a fellow in Sing Sing called Johnnie Stabler," Sieg went on. "He'll be out in a couple of weeks. Said his parents are dead and his wife has divorced him and is living under an assumed name. He has no place to go. Johnnie is an educated fellow. Used to be a clerk in Wall Street."

"Young?" asked Sandra.

"In his thirties."

"That's the sort of man we want. We could help him get a fresh start."

"I'll write to him."

Flat-footed Mary, breathing heavily as she moved around the table, put in her word. "I've got a brother over in Jersey who is down on his luck. He . . ."

"Pipe down, Mary!" said Sieg brusquely. "I know all about him."

A bell sounded in the kitchen and Soup Kennedy plodded upstairs to open the front door. He presently returned saying: "It's a guy to see Sieg."

"Who is it?"

"He's been here before."

Sieg's eyes narrowed. "Is it Jimpson Souter?"

"That's right."

Sieg threw down his napkin, and pushed back his chair. "Don't see him!" urged Sandra nervously. "Let Soup send him away."

"He'd only hang around outside. I'll get rid of him once and for all. Back in half a moment."

Sieg went up the stairs two at a time. The others stopped eating and listened. An indefinable fear crept into their faces. For a long time they could hear only a vague murmur of talk in the hall above.

"Why doesn't Sieg send him away!" murmured Sandra nervously.

Suddenly the two voices broke out in angry cursing. There was the sound of a blow, a fall, followed by a terrifying scramble and stamping to and fro on the floor above. Hattie started to scream and pressed her napkin against her mouth. All sprang up; a chair fell over. Letty, as pale as paper, was the first to reach the bottom of the stairs. Lee thought with a sinking heart: Not another ablebodied man in the house! Nevertheless, he, Soup and little Joe Spencer all clambered up the enclosed stair as fast as they were able. Sandra and Hattie were at their heels.

In the entrance hall Sieg and Jimpson, locked together with crimson faces and starting eyes, lurched heavily from side to side. Sieg's sleek hair stood out from his head, his collar was torn open; there was a small cut over his eyebrow and blood was trickling down his cheek. Lee saw a gun lying on the threshold of the front room and secured it. Sieg slammed Jimpson against the wall. Jimpson's hand stole up between them and fastened around Sieg's throat. Sieg shook himself like a terrier but Jimpson hung on. Sieg turned him halfway round, drew up a knee between them and, thrusting out, sent Jimpson crashing to the floor on his back. Sieg flung himself on the prostrate figure and, gripping his shoulders, beat his head savagely on the floor.

"He'll kill him!" murmured Letty. "Oh, stop him! Stop him!"

Lee and old Kennedy seized hold of Sieg and dragged him off. Jimpson lay on the floor inert.

"Telephone for the police!" cried Sandra hysterically.

The struggling Sieg went quiet in Lee's arms. "No!" he said. "I can handle this!"

Sandra ran into the front room where the telephone was.

"Let me go!" said Sieg urgently. "I'm not going to touch him again."

They released him and he ran after Sandra. Flinging an arm around her, he drew her back from the phone with a grin on his bloody face, as one might grin at a passionate child. "Don't bring in the police," he urged soothingly. "It would be bad for the house."

"He'll kill you!" wailed Sandra. "I saw a gun."

"I have it safe," said Lee.

"He'll never rest until he kills you!"

Sieg laughed. "I'm not afraid of that poor punk. He can't touch me. If there was a new charge laid against him, he'd get ten years. I don't want that on my conscience."

Lee looked at Sieg in surprise. He hadn't suspected him capable of such compunctions.

Sieg deposited Sandra in a chair where she broke into hysterical weeping. Lord! thought Lee, if the world could see the famous Mrs. Cassells now! Little Hattie also was weeping noisily, but Letty was white and stony.

Out in the hall Jimpson lay with an arm flung over his face. He was conscious but he didn't want to stand up to Sieg again. They dragged him to his feet and jammed his hat on his head.

"Now get!" said Sieg.

"Give me back my gun!" whined Jimpson.

Sieg roared with laughter. "That's likely!" he said.

"You can unload it," whined Jimpson. "It took my last cent to buy it. I've got to pawn it in order to eat."

"That's your bad luck," said Sieg. He opened the door. "Get out!"

Jimpson went out of the door crab fashion, as if he expected to be helped with a kick from behind. His face was ashy now with darker streaks. It bore a horrible look of craven fear and rage. He paused for a moment on the threshold and cursed Sieg thickly.

"I'll get you! It may be soon and it may be late, but I'll get you if I burn for it!"

Sieg made a threatening move, and Jimpson went shambling down the steps. Sieg closed the door.

"He shouldn't go free! He shouldn't go free!" wailed Sandra.

"He can't reach me!" said Sieg scornfully.

"You must be armed. You must always be armed now!"

"All right," said Sieg laughing. "Just to please you, I'll take out a license."

Letty led him upstairs to have his face washed and his hair combed. Lee suggested that everybody else needed a stiff drink to compose their nerves.

Later, Sandra and Lee were driving uptown in the Cassells limousine, each sunk in a corner silently thinking over what had happened. Sandra was the first to speak.

"Sometimes I think Letty isn't worthy of a man like Sieg."

"Eh?" said Lee. "In heaven's name, why not?"

"She's so passive! Not a sound out of her the whole time!"

"You never can tell," said Lee. "Still waters, you know."

"Still waters are often stagnant," said Sandra scornfully. There was another long silence.

"Wasn't Sieg magnificent in his rage!" she breathed.

"I can't say that I was impressed, darling. I myself could almost have handled a broken creature like Jimpson."

"Flashing like a meteor!" she murmured. "Awful! Irresistible! . . . I am so fed up with tame men!"

Lee took a pinch of snuff.

# CHAPTER FOUR

THE THIRD BOARDER they took in was Spanish Jack D'Acosta, usually called Spanish around the house. He had been a croupier at Sam Bartol's El Mirador across the river until that showy establishment was closed. Afterward, when he and another man had attempted to open a house in New York, they were raided by the police and sent to Welfare Island for six months as common gamblers. Spanish had just been released. He was a small man, very trimly made, who dressed in a style of quiet elegance. He had a pale, masklike face and ever-watchful eyes, as befitted his profession. His age might have been anything between thirty and forty-five. He said little and was polite to all. Sieg Ammon, who had worked with him at Bartol's, enthusiastically endorsed him.

Lee, from the beginning, felt a vague distaste in the presence of Spanish that at first he could not account for. Spanish, for his part, was a student of Lee's books and professed a great admiration for their author. He brought the books to Lee to be autographed, and was forever seeking his opinion upon this question or that. Spanish had his features under control and his expression never changed—yet somehow it *did* change. Lee presently perceived that it lay in his eyes. While he was looking at you and talking pleasantly, the pupils had a trick of contracting suddenly. You could not see what had happened but it caused a little shiver of primal fear to creep down your backbone. Spanish had the topaz eyes of a cat animal—or a killer.

Whenever Lee appeared at the Henry Street house, Spanish attached himself to him. The first time Lee saw him, Spanish said:

"Mr. Mappin, I don't want to go to jail again."

"Naturally," said Lee.

"But what future is there for a gambler in America?"

"None whatever."

"Then what *can* I do? I have nerves of steel and perfect self-control. I can read human nature. Nothing escapes my observation. Surely those qualities ought to be salable somewhere."

"I haven't a doubt of it," said Lee. "Be a little patient and we'll find an opening for you."

Spanish cast down the telltale yellow eyes. "I suppose a psychologist would call me a callous or unfeeling character," he said deprecatingly. "On that account I need a strong stimulus of excitement to make me feel that I'm alive. In a monotonous job the same day after day and year after year I'd go off my nut."

"I can sympathize with that," said Lee.

"Is there such a thing as honest excitement, Mr. Mappin?"

"Oh, I find it occasionally," said Lee, smiling. "Sometimes too much!"

"I was hoping," Spanish went on, "that you might find some occasion to employ me in one of your investigations. I can say I am a cool hand."

"I can see that," said Lee. "Such a man might be very valuable to me some time or other." Privately he was thinking: I would as lief employ an adder! He took a pinch of snuff.

Lee thoroughly disapproved of the house on Henry Street, but it had an undeniable fascination for him. He was fond of dropping in for a while before dinner to chat with the inmates in the game room. A few nights after his talk with Spanish, he happened to be standing alone by the fire when Letty approached him with a bright smile. He had just time to note that her smile had a strained effect when he heard her saying:

"Don't look surprised at what I'm going to say, Mr. Mappin. We are watched."

Lee smiled brightly back at her. "Nothing you could say would make me look surprised, my dear."

"Are you ever at home in the evenings between half past seven and half past nine?"

"I would be if you wanted to see me."

"I do, but I don't want you to put yourself out. I mentioned those hours because I could tell everybody I was going to the movies. We can't talk in this house because if it was suspected that there was any understanding between you and me it would spoil everything."

"How about tonight?" suggested Lee.

"Thanks," she said quickly. "I'll be there." She went on in a slightly raised voice: "I do wish I could persuade you to stay to dinner."

Over her shoulder, Lee saw Spanish approaching. "I'm sorry, my dear, but I have an honest-to-God date tonight."

LEE WAITED FOR HER at home in no little curiosity. She came a little before eight. When Jermyn brought her into the big living room she dropped into a big easy chair and let her head fall against the back. Lee saw that her beautiful face was white and drawn as if from fatigue, and his heart was soft for her. Past experience had taught him that only too often it was the wistful, fragile type like Letty that furnished the material for tragedy.

"Have a small coffee and a liqueur with me," he urged.

She shook her head.

"A highball, then?"

"No, please," she murmured. "I don't want anything. It's so peaceful here. I feel safe."

Lee was deeply moved. "My dear girl!"

Tears gathered under her lowered lids and rolled down her cheeks. "You mustn't . . . you mustn't sympathize with me," she said with a twisted smile, "or I'll begin to bawl. I can't stand sympathy."

Lee bustled around the room affecting to ignore her. "This room is too damned hot!" he grumbled. He flung a window up and presently flung it down again.

Letty in the chair began to laugh weakly. "You're so kind!" she murmured. "So very, very kind! I've never known anything like it!"

"Don't talk that way," said Lee gruffly, "or you'll have me bawling presently."

"My tears don't mean anything," she said. "It's only that I can relax here. I'm under such a strain all the time."

"Tell me about it," said Lee. "And perhaps we can find a way to ease it . . . And cry all you like if it's a relief. I have a whole drawer full of handkerchiefs when yours gives out."

She shook her head. "I'm not going to cry any more. I'll tell you all I can—but I can't tell you everything. You're the first person I ever knew that I felt I could trust."

"My dear child!"

"I've had a rough life. I was born over on San Juan Hill—you know what that's like; where the Irish and the negroes fight in the streets. Most of my childhood was spent in different orphanages."

"You don't show it," said Lee.

"I know I don't," she said with her painful smile. "I've had a hard life but it hasn't made me hard. I wish it had. I'm not a brave woman! I only want to live quiet."

"I thought you were happy with Sieg," suggested Lee.

"I am!" she said quickly. "That is, I love him terribly. I love him too much. That's not exactly the same thing as happiness, is it? Happiness is peace. I never know a moment's peace!"

"Why not?"

"Sieg is too attractive to other women. Nearly every woman flings herself at his head. Even when I am present."

Lee thought of Queenie Deane.

"And Sieg is only human," Letty went on. "He loves flattery as much as any man. I live in dread that one of these women will take him away from me."

Lee said: "He married you because you were different from any woman he had even known. And you're still different."

"Oh, I suppose he would always come back to me," said Letty wearily. "But it would kill me to share him with other women."

Lee pictured the little scene he had witnessed in Le Coq Noir and lowered his eyes to hide the grimness he felt.

"When I married Sieg," Letty continued, "I was hoping that he would be content with a quiet life. He swore to me that he was going straight and I'm sure he means to. But Sieg can't be satisfied to live quietly. He must always have people around him and plenty of excitement. The house in Henry Street is so bad for him! All those convicts start talking about the exciting jobs they have pulled off in the past, and Sieg gets restless. If we could only live among nice people!"

"You're right," said Lee. "This Henry Street scheme is absolutely unworkable. My hope is that it won't be long before Mrs. Cassells sees that for herself and closes the house."

"If only we don't have a smash first!" murmured Letty. ". . . And if she does close the house, what will become of Sieg and me?" she presently added. "Mrs. Cassells is kind, but rich women never stick to anything long."

"If Mrs. Cassells forsakes you, I pledge myself to see that you and Sieg get a fair start," said Lee.

She smiled at him enchantingly. "That's a load off my mind," she said. "Because I know I can depend on what you say."

Lee studied her shrewdly. "This isn't what you came to talk about."

Letty, quickly looking away, shook her head.

"There is something special and particular that is troubling you."

She nodded. "It's Spanish Jack," she said very low.

Lee grunted. "I might have guessed as much. He's a bad egg."

Letty shivered. "He's the worst of all!" she murmured. "He doesn't care what he does. He has neither fear nor pity nor any natural feelings. He's inhuman!"

"What do you know about him?" asked Lee.

"I worked with him at Sam Bartol's for over a year," she said evasively. "He is a man who would stop at nothing."

Lee scowled. "Is he persecuting you?"

She nodded. "I had trouble with him before. He . . . he threatened me. Now he's threatening me again."

"How do you mean, threatening you? Threatening you with what?"

"I can't tell you the whole story, Mr. Mappin. It's too dangerous . . . too dangerous!"

"You said you trusted me, Letty. How can I act intelligently if you don't tell me the whole story?"

Letty began to tremble pitifully. "I *do* trust you, Mr. Mappin. It's not that. It's too dangerous! For you, for all of us. It's not only Spanish himself. He belongs to a gang whose members have sworn to stand by each other. If you succeeded in putting him away, there would be a dozen to take his place!"

"Do you know any of the other members of this gang?"

"I know one of them. His name is Piero Mendes and he lives at 223½ Sands Street, Brooklyn."

Lee considered what she had told him. "Putting him away" had a significant sound. He said: "You must let me be the judge of the danger, Letty. When a danger is faced out, it is never so bad as it seems."

"This is! This is! This is!" she wailed. "I dare not tell you!"

"At least tell me plainly *why* you can't tell me the whole story."

"Because then you would be forced to take a line that would ruin us all. We would be killed!"

Lee shook his head in perplexity. "How did you expect me to help you if I am to be kept in the dark?"

Letty clasped her hands. "Oh, get him out of the house without his suspecting that I have been to see you! To have him there all the time . . . all the time . . . frightens me so I can scarcely know what I am doing. He plays with me like a cat with a mouse! I am afraid of giving something away. If Sieg should suspect . . . !"

"I think I see a way of getting him out of the house temporarily," said Lee slowly. "But when you've quieted down and got a grip on yourself, you must tell me the whole story, and leave it to me to decide how to act. It's not fair to ask me to act in the dark."

"If you can only get him out of the house, I'll do whatever you say!"

"Can you stand him for a couple of days longer? I don't want to act too precipitately, or he might suspect something."

"I can stand anything if I know there is a hope of release!"

THREE NIGHTS LATER Lee had Spanish Jack to dinner in his apartment. Spanish glanced around the wide living room with mixed approval and envy in his pale eyes. He went out on the balcony and looked down at the passing boats in the East River and the lights on the farther shore. Coming in, he said:

"What a swell joint, Mr. Mappin! And no woman around to mess things up. A man needs a place where he can get away from women!"

Lee smiled. "It's all a matter of temperament!"

Spanish was accustomed to the good things of life and Lee took care to give him a superior dinner. He had some of his best wines served. It was clear that Spanish was enjoying himself to the full, yet more than once, when his mouth was full of friendliness and flattery, Lee saw that baleful change take place in his eyes. Lee thought: He hates me. I suppose he hates everybody on earth. There is no room in his breast for any feeling but hatred.

Meanwhile he set himself in friendly guise to draw out his guest. Spanish, perfectly aware of it, talked freely and well, but divulged only the obvious facts about himself. He was born in Rio, he said, and drifted down to Argentina at an early age, where he was first employed in a gambling casino. From Buenos Aires he progressed to Bucharest and, gradually making his way across Europe, finally landed the job of croupier in the swanky Sporting Club at Monte Carlo. When the upheaval took place in Europe, he was forced to return to America, where he had experienced various ups and downs—mostly downs, he said with a wry smile. He had no family complications. "I'm a bird of passage," he said. "I would begin to hate a woman as soon as I was tied to her."

It was a cool evening and Lee had a fire lighted in the living room. As they sat in front of it later with highballs, he said:

"I suppose you've been wondering why I asked you up here tonight."

"I've been hoping there was something good in it for me," Spanish answered, smiling with his lips.

"Well, it may prove to be a beginning. You put the idea into my head by suggesting that you might be able to help me in some of my investigations. I led you to suppose that I rarely undertook an independent investigation. That was not true. I have cases from time to time, but they are all of the sort that calls for absolute secrecy. A breath of publicity would ruin me. Consequently it is easier for me to make out that I am just an amateur."

"I suspected as much," said Spanish.

"You're a smart fellow! . . . You can see, then, that if you are going to be of any help to me, you must act with complete discretion."

"You needn't have any fear of that, Mr. Mappin. If I hadn't learned to keep a close tongue in my head I would have died much younger."

"Good! There's another warning I must give you in advance. It will not be possible for me to take you completely into my confidence. It is a rule that I have adopted toward everybody."

"That's all right with me. You just give me my line and I'll stick to it."

"Something has come up concerning a prominent man in Boston. He is a distinguished member of the Harvard Faculty and bears a blameless reputation. For this reason you must proceed with the greatest care. There is some evidence that he is leading a double life. If he *has* turned to crime, he is a very dangerous man because he possesses one of the most remarkable brains in the country. I want you to keep him under surveillance for a while and find out what he is up to."

"What do you suspect?" asked Spanish.

"I shall not tell you that, because there is no proof. I want you to start with an open mind. It is up to you to lay bare the facts. This man and I are supposed to be friends. For that reason I cannot help you to approach him. You must find your own way. You must not allow him, of course, to suspect that he is being watched, for then your usefulness would be at an end."

"I get you," said Spanish. "What sort of a screw will I get?"

"To start with I'll pay you fifty dollars a week over and above expenses. As soon as you make yourself valuable to me I'll pay more."

"I'm satisfied, Mr. Mappin."

"Call yourself George Alvarez," Lee went on. "That will account for your slight accent. Take a room at a small hotel called the Charles on lower Tremont Street. It is run by a man called Simon Fussell. He's a friend of mine and he will know that you are working for me. He'll help you in any way that will not compromise his position. Your quarry is Professor Henry Stonestreet, the head of the Department of Paleontology at Harvard. Do not, of course, name him in your reports to me."

"When do I start?" asked Spanish.

"The sooner the better."

Spanish glanced at his watch. "I can take the midnight to Boston."

"Very good. I'll give you a note of introduction to Simon Fussell and a hundred dollars on account for expenses. Send me daily reports of progress."

As soon as Spanish had left him, Lee sat down to write to Professor Stonestreet:

> Dear Henry:
> It was necessary for me today to invent a job on the spot for a man in order to get him out of town, and I have taken the liberty of setting him on your trail. I hope you will forgive me for using you as a kind of fall guy. I am hoping you may get a little humor out of the situation.
>
> The fellow will call himself George Alvarez. He's a slick little guy of Brazilian extraction with a face as smooth as wax and keen yellow eyes. You can't help but recognize him when you see him. He's a bad egg. Do not let him guess that you are on to him, but

string him along. If he annoys you in any way, let
me know at once and I'll call him off.

Yours ever,
Lee Mappin.

P.S. Destroy this as soon as you have read it.

# CHAPTER FIVE

INSPECTOR LOASBY, the chief of the New York City detective force, stopped in at Lee's office on his way down to Headquarters. They had been engaged together in investigating various cases in the past and were excellent friends. Today the Inspector's handsome face bore a frown, and when he was seated opposite Lee in the latter's private office he lost no time in coming to the point.

"Mr. Mappin, what is this crazy idea of Mrs. Nick Cassells' to open a home for ex-convicts on Henry Street? Of all the crack-brained, immoral schemes I ever heard of! And I'm told you're in it, too. I must say that's hard to believe of a sensible man like you. How on earth did she rope you in?"

Lee leaned back in his chair with a smile and placed the tips of his fingers together. "A crack-brained scheme, I agree, Inspector. I have pointed that out to the lady with all the force at my command, but uselessly. However, I don't see why you should look on it as immoral."

"Yes, sir, immoral," insisted the Inspector. "Herding a lot of hardened criminals together under the same roof. Making things easy for them. Who can tell what plots may be hatched there?"

"You, of course, believe in making things as hard as possible for released convicts."

Loasby perceived no irony. "Certainly! And above all in keeping them on the move!"

"I assure you that the lady is acting from purely philanthropic motives."

"Sure! Sure! I know these rich and idle women. Morbidly interested in crime! If you agree that it is a crazy scheme, why are you in it?"

"Well, Mrs. Cassells is an old friend, and I want to protect her as far as I can from being victimized. I have a feeling that it won't last long, my friend."

"Certainly it won't last long. You can't house a lot of criminals together without something ugly happening. But what am I going to do in the meantime?"

"I don't see that you're called on to do anything."

"Certainly I've got to do something. It's a public scandal, pampering criminals like that. Even Henry Street is complaining of such neighbors, and they're not too particular."

"What do you propose doing?"

"I don't know. I was hoping that a quiet word to you would be sufficient. It's just a headache. Mrs. Cassells is a rich and influential woman. If I closed up her house the newspapers would get after me like a pack of hounds."

Lee, who knew his Inspector, murmured: "I'm afraid they would."

"Can't you say something to her, Mr. Mappin?"

"I have said plenty, Inspector. It falls on deaf ears!"

"It's only an idle woman's whim!"

"Sandra Cassells has a whim of iron!"

"Well, I'm going to keep a close watch on them, I can tell you," said the irritated Inspector. "If the worst comes to the worst, I'll put a man inside the house. I have plenty of genteel crooks on my payroll."

"Don't do that—yet," urged Lee. "Think how difficult it would make my position. Look here, would it be sufficient for the present if I watched for you? I am a frequent visitor there and my eye is not untrained. I will promise to let you know at once if I see anything going on that looks suspicious."

"Well, that's very decent of you, Mr. Mappin," grumbled the Inspector. "I accept for the present. But just the same, the place ought to be closed up! A house of crime like that!"

"I'll keep in touch with you," said Lee.

When he saw Sandra later in the day, he told her of Loasby's complaints. Sandra was indignant.

"It's none of his business as long as they behave themselves."

"Of course not," said Lee. "Look, here's an idea. Loasby is a handsome fellow and a ready talker. As the chief of the detective force he ought to be a good drawing card at one of your parties. Why not ask him?"

Sandra smiled comprehendingly. "Sometimes you display almost human intelligence! I'll ask him for Monday night."

On Tuesday morning Loasby dropped in at Lee's office again. "I had supper at Brookwood, the Cassells place, last night," he said carelessly.

"Really," said Lee, registering envy. "You *are* favored!"

"Some party!" said Loasby solemnly. "A hundred people or more, sitting at little tables in what they call the conservatory with tropical palms and big ferns and orchids growing all around. Mrs. Cassells made me sit beside her."

"So you made a hit!"

"That house is like a king's palace," Loasby went on. "And such eats and drinks! Beautiful women and dresses and jewels! Mrs. Cassells was the finest lady there! She's a lovely woman, Mr. Mappin. Why didn't you tell me?"

"Well, now you have found it out for yourself."

"Not at all what I expected," said Loasby enthusiastically. "Was as easy with me as if I was her brother. A very intelligent woman, too. Has a real interest in my profession."

SANDRA AND LEE were again dining at Hope House. Thus the establishment on Henry Street had been christened. Sandra went up to Letty's room to powder her nose while Lee drifted back to the game room to talk to the boarders. There were two new men in the house; Johnnie Stabler, the ex-Wall Street clerk, a tall, pale, weedy young man, and Duke Engstrom, an older and rougher specimen with a quiet face that seemed to have been ravaged by passion. Lee didn't care for either man; Johnnie was a feeble creature, always trying to impress you with his superiority, while the brawny Duke Engstrom was never at his ease. He had immense hands that he didn't know what to do with. Duke was Sandra's choice, his quiet, terrible face fascinated and terrified her. He was said to have held up a train single-handed and escaped with two pouches of registered mail.

Hattie and Joe Spencer were also in the room. Lee went from one to another with a word or two of greeting. Each spoke to him with a lowered voice and side glances at the others. Lee was beginning to hate the place. Nobody trusted anybody else. It was impossible to relax in such an atmosphere, to have a good time. It seemed to him that there was an exquisite irony in the name Hope House. He had no part in bestowing it. Sandra's impulse in starting it had been a kindly one, but it just didn't work. Notwithstanding all the fresh paint and bright wallpaper, it seemed to Lee that there was a bad smell in the house—was it the smell of old crimes?

The slender figure of Sandra appeared in the doorway of the game room, clad in one of the elegant black dresses she affected. This one had touches of pale blue. Sandra always wore her prettiest clothes and her jewels when she came to Hope House, "for the psychological effect," she said. That was a kindly impulse also, but a mistaken one, for the boarders, in awe of her expensive presence, became more self-conscious than ever. At the moment Lee perceived from Sandra's widened, shortsighted eyes, helplessly searching the room for him, that something new had happened to upset her. He went to her and she murmured:

"Come into the front room. I must talk to you."

The front room on the ground floor was used for a reception room and office. Sandra carefully closed the door.

"Lee," she said, "I'm afraid we're in for bad trouble."

Lee smiled grimly and refrained from saying: I told you so.

"When I went into Letty's room," she continued, "her handbag was lying on the bureau. It had come open and a letter had partly slipped out. I recognized Blondy's handwriting. Oh, I know he's a favorite of yours, but I have always distrusted him and I thought I had better read it, for all our sakes. I knew Letty was down in the kitchen."

"Well?" said Lee.

"Oh, Lee, there is something going on between those two!" she said distressfully. "It's a good thing I did read it! Letty is *inciting* Blondy to something; I don't know just what!"

"You must be mistaken," said Lee soothingly. "If there was ever a woman in this world who was infatuated with her husband, it is Letty!"

"She is fooling you, Lee! Those quiet women are always the most dangerous. You can't tell what is going on behind their smooth faces!"

"What was in the letter?"

"I didn't dare take it, because Letty would have missed it and the fat would have been in the fire; but I copied it down for you."

She unclasped her hand and Lee saw a crumpled scrap of paper on her palm. Smoothing it out, he read:

> Dear Letty:
> Your letter drove me near crazy. I don't understand it. For God's sake write again and tell me plainly what it's about. I thought that Sieg meant everything in the world to you and so I held myself in and I would always have held myself in if it killed me. Now you write me this letter. Ever since I came out of stir I've been living in hell. I got out of New York to try and forget you but it only made it worse. It's awful not to see you any more. I hate my life. Your face comes between me and everything I do. And now you write me this letter. What am I to think from that? Have I been mistaken about you and Sieg? Oh God! how I love you! It is a pain in my breast that gives me no rest day or night. It saps my strength. I am good for nothing. Write me quick what do you want of me?
>
> > Yours,
> > Blondy.

"I don't understand it!" said Lee, shaking his head. "If ever I saw love in a woman's eyes . . ."

Sandra took the paper from him and prepared to burn it in an ash tray, but Lee recovered it.

"We may need this later. The original will be destroyed. It will be safe in my wallet." He put it away.

"What are we to do?" faltered Sandra. "If Sieg knew about this he would kill Blondy."

"Provided Blondy doesn't kill him first."

"Oh, why did I give him a car? It's only a twelve hours' drive from Cleveland."

"I'll write to him," said Lee. "May not do any good, but it can't do any harm either. I believe in that lad."

"I'll tell you what I'm going to do," said Sandra. "I'm going to engage detectives in Cleveland to watch Blondy and to let me know if he starts for New York."

"Well, that can't do any harm either."

A bell for dinner sounded through the house.

"Come on," said Lee. "We must put a good face on it. Perhaps it's not as bad as we think. Lots of foolish letters are written."

"It's all that woman's fault," said Sandra. "Such women ought to be locked away from men. How can I sit down at table with her and be polite?"

"Watch me," said Lee.

They descended the stairs.

Dinner was a pretty gloomy affair. Lee got out of the house afterward as soon as he could. He wrote a brief letter to Blondy, dispatched it by air mail.

> Dear Blondy:
> Do you remember what I said about getting in a jam? Has it come? If so, give me a chance to talk things over with you before you take any action on your own. Very often when a case seems absolutely hopeless to a young head, an old one can see a way out.
> Always your friend,
>     Lee Mappin.

No answer was ever made to this note.

On the morning after he had sent it, Lee dropped in at Police Headquarters and proceeded to Inspector Loasby's office.

"Loasby," he said, "if you have the right man to put in as a boarder at Hope House, I believe the time has come for it."

"What's the situation, Mr. Mappin?"

Lee put him in possession of the facts as far as he knew them.

"Does it have to be an ex-convict?" asked the Inspector.

Lee said: "I doubt if you've got a good enough actor to play the part."

"You have always underrated my force," said Loasby sorely.

"I'm willing to be shown," said Lee. "If you have a man who can get away with it, send him up to me without loss of time. There are still a couple of vacant rooms at Hope House, and I can get him in. But I don't need to tell you that he will be closely watched. He ought to be a husky guy, too, in case of trouble."

"I'll have him at your office before twelve o'clock," said Loasby.

THE INSPECTOR WAS AS GOOD as his word. The man gave the name of Harry Boker, his age as forty-two. Lee took to him at once, for not only was he a muscular fellow with an air of quiet assurance, but there was a glint of humor in his gray eyes. A little humor wouldn't come amiss at that gloomy dinner table, thought Lee. Boker had a good command of prison slang, which he accounted for by saying he had spent a couple of months in a cell at Sing Sing on police work. Lee spent a couple of hours with Boker, composing the story he was to tell at Hope House and rehearsing him in it.

"You mustn't have come out of Sing Sing now," said Lee. "Sieg Ammon knows the place too well. Are you acquainted with Philadelphia?"

"Sure," said Boker.

"Then you have just been released from Moyamensing Prison, see? and you have come to New York to get a start in fresh surroundings. Your name is George Tappan, but your friends call you Jidge. You're a younger man than the real Tappan, but as none of those people on Henry Street ever saw him, that will be all right.

He died a couple of years ago, shortly after his release from prison, but as he was then living under an assumed name, they can't have heard about that. Ten years ago, Jidge Tappan went to prison for accepting bribes in connection with paving contracts. In fact, I helped to send him there. It was a famous case in its day with widespread ramifications. I wrote it up and if you'll study the book, you can get Jidge Tappan's whole career by heart from the cradle to the grave."

Lee gave Boker—or Tappan—a letter recommending him to Sieg Ammon. Before the day was out he had the satisfaction of hearing from Sieg himself that Tappan had been accepted as a member of the Hope House family.

# CHAPTER SIX

SANDRA CASSELLS AND LEE MAPPIN had got into the habit of dining at Hope House every Wednesday night, and afterward sitting down in the office to hear Sieg Ammon's report for the week and to okay his accounts. There was no reason why Lee should have imposed this duty on himself, since he had been against the project from the start, but he could not bear to let Sandra enter that den (as he called it to himself) alone. In Sandra, along with her worldliness and sophistication, there was a certain innocency that made Lee feel toward her as to a willful little girl who must be protected from the consequences of her own folly. Notwithstanding all the people who surrounded her, Lee doubted if she had a single disinterested friend in the world except himself. She was too rich.

On this particular Wednesday night there were nine people at the dinner table. They now had a young stick-up man to assist Mary in waiting. Lee, looking around at the faces, thought to himself: What a crew! Tappan, who had been in the house a week, had become popular with everybody in the house. Owing to his efforts, the table talk had taken on a more cheerful tone. He told the story of his paving operations in Philadelphia with a sly humor that set them all laughing.

Only Letty's smile was strained and painful. Lee was shocked by the change that had taken place in the girl since he had last seen her. Her make-up stood out in ghastly fashion against the livid pallor of her skin. Her hands were shaking. She scarcely seemed to know what she was doing. Spanish was safe in Boston; Tappan's reports had given Lee no further light on what was happening in the house. Lee watched the girl without appearing to. At moments when she thought she was unobserved, her glance still crept to Sieg's face in the manner that suggested she had utterly lost herself in her husband. Lee was baffled. If that look lies, he said to himself, I shall have to begin at the A.B.C. of my profession again. He determined to have another heart to heart talk with Letty.

After dinner, Lee and Sandra went up to the office to wait for Sieg. A few minutes later the Cassells butler, Dunstan, arrived at the house with a telegram for Sandra. He said:

"I opened it according to instructions, madam, but the contents was such as I didn't think you would want it telephoned, so I brought it down by car."

Sandra, reading the message, bit her lip. She said: "There's no answer, Dunstan. You needn't wait. You did right in bringing this to me."

"Yes, madam. Thank you, madam." He bowed himself out.

Sandra had handed the telegram to Lee. It read:

> Your party left Cleveland at 5 A.M. today in his own car. It is not known which way he was heading. His absence was not discovered until the day shift at the mill came off work this afternoon.

"You can't depend on anybody," said Sandra bitterly. "I've been paying these people a hundred a week and they fell down on the job. Blondy is in New York by this time."

"That would account for Letty's agitation," said Lee.

Sieg came into the room briskly and Lee quietly folded the message and slipped it into his pocket. There was nothing on Sieg's mind. He displayed his usual smiling, self-confident air.

"Where's Letty?" asked Lee.

"She has no head for business," said Sieg smiling. "She's gone to the movies. She'll be back by the time we're through our work."

Lee felt his face growing grim. "What movie?" he asked.

"She didn't say. I suppose it's the neighborhood house down the street."

Sandra said: "Letty shouldn't be out on the streets alone after dark."

"Safest place in the world," said Sieg, smiling. "I have heard you say so yourself." He spread his bills on the desk.

Lee felt that to sit there doing nothing while the time passed would be more than he could bear. Anyhow, the bills were no business of his. "I'm going out for a walk, while you do your work," he said. "I need air."

A brilliant electric sign advertised the motion picture theater two blocks away. Lee paid his way in. It was dark inside and he could distinguish only a few faces sitting close to the aisle. He sat down far in front and waited while a distorted picture unrolled itself in front of him. He never knew what it was. At the end of the feature, when the lights went up, he rose and studied the faces in the audience row by row. Letty was not in the house. He hadn't expected to find her there.

He returned to Hope House. Sandra and Sieg were still at work in the office. "Has Letty come back?" he asked. But Sandra's face had told him she had not without his asking.

Sieg glanced at his watch. "Not time for her yet," he said.

When the bills were okayed they had a drink. The suspense was cruelly hard on Sandra. Her hands began to tremble as Letty's had done earlier, and Lee was afraid that she might blurt out something that would precipitate a catastrophe.

When ten o'clock came and went, Sieg began to grow uneasy. "She never stayed as late as this," he said. "She has had more than enough time to see the program through. I'll go down to the theater and walk home with her."

When he had left the house, Lee urged Sandra to go home. "There is nothing you can do here."

She shook her head. "I can't go until I know what has happened."

In a quarter hour Sieg was back. He was worried now. "Has she come home?" he demanded.

"No."

Sieg gripped the back of a chair for support. "I can't understand it," he said brokenly. "She wasn't in the theater. I went in to make sure. The ticket seller knows Letty but she had already gone home. Letty must have gone to some other theater." He ran out of the house distractedly.

"Should we tell him about Blondy's letter?" asked Sandra.

"No!" said Lee quickly. "Let that come out through other sources."

They spent another wretched half hour. When Sieg came in again he was like a broken man. He did not ask if Letty had returned; a look in their faces was sufficient. He dropped into a chair and covered his face.

"She's gone!" he groaned.

"What have you learned?"

Sieg didn't hear. "Oh, God, if I've lost her I'm done for!" he said hoarsely. "Letty was everything to me! She made me go straight. She gave me something to live for!"

"Why do you say you've lost her?"

Sieg lifted a tormented face. "I found the ticket seller. She told me Letty did not go in tonight. Then I walked the streets not knowing where to look. I met McArdle, the cop who patrols our street. He told me . . ." Sieg clutched his hair as if he would tear it out. "He told me Letty got in a car with a man and drove away! . . . I thought . . . I thought he was pulling my leg. I laughed at him. But his story was so detailed I had to believe it. I wanted to kill him then . . ."

"What was his story?"

"God! it drives me mad! . . . He said . . . he said he had seen this car waiting for an hour in Scammell Street just off Henry. He noticed it because it was a fine new car, a maroon-color Chevvy convertible with a khaki top."

"Did he get the license number?"

"No. He thought nothing of it. He never looked at the license. . . . There was a man sitting in it, but the top was up and he didn't get a good look at his face. . . . At about half past seven—that would be just after she left the house—Letty came along and got in and they drove away! She expected to find the car there, he said. She looked scared . . ."

"Funny he didn't take the number."

"No. If Letty was stepping out it wasn't none of his business, he said. . . . Letty! Letty! Letty! I can't understand it! I thought she was crazy about me. I made her happy. She never looked at another man. I thought I knew her! Oh God, I would have staked my life on Letty! That's why I married her . . ."

Sandra could not bear to look at the broken man. "I'll go," she murmured to Lee. "I can't help him now."

"I'll see you to the car," said Lee.

On her way out, Sandra laid a hand on Sieg's shoulder. Her tender heart was torn by his cries of pain; her eyes filled. "Don't give up," she said. "There may be some perfectly natural explanation. After all, it's not late. Perhaps she met a friend . . ."

"She has no friends in this part of town," groaned Sieg. "No! The man was waiting for her!"

Sandra's words of comfort sounded halfhearted in her own ears because she knew they were false. She hastened out of the room. Lee followed.

As she dropped back in her car, she said: "Call me up whenever you hear anything. At any hour. I shan't be able to sleep."

Before returning to the house, Lee entered the drugstore at the corner and, after some telephoning from a booth, succeeded in running down Inspector Loasby at a smoker on Washington Heights. He told Loasby the story.

"Well, they're free, white and twenty-one," said Loasby. "It's not a case for the police."

"You'd better look into it," said Lee, "or worse will follow."

"Very well. I'll send out an alarm."

"Keep it out of the newspapers."

"Sure!"

"Blondy is still carrying New York license plates." Lee gave Loasby the number. He then returned to Sieg Ammon. The young man was pacing the office in a half-crazed state. He alternately mourned the loss of Letty and cursed the man who had taken her from him.

"By God! as soon as I get a clue I'll follow them! I'll follow them to the ends of the earth. And I'll kill him! I'll kill him slowly."

"That wouldn't win Letty back," suggested Lee dryly.

Sieg, paying no attention, continued to rage and to describe the fiendish tortures he would inflict on the man who had wronged him. Suddenly he said: "Maybe it was Blondy!"

"What put that into your head?" said the startled Lee.

"Letty told me once that Blondy was crazy about her. But, she said, he hid it so close it was only by her woman's instinct that she knew it. Blondy was so loyal to me, she said, there was nothing to fear from him. And I believed her . . . By God! if it's Blondy . . . !"

"Wait and see," said Lee.

For two hours Lee bore patiently with his ravings. Shortly before two o'clock, the telephone rang with startling suddenness. Sieg leaped to the instrument, wild with eagerness.

"Yes, this is Sieg Ammon. Who are you? . . . Well, what do you want? What? . . . Well, spill it! Spill it! What has happened? . . ."

With a wild cry, Sieg started back, dropping the instrument and clapping his hands to his head. "No! No! No!"

Lee picked up the telephone. "What is it?"

Loasby's voice came over the wire. "That you, Mr. Mappin? Thank God! The young fellow sounded out of his head."

"Can you blame him? What has happened?"

"Well, it's bad enough. I'm speaking from Police Headquarters in White Plains. The body of a young woman has just been brought in here. She was picked up alongside Wilkens Avenue about eight miles north of the city line. Had evidently been thrown out of a car. She has a bullet hole through her head. The doctor says she has been dead about four hours."

Lee moistened his dry lips. "Are you sure it's Mrs. Ammon? Describe her."

"A natural ash blonde, about twenty-five years old; five feet eight tall; slenderly made; weight about one hundred and twenty-five. Clothes of expensive materials; a pale green evening dress

with a tight-fitting jacket over it and over that a black wool top
coat. No hat . . ."

"That's enough," said Lee heavily. "It's what she was wearing
when she went out. Any trace of the car?"

"Not yet," said Loasby. "I'll keep you advised."

Lee hung up. He could hardly take in what had happened. Sieg
was crouched in a chair with his arms wrapped around his head,
moaning endlessly: "Letty! . . . Letty! . . . Letty!"

Everybody else in the house had been in bed for some hours
except Tappan. Lee found him in his room reading. Lee told him
briefly what had happened and, bringing him downstairs, left Sieg
in his care.

"Try to get him to go to bed," said Lee.

Stopping at a Western Union office on his way home, Lee sent
a telegram.

> George Alvarez
> Hotel Charles
> Boston
>
> Return by first train and get in touch with me.
> Mappin.

A couple of hours later, Jermyn aroused him from sleep to hand
him the answer.

> Amos Lee Mappin
> East 54th Street
> New York
>
> Alvarez checked out early this morning. Told me it
> was by your orders.
> Simon Fussell.

# CHAPTER SEVEN

AT DAWN THE MAROON CONVERTIBLE CAR was found standing alongside a highway near Utica, New York. The driver had run her out of gas. The top was down when found; there were plentiful blood stains on the steering wheel and the upholstery; the gun with which Letty had presumably been shot was still lying on the floor. It had been discharged once. An hour later, Blondy Farren was picked up wandering blindly in the fields near by. There was blood on his hands, on his clothes; he was like a man completely distraught and could give no coherent account of what had happened. Detectives were dispatched to Utica to bring him back. He was expected to arrive at Headquarters in White Plains at five in the afternoon.

Early in the morning Lee and Sieg Ammon drove up to White Plains for the purpose of identifying the body. Sandra met them in the little mortuary. Lee begged her not to subject herself to this ordeal, but she insisted. Every detail of the affair had a gruesome fascination for her.

"I feel partly responsible," she said.

When the sheeted body was wheeled in and the cover drawn down a little, a glance into the beautiful waxen face was sufficient.

"That is Mrs. Ammon," said Lee. He marveled at the serenity of the dead face. The unfortunate, harried girl had found the peace she longed for in life. When the attendants started to wheel her out, Sieg flung himself across the body with wild cries.

"Letty! Letty! Letty! I can't let you go!" When he was dragged away, he collapsed on a bench.

Lee made a further examination of Letty's wound in private. She had been shot in the right temple. Deep powder burns in the skin surrounding the wound indicated that the gun had been discharged close to her head. The bullet, after having passed through her brain obliquely, had been found lodged under the scalp on the other side. No further autopsy was considered necessary. It was a bullet of .25 caliber. Letty's pretty clothes were soiled with blood and earth. Her handbag was missing.

They were back in Henry Street before eleven o'clock. All the boarders were gathered in the game room talking over what had happened in subdued voices. Little Hattie Oliver's eyes were as big as saucers. Drawing Lee aside, she whispered:

"I must speak to you outside." In the hall she said with her old head nodding like a china mandarin's: "Spanish Jack was here an hour ago."

"Hey?" exclaimed the startled Lee. "What was he after?"

"Nobody saw him but me, Mr. Mappin. He must have let himself in with his latch key. He knew everybody would be in the back of the house. It was just by chance that I was in my room which is next to Letty's. I heard somebody moving in her room. Nobody had any right to go in there but Mary Kennedy, and I knew it wasn't Mary because it moved too soft. It moved like a thief. I heard a bureau drawer pulled out. I was afraid to go and look. I set my door open a crack and waited. And bye and bye Spanish come out. He run down the stairs as quiet as a cat and let himself out the front door."

Lee said: "Sieg must know about this." He called Sieg out into the hall. "Sieg, Spanish Jack has been here while we were out."

"What of it?" growled Sieg apathetically.

"Judging from his actions, he was up to no good. When he went away, did he surrender his latch key?"

"Sure."

"Then he has had a duplicate made. He appears to have been ransacking Letty's things. Come and see if anything is missing."

Sieg clapped his hands to his head. "God! don't ask me to go through Letty's things now! I couldn't bear it!"

"If we have a thief to deal with, we've got to know it."

Sieg was persuaded to go upstairs. When the first drawer of Letty's bureau was pulled open, the contents seemed to be in good order, but Sieg said at once: "Somebody's been in here. Letty would spend an hour tidying it up and when she left it, it was like a pin."

"Look over her valuables," said Lee. "You must know pretty well what she possessed. Let me know if anything is missing."

Letty's valuables were not very many nor very costly. Sieg reported that so far as he knew nothing had been taken. Nor had the drawers in his own chiffonier been disturbed.

"Then it was something else he was after," said Lee.

"If you ask me, old Hattie is loco," growled Sieg. "Spanish, whatever you may say, is no sneak thief."

From the office downstairs, Lee telephoned to Loasby at Headquarters and told him what had occurred. "I happen to know that one of Spanish Jack's best friends is living at 223½ Sands Street, Brooklyn, under the name of Piero Mendes. You may be able to pick Spanish up there."

"Is it your idea that this has got something to do with the girl's murder, Mr. Mappin?"

"I don't know."

"How could it? There's a perfect case against Blondy Farren."

"Just the same, this ought to be investigated."

"Okay, Mr. Mappin. Just to oblige you, I'll send men right over."

In quarter of an hour, Loasby called back to say that Spanish Jack had been found in the Sands Street flat of his friend. The coming of the police had given him an unpleasant surprise, Loasby said, but he had submitted quietly. Thinking that Mr. Mappin might want to have the premises searched, Loasby had ordered his men to hold the prisoner there until they could get over.

"Very good!" said Lee. "I'll be with you in five minutes."

Lee and the Inspector made fast time across Brooklyn Bridge in a police car with a siren. Sands Street starts at the Brooklyn end of the bridge. On the top floor of a cheap flat above a hardware store, they found Spanish, his friend Piero, and Piero's girl. The last two were a coarsely handsome young couple who described themselves as teachers of the tango and the rumba. All three had regained their equanimity. Spanish greeted Lee impudently.

"How are you, Mr. Mappin?"

"What are you doing in New York?" asked Lee mildly.

"Why were you so anxious to get me out of New York?" countered Spanish.

"I don't understand you."

"Oh, yes you do!" sneered Spanish. "I don't like to hear you lie, Mr. Mappin. I have too much respect for you. You ordered me to get next to Professor Stonestreet, didn't you? Well, I obeyed your orders. I obeyed them a little better than you counted on. I examined the private letters in his desk and I found what you had written to him about me!"

Lee, silently cursing the Professor's failure to destroy his letter, let it go with a shrug.

"You haven't answered my question," sneered Spanish.

His impudence was too much for Loasby. "Shut your mouth!" commanded the Inspector. "It's not your place to ask Mr. Mappin questions."

Spanish laughed silently.

"Has he been searched?" asked Lee.

"Yes, sir. In his pants pockets all we found was a handful of loose change and a latch key."

"That's the key to the Henry Street house," said Lee. "Mark it and keep it for evidence."

"In his breast pocket we found a wallet containing fifty-four dollars in bills and a note which refers to you, Mr. Mappin. Nothing else."

"Let me see the note, please."

It was in Letty's handwriting. It consisted of four lines only, and bore neither date nor salutation.

> I shall never tell what I know as long as you stay away
> from me. If anything happens to me I have fixed it
> so that Mr. Mappin will be informed of what took
> place, and you can't prevent it.
>                                             Letty.

Lee was baffled. All the policemen were looking at him and he was forced to appear wise and knowing. "An important piece of evidence," he said. "With your permission, I will keep it for further study, Inspector."

"Certainly, Mr. Mappin."

"Much good may it do you!" sneered Spanish with his soundless laugh.

"Shall we search the place?" asked Loasby.

"Yes."

"You can't do that!" blustered Piero. "It's my place. There's no charge against me! You have no warrant."

"You're harboring a thief," said Loasby with a hard smile. "I'll take a chance on it."

"You haven't proved me a thief," said Spanish.

"You were seen and heard ransacking Letty's room," said Lee. "That will be sufficient evidence."

Spanish was momentarily taken aback. "I didn't take anything," he growled.

Spanish, Piero and the girl were lined up in three chairs in the kitchen placed too far apart for anything to be passed between them, and left under the watchful eye of a plainclothesman. Lee, Loasby and the other detective searched the three rooms.

"What do you expect to find?" asked Loasby.

"That's the rub," said Lee dryly. "I don't know. . . . A letter, perhaps. Show me anything that does not seem to belong here, anything that does not explain itself."

Evidently the dancing business had not been too good lately and the flat was but meagerly furnished. Nothing was locked away. A couple of trunks full of theatrical costumes delayed them for a while, but they contained nothing except what went with the costumes. Spanish Jack's suitcase was under the sofa in the living room. Its Contents gave Lee nothing to go on. There was not a scrap of writing anywhere in the flat. In short, the search was futile.

When Lee returned to the kitchen, Spanish asked him with a grin, "Well, did you find what you were looking for, Mr. Mappin?"

Lee made no reply.

"I'm afraid you're slipping, sir. You're slipping badly. Your numerous admirers will be disappointed in you."

"Shut your mouth!" shouted Loasby. "This isn't doing you any good! . . . You come along with us!"

"With pleasure, Inspector!"

On the return to Manhattan, Loasby and Lee occupied the rear seat of the big police car. Spanish sat on one of the folding seats in front of them with a detective beside him, and the second detective rode with the chauffeur. The day was warm and the windows fully open. They bowled across Brooklyn Bridge at a high rate of speed. When they were over the middle of the river at the highest point in the arc of the bridge, Spanish stooped down to scratch his ankle. When he straightened up he had a thin, small key in his hand to which was attached a shipping tag with writing on both sides.

Lee, Loasby and the detective flung themselves on Spanish simultaneously, but they were too late; they only collided with each other. Spanish half rose, swung his right arm; the key with its fluttering tag sailed over the steel parapet of the bridge and went dropping into the river far below. Lee had glimpsed the writing on one side of the tag. It read: "For Mr. Mappin." On the other side were several lines of writing, too small for him to decipher a word.

Spanish dropped back in his seat and laughed in his silent fashion. It was a bitter pill for Lee and the Inspector to swallow.

Lee left them at Headquarters. From the expression of Loasby's face, he guessed that Spanish was due to undergo a severe sweating; very reprehensible, of course, but after all it was none of his business. He said nothing.

# CHAPTER EIGHT

WHEN LEE RETURNED to Henry Street, Sieg roused himself to ask many shrewd and anxious questions about the relations between Letty and Spanish. Lee could throw little light on the subject. Sieg was greatly disturbed to learn that Letty had been to Lee to confess that she lived in terror of Spanish.

"Why didn't she come to me?" Sieg demanded. "I was her natural protector."

"That's easy," said Lee. "She didn't want to involve you in a fight with Spanish."

"That little rat!" said Sieg contemptuously. "I could take him on with one hand!"

"Surely!" said Lee. "And afterward he'd shoot you in the back."

"I can't understand it!" said Sieg scowling. "I thought Spanish was my friend. What could there have been between Letty and him?"

"Whatever it was," said Lee, "no blame attaches to Letty. She was all yours!"

Sieg flung up his arms. "God! what does it matter now!" he cried. "She's gone!"

Later in the afternoon Loasby called for Lee and Sieg in the big, red police car and they returned to White Plains to await the coming of Blondy. There was little talk during the long drive. Sieg had relapsed into torpor; Lee and the Inspector were busy with their own thoughts. Loasby remarked briefly that he had not got anything out of Spanish. At the Westchester police office, they found Sandra waiting for them. Lee, Sieg and Sandra sat down in the outer office while Loasby conferred with the local chief.

Blondy was brought in between two stalwart policemen. Grief, remorse or other passions had so changed him that he was hardly recognizable. He looked at his friends without seeing them. The police had put him into clean clothes for the railway journey, and were saving the bloody ones for evidence. At sight of Blondy, Sieg sprang up with a bellow of rage.

"I'll kill him! I'll kill him!"

A couple of policemen flung their arms around Sieg and held him. Blondy never even flinched from the attack, but only looked at Sieg with a strange remoteness, as if the outburst had nothing to do with him. He was led into the private office and Sieg dropped back in his chair.

Lee was the only one of their party to be admitted to the examination. In addition to the two men who had brought Blondy, Inspector Loasby and the local chief were in the room, and a third officer to take down Blondy's statement. The privilege of interrogating the prisoner was yielded to the City Inspector. Lee took a seat in a corner of the room where he could watch and listen without being conspicuous. Loasby, behind a flat-topped desk, surveyed Blondy from hand to foot before addressing him. Blondy bore it with complete indifference.

"Are you ready to make a statement?" asked Loasby.

Blondy moistened his lips. "I'll try. My head isn't very clear."

"Have you been drinking?"

"Not since last night."

"Well, tell your story."

Blondy put a hand to his forehead. "You'll have to question me," he said dully. "My head don't feel right. I can't tell a straight story."

"Why did you shoot Letty Ammon?"

"I didn't shoot her."

"Don't waste my time," said Loasby coldly. "Come clean or go to a cell. Do you expect me to believe that?"

Blondy sighed. "It's nothing to me whether you believe it or not. I didn't shoot her."

"How did you get blood on your hands? On your clothes?"

"When I found her shot I took her in my arms. I was wild."

"When you found her, you say. Where were you when she was shot?"

"Right there on the seat beside her. I had fallen asleep or passed out. I can't remember anything."

All the policemen laughed a little. "Is that the best story you can tell?" said Loasby. "That old gag!"

"I loved her," said Blondy, very low. "It would be impossible for me to hurt Letty."

"That's what they all say," said Loasby. "Where did it happen?"

Blondy passed a hand wearily over his face. "I can't tell you exactly. When I came to myself the car was standing by a house. The house had been burned out recently. It was deserted. The car had been run into these private grounds. The highway was fifty yards away."

"What about Letty?"

Blondy's head went down. "She was leaning over on the wheel. Her hands were caught under her. She was dead. She was cold already."

"Do you mean to say her hands were still gripping the wheel?"

"No. Her hands were turned palms up."

Loasby smiled contemptuously. "And this happened while you slept beside her?"

"That's right."

"What made you fall asleep or pass out or whatever it was?"

"I don't know. I had been drinking some. But not enough for that. I never passed out like that before."

"What did you do then?"

"For a while I didn't know what I was doing. When my head cleared, my first thought was to get help. I shoved Letty over and took the wheel. I drove out on the highway. I didn't know where we were. The sky was cloudy and no stars were showing. I started driving blind. My head wasn't right; I can only remember what happened in spots. In a little while, when I went over a hill, I saw by the reflection in the sky that the city was behind me, so I turned around and drove the other way. Then when I got near the city it suddenly came over me that I would be charged with shooting Letty. And what kind of a story could I tell? Nobody would believe me. Not with my record. So I turned around again and drove away from the city. I was out of my head, I guess. I stopped the car. I put Letty out beside the road. I drove on blind until I ran out of gas. That's all."

"You had a gun?"

"Yes. Letty had asked me to bring it."

Loasby's eyebrows ran up. "For God's sake, why?"

"I don't know. She said there was a danger threatening her. That was enough for me."

"Where was the gun when you, as you claim, passed out?"

"At first it was in my pocket. Letty asked me if I had it and I showed it to her. Then I put it in the compartment on the dashboard."

Loasby exhibited a gun on the desk. "Is this it?"

Blondy gave it an indifferent glance. "How do I know? I reckon so. It was a gun like that."

"Start at the beginning now," suggested Loasby, "and tell us how you first became acquainted with Letty."

"It was over two years ago," said Blondy in his toneless voice. "Sieg and I met her when we went to work for Sam Bartol over in Jersey. Letty worked in Sam's place. They called her Anita Western over there. Her real name was Letty Stair. She was so different from the other girls there, different from any girl we had ever known, and Sieg and I both fell for her hard. But of course she couldn't see anybody in the world but Sieg, and I never said anything to her. For near two years she waited for Sieg while he was doing his stretch in Sing Sing. I was released a month ahead of him and I looked her up. I saw right away that she hadn't changed any; all she wanted was to hear about Sieg. So I never said nothing. We talked about Sieg all the time. I was crazy about Sieg myself. Always had been up to now. That was the worst of it. Just my bad luck, I thought, that I had to fall for my pal's girl."

"Just a moment," interrupted Loasby. "You said 'up to now.' What has changed your feeling toward Sieg?"

"Well, I got the idea from Letty that he had been ill-treating her. Nothing definite."

"Proceed with your story."

"As soon as Sieg was released from Sing Sing he married her. I stood up with them. It was like . . . like watching my own funeral. I thought I would get over it, but I didn't. She spoiled me for other women. It was worse after they got married—being with them all the time. Mr. Mappin saw how it was with me, I guess. He's been a good friend to me. He got me a job out in Cleveland, and I was glad to take it. But I couldn't forget her."

"What brought you back to New York?"

"Letty wrote to me."

"In answer to a letter of yours?"

"No. I had never written to her up till then. Her letter was out of a clear sky. I had quieted down some, and it got me all stirred up again."

"What did she say?"

"It was only a short letter. All mixed up. I couldn't rightly get the hang of it except that she was in some kind of trouble and wanted help."

"And that brought you to New York?"

"No. I wrote to her first, asking her for God's sake to tell me plainly what was the matter and what she wanted of me."

"And then?"

"She wrote again and asked me to come. It was just as wild as the other. Said she'd be waiting for me at the corner of Henry and Scammell Streets at half past seven Wednesday night. That was last night. So I was there."

Lee intervened at this point. "Inspector, may I ask a question?"

"Certainly, Mr. Mappin. As many as you like."

"Blondy," said Lee, "have you got the two letters she wrote you?"

"No, sir. She asked for them back again when we started out last night. She put them in her handbag."

Lee addressed the Inspector: "And the handbag is missing?"

Loasby smiled. "Unfortunately for the prisoner, yes." He shot a forefinger at Blondy. "What did you do with her handbag after her death?"

"Me?" said Blondy with an astonished glance. "I never saw it after."

Loasby sneered. "That's just too bad! . . . Go on with your story."

Lee quietly put in: "Still, she *did* go to meet him."

Said Loasby: "Very likely he had threatened her with harm if she didn't."

Blondy plucked up a little spirit. "That's foolish!"

"Stick to your story!" said the Inspector angrily.

"She was excited and nervous when she got in the car," Blondy continued. "She was shaking like a leaf. She said: 'Drive away! Drive away quick!' 'Where to?' I asked her. 'Anywhere!' she said. 'That cop on the corner knows me. What a rotten piece of luck!'"

"The patrolman's name is McArdle," put in Lee.

Loasby made a note of it. "Go on!"

"I drove north, uptown," said Blondy. "When I tried to get her to talk she only burst into tears. So I gave her time to quiet down. I never did understand women. She said she wanted to drive out in the country and I suggested driving over the Queensboro Bridge to Long Island, but she said no, we could get into the real country quicker by driving north. So I kept on through the Park, up Seventh Avenue and on up through the Bronx. She still wouldn't tell me what was the matter and I got sore. 'I've driven seven hundred miles to find out,' I said, 'and I'm entitled to know what it's all about.' But it only made her cry. I couldn't stand to see Letty cry. I was half crying myself."

Blondy had warmed to his story now and required no further prompting. His eyes were fixed on Lee as he talked as if he felt sure of finding understanding there. The policemen did not exist for him. "I couldn't tell you everything that was said. She would say such things as she wished she was dead; she was the unhappiest woman in the world, and all like that, but nothing I could get hold of. I asked her plain if Sieg was mistreating her and she would only say she loved him still, she couldn't help herself. What was I to make of that? Another time I mind she said she wished we could drive on and on forever and never turn back, and I said that would be all right with me. I told her I loved her. I never told her that before. I told her I'd cut off my right arm to serve her, and I wasn't counting on any return either. Then she cried and cried and told me I mustn't say such things because it only made matters worse. We were getting out in the country now. I pulled out of the road in a quiet spot and she let me take her in my arms and kiss her. It was the first time . . ."

"You were happy then?" said Loasby sarcastically.

Blondy glanced at him somberly. "Nothing to it," he said with a kind of contempt. He looked at Lee again for understanding. "I could see she was in bad trouble of some kind, but it didn't have anything to do with loving me. It wasn't me that she wanted. A man can tell. She lay cold in my arms. She was glad when I let her go. Letty was a one-man woman. Sieg was her man."

"And that's why you killed her," suggested Loasby.

"I didn't kill her," said Blondy. "I could easier have killed myself."

"Go on with your story."

"Well, Letty asked me if there wasn't a big roadhouse called Schanze's near where we were. She said she wanted a drink. I knew Schanze's and I took her there. It wasn't like Letty to ask for a drink. God knows, I didn't want to go into that place with all the lights and the noise and the crowd, but she said she wanted a drink, so we parked the car in the yard and went in. We had a couple of drinks. I was uneasy in that place because there was a woman came in who knew us and she was watching us."

"Who was that?" asked Loasby.

"Her name is Queenie Deane; she sings at Le Coq Noir."

Lee pricked up his ears. "What was she doing up in Westchester County?"

"How do I know? That was about eight-thirty. She don't go on in her show until midnight."

"Why were you afraid of her?"

"She's a troublemaker. She and Sieg Ammon were teamed up in Chicago a few years ago. Queenie was crazy about Sieg, and may be still for all I know. All the women are."

"Well, go on."

"After she came, I got out of Schanze's as quick as I could. It was a mild night and Letty said to put the top down, so I did, and we drove on. At McGovern's place she wanted to stop again. Seemed like it was a relief to her to get into one of those joints; I had to hold myself in when there were people around. We had a couple more drinks. Letty swallowed hers like an old hand. I never saw her do that before. 'Helps me to forget!' she said. I mind saying to her in McGovern's: 'Letty, why don't we keep on driving until we get to Ohio? I don't know what kind of a jam you're in, but I'll save you from it if a man can. And you don't have to take me, either. You'll still be as free as air!'"

Blondy seemed to have forgotten that he had listeners. "She shook her head and smiled. God! what a smile! Like a knife through my breast. 'No can do, Blondy,' she said. 'For God's sake, what *are* we going to do,' I said. She asked me what time it was—she was always asking the time. Nine-thirty, it was then, and she said, still smiling: 'An hour of forgetfulness, Blondy, then we part!' And then she said: 'Do you know why I sent for you, Blondy?' And I said, 'No.' And she said: 'I wanted to restore my belief in human nature' . . ."

Blondy looked across at Lee. "What do you make of that, Mr. Mappin?" he asked pitifully. "I can't make nothing of it."

Lee shook his head.

Blondy continued: "So we drove on and when we came to that big joint they call the White Goose, Letty wanted to stop again. I ordered three rounds in that place. Letty wouldn't drink hers."

"You said she wanted to stop."

"She did. But when the drinks came she wouldn't take hers. I drank mine and hers, too."

"That would be six slugs," said Loasby grimly. "And you had had four before. And do you still say you weren't drunk?"

"If I was, I wasn't aware of it," Blondy said indifferently. "I felt as sober then as I do now. I don't think I was drunk because when a man is as worked up and excited as I was, whisky don't have any effect on him."

"Go on."

"Letty wanted to drive, so I said okay. She asked me what road we were on and I didn't know, so we stopped to read the name on a lamppost. It was Bicknell Avenue . . ." Blondy's voice faltered. "That's about all. Letty said, . . . Letty said: 'If I could have loved a man like you, Blondy, we would have been good to each other. And it wouldn't have come to this!' 'Come to what?' I said. But she never answered me . . . That's all I can remember."

For an hour longer, Loasby went over the story point by point with the stabbing forefinger for emphasis. With all the skill of his long experience in cross-examination, he gained nothing by it. Blondy stuck to what he had said in every particular. His apathetic air was his defense. He didn't appear to care whether or not he was believed.

"You threatened Letty," stormed the Inspector. "You wrote her that if she didn't meet you, you'd lay for Sieg Ammon and shoot him."

"That's silly," said Blondy. "I had nothing against Sieg. Sieg was my pal. Sieg didn't take her from me. She was always his. For Letty I didn't exist as a man."

"You cared nothing about that," said Loasby, "so you could enjoy her once."

Blondy looked at him with contempt. "Then why didn't I enjoy her last night? I could have."

"Don't bandy words with me! I'm asking the questions . . . Do you realize that you are faced by the chair?"

"The sooner the better for me," murmured Blondy. "Letty's gone."

"You drove into those private grounds to accomplish your purpose."

"I told you Letty was at the wheel. I didn't know that place. When I came out into the highway afterward I drove up and down like a crazy man."

Finally, Loasby gave up and Blondy was taken away to a cell. The Inspector lit a cigarette.

"It's an open and shut case," he said. "We'll send him to the chair as easy as rolling over in bed! His own story is enough to convict him. He was mad about the girl and he killed her."

Lee had to admit to himself that it had the features of the classical crime of passion; still he was not satisfied. In Blondy's story there were too many curious and inexplicable details. These details were not of the sort that could help Blondy; many of them were damaging; nor were they the sort of things that a man would naturally invent. Suppose, then, that Blondy was telling the truth—or most of the truth. What was the explanation of Letty's extraordinary behavior? It sounded as if she had been leading Blondy on—only to be killed herself. The letter from Blondy to Letty, that Lee had seen, bore out that theory.

Was the fear that Letty had expressed to Blondy during their drive her fear of Spanish? Spanish was supposed to be safe in Boston, but he might have threatened to return. Since he had left Boston in the morning, he had had ample time to be on hand at the spot where the shot was fired. Suppose Spanish had forced Letty to agree to an assignation in the grounds of the deserted house, and Letty had taken Blondy there to protect her from Spanish and, if necessary, to shoot the man who made her life a burden to her. This would account for Letty's concern to make sure that Blondy had a gun.

This theory had a plausible sound and Lee for a while turned it over in his mind, only to reject it in the end. If Blondy and Letty had come upon Spanish at the meeting place, and there had been a fight and Letty shot, perhaps by accident, what reason on earth could Blondy have for concealing the truth? His story of having "passed out" was hard to believe. If he had passed out, why should Letty have driven him to the spot where the dangerous Spanish was waiting? At this point Lee flung up his hands, figuratively speaking. No piece of his puzzle fitted any other piece. He had to search for additional pieces before the main design would begin to shape itself.

# CHAPTER NINE

ADDITIONAL EVIDENCE piled up against Blondy. The bullet extracted from the dead woman's skull was proved to have been fired from the gun found lying on the floor of the murder car. And through its serial number this gun was established as belonging to Blondy. Blondy's fingerprints were on it.

"That last fact doesn't advance you any," Lee pointed out to Loasby, "because Blondy has already stated that he handled the gun when showing it to Letty."

"I doubt if she ever saw the gun until it was fired."

"The girl might have killed herself," suggested Lee. "That would account for her interest in the gun. And certainly Blondy's story suggests that she was in a desperate frame of mind."

"If true," said Loasby dryly. "Hardly likely the girl would kill herself and leave Blondy to take the rap."

"No, it's not likely, but there are a lot of things in this case that are still unexplained."

"If the girl had turned it on herself, her prints would be on the gun. She was not wearing gloves when she was found."

"That's right."

"Or if anybody else had handled the gun there would be other prints."

"So it would seem. Are you having a search made for Letty's handbag along the roads? You should offer a substantial reward for the return of the handbag in case it has been picked up. I have a feeling that the explanation of this case would be found in that handbag."

"Assuming that we do not already know the explanation," said Loasby with a smile. "Make your mind easy; I am not overlooking the handbag."

As a matter of fact, the handbag was not found, and the police, satisfied that they already had a complete case against Blondy, did very little further work on it. Lee pursued his own private investigation. Loasby did not resent it, because he assumed that if Lee was going to write up the case later, he needed all the details he could dig up. Spanish was held for the time being on a charge of unlawful entry.

By the next morning the murder car had been brought back to White Plains and was stored in the police garage. As far as possible, it was left in the exact state in which it had been found. Lee was on hand early to examine it. The police ran it out in the yard to give him plenty of light.

He saw at once that it was the maroon convertible coupé that he had helped Blondy to buy. Quite a lot of blood had dropped on the steering post and had run down to form a little pool on the floor. This confirmed Blondy's statement that Letty was sitting at the wheel when she was shot. She had been shot in the right temple, that is to say, the side on which Blondy said he was sitting, but that fact by itself didn't prove anything. The car, it could be assumed, was standing at the moment she was shot; if Blondy *had* passed out, anybody could have reached past him and shot the girl. Lee tried to reconstruct the scene. Letty had fallen forward on the wheel and had died instantly, according to the medical examiner. Her hands were caught under her with the palms turned upward. That was a detail which Lee could not account for under any hypothesis. Yet surely Blondy could not have thought of such an odd little detail unless it was something he had seen. The left front fender of Blondy's car was scraped and bent.

The police assured Lee that at the time the car was found there were no fingerprints anywhere upon it except those of Blondy and Letty herself. Blondy's suitcase was in the luggage compartment;

it contained nothing but a change of clothing and a man's toilet articles. In the little locker on the dash he found maps of Ohio and New York state, showing Blondy's route to the East, also a map of New York City with a penciled cross marking the corner of Henry and Scammell Streets.

The car had not been driven far since it was purchased, and the imprint of the tires was still fresh and sharp. On the rear right tire, there was a cut on the tread which left a distinguishing mark. Lee took a careful impression of it in a piece of modeling clay that he had brought for the purpose.

Lee and his chauffeur then set out to look for the scene of the murder. Taking the resort called the White Goose for a starting point, they systematically searched the roads in the vicinity and within an hour found the melancholy burned house standing in its own grounds beside the road. It was a north and south highway not much frequented, known as Woodhull Avenue. The house was an old-fashioned wooden one; the roof was burned off and the lower floors gutted. It had not long been abandoned, for the grounds were still in good order. Only a couple of weeks had passed since the grass was mown.

Leaving his car alongside the highway, Lee went over the circular driveway inside the entrance gates with keen eyes. By degrees he was able to establish that this was certainly the spot. It was a hard-surfaced driveway and the tracks of the car only showed here and there where a little film of mud had been deposited. Blondy's car had entered there. Lee could even identify the spot where it had stopped for a while because in starting again Blondy had let in the clutch with a jerk and the rear wheels had scuffed the surface of the drive. On the spot where the car had stood he found several spots of blood. This tended to confirm Blondy's story that some time had elapsed before he came to and found Letty dead beside him. Lee couldn't imagine any other reason why Blondy should have remained there after Letty had been shot.

Lee looked around him with a slight shiver. In this dismal spot, Letty's young life had been snuffed out. There was a heavy smell of drenched, charred wood on the air. All the trees close to the house were scorched and brown on that side. Inside, the house presented a scene of complete ruin, the floors caved in, the roof open to the sky. Off to the left, as you faced the house, was a grove of gloomy pines extending to the highway, evidently planted long ago as a windbreak for the old house.

Lee, with patient searching back and forth in the driveway, found something else: another car had entered and left the driveway since the last rain. It was only here and there that he was able to pick out traces of its track. It had come and gone *before* Blondy's car, which didn't help any. Nothing in it, perhaps; any curiosity-seeker might have driven in to get a look at the wrecked house, the former occupants, maybe. Still, it was a fact to keep in mind. The rear tires of the second car were shod with tires having a peculiar wavy pattern in the tread. This car might have come here before Blondy's car, have been waiting here, and have left before Blondy, Lee figured, but he could not establish it by any evidence.

Lee went over every foot of the grounds before leaving. There was a screen of ornamental bushes in front of the pine trees. Behind these bushes he found a scrap of paper, the wrapping from a stick of chewing gum of a widely sold brand; Triple X. The paper was dry and fresh. Obviously no rain had fallen since it was dropped there. Had somebody been waiting and watching through the bushes two nights before? Somebody whose mouth had gone dry from excitement? The finding of the paper aroused Lee but did not help him any. Millions of people chewed that brand of gum. He carefully stowed the wrapper in his wallet. Unfortunately the springy carpet of pine needles retained no trace of any footprints.

There was no other house in the near neighborhood. Perfect scene for a murder. A shot could have been fired there without having been heard by anybody in the world.

On his way back to town, Lee stopped at Schanze's big roadhouse, and introduced himself to the proprietor, a fat, good-humored innkeeper who certainly partook largely of his own beer. "Do you know a night-club singer called Queenie Deane?" Lee asked.

"Sure, I know her. She has sung at my place."

"She was here night before last."

"That's right. She was here for a while."

"Who was she with?"

"She was by herself."

"Isn't that rather unusual? A handsome woman like that."

"Sure, Mr. Mappin. Queenie come to me and said she had a date to meet a fellow here. He was late and she didn't want to sit down by herself; too many single guys around, looking for a pick-up. So I sat down with her myself and we had a Martini."

"What time was this?"

"About eight-thirty."

"Did her date come?"

"No, sir. And after about fifteen minutes—she hadn't even finished her drink—she jumped up in a rage and left. Said she wasn't going to wait for the best man on earth. She didn't have to. Said if I saw him looking around for her, I could tell him to go plumb to hell!"

"Did he come after she had left?"

"Not to my knowledge."

"So she left pretty abruptly?"

"Abruptly! And how! She fairly run out of the place."

"What did you two talk about during those fifteen minutes?"

"How can I say, Mr. Mappin? Just passing the time. I ask her how she was doing and all."

"Did she appear to be interested in anybody who was here at the time?"

"Not that I mind."

"Was the place crowded?"

"No, sir. We don't fill up until after eleven."

"Did you happen to notice another couple who were here at the time? The girl was a tall, slender, natural blonde, wearing a black coat over a pale green evening dress; no hat. A conspicuously beautiful girl. She was with a blond young man about twenty-six years old."

"Sure! Now that you speak of it. I took note of that girl. She was a beauty. And she had class." Schanze's eyes widened. "And by God! now I mind, Queenie herself called my attention to them! She ask me how long they been sitting there."

"And what did you answer?"

"I said half an hour or more. You see, at eight o'clock, when this couple come in, there was only a few here and I took good note of them."

"You know who that couple were?"

"No, sir. I never seen them before."

"It was Letty Ammon and Blondy Farren."

"My God!" gasped Schanze. "What am I getting myself into! Sure! Sure! Their pictures was in the paper but I didn't recognize them for the same two! Gee! Mister, I don't want to get mixed up in no murder case!"

"You won't," said Lee dryly, "if you keep a close tongue in your head."

"They said it was the fellow smoked her. What's Queenie Deane got to do with it?"

Lee took a pinch of snuff. "That's just what I'd like to know, Mr. Schanze. Did the couple leave at the same time Queenie did?"

"I took no notice of that. Surprised me so when Queenie jump up and run, I wasn't thinking about them." Schanze thought it over. "They must have left about that time, because I didn't see them any more."

"How did Queenie get here?"

"I couldn't tell you that, Mr. Mappin. Taxi, maybe."

"If she left in a hurry, could she count on picking up a taxi outside?"

"She couldn't count on it. They come and go."

"Do you know if she drives her own car?"

"She had a car when she worked for me. I don't know if she come in it Wednesday night."

"Can you tell me anything further about the couple?"

Schanze cast back in his mind. "I can tell you this, Mr. Mappin; they wasn't having a good time like most of the couples comes here. The girl look like she might a been crying and the fellow was glum."

"Who waited on them?"

"They sat by the window yonder. That's Emil Foltz' table."

"Where can I find him?"

Schanze frowned. "Have you got to bring him into it?"

"It's bound to be published that Letty and Blondy stopped here for a drink on Wednesday. It doesn't have to go any further unless you talk. I'm only going to ask Foltz one question: Did he hear anything that passed between that couple?"

Schanze reluctantly gave Lee the address. "Keep me out of it, Mr. Mappin," he begged. "I run a decent place here; all I've got is invested in it. And it's so easy for a roadhouse to get a bad name!"

Lee assured him that he had nothing to fear.

He had himself driven to the cheap East Side flat where Foltz lived, but he had no success there. The waiter, a thin, worn individual with a prominent Adam's apple, was eager to talk but he could tell Lee nothing that he didn't know already. Foltz had recognized Letty and Blondy by their pictures in the papers.

"They were down in the mouth," he said. "You couldn't help but see it."

"Quarreling?" suggested Lee.

"No, not quarreling, exactly. The fellow was crazy about her, and I couldn't blame him. She was a lovely girl. And to think a couple of hours later!" Foltz shook his head heavily.

"Were they silent while sitting there?"

"No, they had plenty to say, but whenever I came to the table they dried up until I moved away. All I heard him say was: 'I can't make you out!' A fellow often says that." Such was the extent of Foltz' information. Lee tipped him generously, saying: "Better not talk too much about this case or you'll find yourself out of a job. Say nothing about my coming to see you."

"You can depend on me for that, Mr. Mappin!"

# CHAPTER TEN

LEE PROCEEDED DOWNTOWN to Le Coq Noir where he was told that Miss Deane lived at the Hotel Amsterdam. He also procured the address of the woman who dressed Queenie at the night club. It was about ten-thirty when Lee reached the Amsterdam. They told him at the desk that Miss Deane had left a standing order that she was not to be disturbed before noon. Lee insisted on having his name sent up and Queenie finally consented to see him.

In her sitting room a heavy scent of chypre met his nostrils. He doubted if the windows had been opened in a month. It was the conventional hotel sitting room further embellished with fancy lampshades, innumerable cushions and lush pictures. At this time of the day Queenie's brilliant beauty was a good deal obscured. She was in a bad humor and she didn't care how she looked.

"You remember, we met at Hope House on Henry Street," Lee said affably.

"Sure, I remember," Queenie said with a cold stare that seemed to add: "What the hell do *you* want at this hour?"

"Little did we guess then what was going to happen!" said Lee.

Queenie laughed shortly. "I'm not breaking my heart over it. If a woman wants to cheat, that's what she must expect!"

"So you think Letty was cheating?"

"Obviously."

Lee said softly: "I understand you saw them up at Schanze's on Wednesday night."

The question took her by surprise. A look of naked terror leaped out of the hard black eyes. "Who told you so?"

"Blondy."

"He's lying!" she cried shrilly. "What's he trying to do? Drag me into this dirty case?"

Lee affected an air of surprise. "What have you got to do with it? He just happened to see you in the place."

"I've got nothing to do with it! And I haven't been near Schanze's in months!"

"But Schanze himself told me he had a drink with you Wednesday night."

Queenie's face was a study. "So you've been following me up!" she sneered. She paced the little room, struggling to recover herself. "Well, what if I did?" she said defiantly. "What's it to you?"

"I just thought you might be able to throw a little light on the affair."

"Well, you've got another guess! . . . Light! You don't need any light! Blondy croaked her. And if she had been playing fast and loose with him I don't blame him!"

"Who would?" said Lee. "How did you happen to be up at Schanze's?"

"I had a date with a fellow there. Didn't Schanze tell you that?"

"Yes, he did."

"Then why are you asking me?"

"Well, eight o'clock seems too early or too late in the evening to make a date."

Queenie said nothing.

"And I can hardly see a woman like you driving all the way up to Schanze's to keep a date with a man."

"That's my business."

"Nor can I see a man breaking a date with you so easily."

"Are you intimating that I'm a liar?"

Lee took a pinch of snuff. He said nothing.

"You'd better get out of here," said Queenie in an uncertain voice, "before I telephone to the office."

Lee made no move to go. "Where did you go when you left Schanze's?" he asked calmly.

Queenie cursed him furiously. It was a novelty from feminine lips and Lee smiled. She was angry: very well; if he made her angrier still, he might learn something. "You haven't answered my question," he reminded her.

"Who the hell are you to ask me questions?" she shrilled. "You're not on the force. You have no standing. I don't have to answer *your* questions."

"Certainly not," agreed Lee, smiling still. "I can easily get the answers from others, but I thought it would be kinder to come to you first."

She quieted down. Lee was a puzzle to her. She paced the room, darting glances of fear and hatred in his direction. Finally, she said: "Are you trying to make out that I had something to do with this murder? That's foolish!"

"You suggested the idea yourself . . . Come to think of it, you had a powerful motive for putting Letty out of the way."

"I couldn't fire a gun."

"It's not difficult if you're close enough to your object."

"You can't prove it on me!"

"All right. Help me to prove it on somebody else. . . . Answer my question. Where did you go when you left Schanze's?"

"I won't answer your questions. Now or any other time. It's none of your damned business."

Lee turned on a little heat. "Sorry! In that case, I'll have to take my story to Sieg Ammon."

Queenie changed color. "What story?" she asked breathlessly.

"That I believe you followed Letty and Blondy up to Schanze's and that you followed them away from there."

"How could I follow them there? They was there half an hour before me."

"Well, say you found them there and followed them away."

"It's a lie!" she cried stormily. "What are you trying to do to me? I never harmed you!" Queenie was breaking now; the hard black eyes filled with tears, but tears of rage, Lee noted, not grief.

"Why do you want to bring Sieg into it? Just to make trouble between us! Promise me to leave Sieg out of it and I'll tell you anything you want to know."

"All right," said Lee. "I'm no troublemaker. I promise to leave Sieg out of it *for the present*. I mean, I shall say nothing to him until I have proof that you were mixed up in this business. That's fair enough, isn't it?"

She nodded. Her eyes were still distrustful.

"Where did you go when you left Schanze's?"

"I came down here."

"Then where did you go?"

"I stayed right here until it was time to go to the club to dress for the first show."

"How did you get up to Schanze's?"

"By subway and taxi."

"You have a car of your own, haven't you?"

"Sure. But when I go out in the evening I let the man supply transportation."

"Naturally. With what man had you a date on Wednesday night?"

Queenie answered glibly—too glibly. "Arthur Burton."

"Who's he?"

"Just a fellow I know."

"Where does he live?"

"I don't know."

"You don't know!"

"I don't know the addresses of all the men I meet at the club!"

"If you can bring forward this Arthur Burton," suggested Lee, "and have him identified, and if he corroborates your story, it will clear you. I'll never have to trouble you again."

Queenie bit her lip. She saw that she had committed an error of tactics. "I don't need clearing," she said defiantly.

Lee looked at her steadily. "In my eyes you do."

Queenie looked at her nails, affecting an indifferent air. "If I see him again, I'll tell him. He doesn't live in New York. He's a Philadelphia boy comes over occasionally for a little fun."

"Well, ask him to come and see me."

"Okay," said Queenie, "but after standing me up, he's not likely to come around me again for a good while."

Lee was more than ever convinced that no such person as Arthur Burton existed. He changed his line. "What can you tell me about Spanish Jack?" he asked.

This time Queenie was not caught off her guard. "Not a thing," she said unconcernedly. "I've heard Sieg speak of him, but I never met the guy myself."

"What did Sieg tell you about him?"

"Nothing much. That he was a guy he knew, who was down on his luck, and he got him a room in the house on Henry Street; that's all."

"Sieg's in a terrible way!" said Lee, shaking his head with deceitful sympathy. "He seems half out of his mind."

This administered a stab to Queenie, but she faced it out. "Naturally," she said, "he was cracked about his pasty-faced doll." She smiled in an ugly fashion. "But he'll get over it. Men always do."

"He needs another woman's sympathy," suggested Lee casually.

Queenie failed to rise. "Oh, yeah?" she said.

Lee tried a shot in the dark. "Later, on Wednesday night, you were seen at McGovern's place in the Bronx."

"You're a liar!" said Queenie. "I never went in."

Lee rubbed his lip to hide a smile. "I mean you were seen sitting in your car in the yard there. Your face is pretty well known, you know."

Queenie cursed him roundly. "I never was near McGovern's. I don't know where the joint is!"

Lee made believe to let it drop with a shrug. "The fellow who told me said he could swear it was you."

He presently got out, leaving a worried and uncertain Queenie behind him.

She would have been more worried could she have followed him during the next hour. Downstairs in the hotel he asked for the manager, and when that gentleman appeared, presented him with his card. Lee affected to be annoyed by the vast amount of publicity that had been thrown on him in recent years, but it had this advantage; his name was so well known to newspaper readers that his card was a passport wherever he went. The gratified manager made haste to show him into his private office.

"What can I do for you, Mr. Mappin?"

"A small service that may prove to be of great help later on. I want to know the hour at which Miss Deane returned to the hotel on Wednesday night."

The manager did a little telephoning. He roused one of the night clerks from sleep. Putting down the telephone, he said to Lee:

"Queenie left the hotel about eight on Wednesday night. She phoned for her car and left in a terrible hurry."

"Good! That checks with my information. And when did she return?"

"About four A.M. That's her usual hour after the last show at Le Coq Noir."

"Thank you very much. One more question. Where does she keep her car?"

The garage was named.

Lee repeated his thanks. "Please do not speak of my inquiries to anybody, and above all, don't jump to conclusions. My investigations lead in every direction, you know, and not all of it turns out to be important. I have nothing against Miss Deane."

The manager bowed him out. "I shall say nothing about this, Mr. Mappin. You can depend upon that, sir."

Lee drove to the garage. Here the information he had received at the hotel was confirmed. Miss Deane had phoned for her car about eight o'clock on Wednesday night. She was waiting for it at the door of the hotel and was in a terrible hurry. She returned the car to the garage about eleven-fifteen and called a taxi to take her to Le Coq Noir.

Lee thought: She must have had to dress in a hurry.

He asked to be shown Queenie's car. The tire treads bore a common, diamond-shaped pattern, not the wavy lines he had half hoped to find.

"Have any of these tires been changed lately?" he asked.

"Not in many weeks, Mr. Mappin."

Lee's last visit was to the woman who dressed Queenie at Le Coq Noir. If this woman was on a confidential footing with her employer she would undoubtedly tell Queenie of his visit, but Lee didn't mind that. It wouldn't hurt to let Queenie know that a little pressure was being brought to bear on her.

"I understand that Miss Deane was very late in reaching the club on Wednesday night," he suggested.

The woman looked at him suspiciously. She was elderly and tight-lipped. "That's right," she said.

"Did she appear to be agitated?"

"Naturally she was upset at being so late. She had less than half an hour to make up and dress for the first show."

"Did she tell you why she was late?"

"No, sir."

"Being late was hardly enough to account for her extreme agitation, was it?" suggested Lee.

The woman hesitated. "What do you want to know for?" she demanded.

"For my own information," said Lee blandly. "What you tell me will go no further. But if you refuse to answer, I shall have to put it in the hands of the police and you will be forced to answer."

She looked at Lee. Every newspaper reader was aware that Lee Mappin enjoyed the closest relations with the police, and she decided that it was not safe to oppose him. "Sure, she was all upset," she answered sullenly. "Had to take a couple of brandies to steady herself before she could go on."

"Didn't she give you some clue to the cause of her agitation?"

"She said a fellow had stood her up and she was mad."

"Do you know a friend of Queenie's called Arthur Burton?"

"Never heard of him, sir."

"If her date failed to turn up, why was she so late in getting to the club?"

"She didn't tell me that."

"That's all," said Lee. "And thank you very much."

As he drove on to his office, he was thinking: "Well, I have gathered some more pieces of my puzzle, but none of them fit together yet."

# CHAPTER ELEVEN

LEE SET HIMSELF the task of tracing Spanish Jack's movements after his arrival in New York on the fateful Wednesday. He read the report of his examination by the police. Spanish had produced an alibi to account for every moment of the day and night, but Loasby, with his long experience of alibis, was not convinced by it, and neither was Lee.

Over in Brooklyn Lee had a bit of luck. The doings of the showy young couple, Piero Mendes and his girl, had excited a good deal of curiosity in the humble neighborhood where they lived, and it was not difficult for Lee to establish that Spanish had arrived at their place in a taxicab during the noon hour on Wednesday. They had all left together in another taxi about two o'clock. This was a local taxi, the driver was known, and Lee found him. He said he had driven the trio to Fossberg's restaurant on Delancey Street, Manhattan. Delancey Street was not very far from the Henry Street house, and was the principal shopping thoroughfare of that part of town. Spanish had not been seen again that day in Brooklyn, but as he was on hand next morning, the neighbors inferred that he had spent the night with his friends. The neighbors had been much impressed by Spanish Jack's fine clothes and his extravagance in taxicabs.

Lee proceeded to Fossberg's. The most expensive place in the quarter, it was the rendezvous of the elite of the East Side. Not a very big place, it was oppressively decorated and upholstered. It had a row of alcoves along each wall and a few tables in the middle.

Since the rush hour was over when the South Americans had arrived, their visit was remembered; the waiter who had served them pointed out the alcove where they had lunched. The older man, he said, had ordered an expensive meal for his young friends with plenty of drinks. On my money! Lee reflected ruefully.

When they had finished eating, the older man had telephoned from a booth in the restaurant. Upon returning to his table, the waiter heard him say: "She's coming." The young pair then left, and the other man, ordering another drink, waited. In about quarter of an hour, a young lady appeared and, after looking into the various booths, sat down opposite the man. He jumped up, very pleased to see her, but she did not smile at him. She looked frightened. She refused to eat or drink anything. They talked together in whispers for a little while; the foreign-looking gentleman had an ugly smile. He was trying to persuade her but she kept shaking her head. Then she left. Lee showed the waiter a picture of Letty that he had in his pocket. Yes, that was the girl, he said. He could swear to it.

After the girl had gone the man looked sour. He had another drink and left. He hailed a taxi at the door. There was no way of tracing that taxi and Lee lost the trail of Spanish at this point.

Lee mulled things over in his mind. If Spanish had been at the spot where Letty was killed, he must have had a car to get there and get away again. No doubt he possessed friends who owned cars, but upon starting out on a criminal errand, so astute a man as Spanish would never risk using a car through which he might be traced. Certainly not when cars were so easy to pick up in New York streets. Nearly every day in the year stolen cars were found by the police in the streets after they had been abandoned.

Lee went to the police bureau that dealt with stolen cars. Here he was informed that three abandoned cars had been picked up during the early morning hours of Thursday. In the case of two, the loss had already been reported and they were immediately returned to their owners. The third car presented an unusual problem, for the license plates had been removed and there was no way of identifying its owner. It was still in the possession of the police.

Lee asked to have the car shown him and he was led out into the adjoining yard. A somewhat battered old sedan was pointed out to him. Instantly he saw that the rear tires left a track of waving lines. It was not conclusive evidence, for many cars must be shod with the same make of tires, but taking into consideration the circumstances in which this car had been found, it was enough to make Lee's heart beat a little faster. The car had been picked up in Varick Street at three o'clock on Thursday morning. This was a district of wholesale houses almost completely deserted after nightfall. The car was a black Buick sedan of a model five years old. The body was in bad shape, the upholstery much worn, but the engine was in good running order, Lee was told. The body had recently been given a hasty coat of paint. In places where the black paint had flaked off, it could be seen that the original color was gray. The right-hand front fender was bashed in. This damage appeared to have been received within the last few days, for in spots where all paint had been scraped off, the steel had not yet started to rust. In searching the car, Lee found a card of matches that had slipped behind the front seat. It bore the imprint of the Eureka Restaurant, Elizabeth, New Jersey.

It now became necessary for Lee to call on the police for help and he went on to Headquarters. Inspector Loasby was still taking the attitude that Lee was looking for a mare's nest in the case of Letty Ammon, but he was willing to indulge him. A list of second-hand automobile dealers was made up from the telephone business directory and divided up among half a dozen plainclothesmen, who were sent out to investigate and report. That ended Lee's efforts for the day.

He dined with Sandra Cassells up at Brookwood. It was one of her small parties, and he got no chance to talk to her privately until the other guests had departed. Sandra, slim and lissom in another exquisite black confection glittering with jewels, sat at the head of her table, delicately fiddling with her food on a golden plate. With her enormous, vague, blue eyes and baby skin, she was like a modern demi-goddess, unearthly and immortal. Watching her, Lee reflected on the inequalities of Life. There was Sandra with a million a year, indulged, made much of, protected since babyhood; and there was poor, beautiful Letty, persecuted, victimized, frightened, foully done to death.

When Lee finally got Sandra alone in her boudoir, he didn't receive much sympathy on account of his day's activities. Like Inspector Loasby, Sandra was convinced that Blondy had shot Letty and would listen to no contrary suggestion. She said:

"I can see your point of view, Lee. This case is so obvious there is nothing for your analytical mind to get its teeth into. So you've got to discover these complications."

"Maybe so," said Lee good-humoredly.

"Consider it from the normal point of view for a moment," said Sandra. "Blondy made a date with Letty to meet him at the corner of Henry and Scammell Streets. He drives her up to this remote corner of Westchester and he shoots her. Could anything be simpler?"

"But the letter from Blondy that you and I read, suggested that he didn't want to come to New York and that she was urging him to come."

"That doesn't matter. He *did* come."

"And Blondy says it was Letty who made the date to meet at that corner. Certainly it was Letty who drove him to the spot where she was shot."

"All right. Letty was playing fast and loose with him and he killed her! On the level, Lee, can you believe his yarn that he had passed out and knew nothing about what happened?"

"I confess it is hard to swallow," said Lee. "I'm not insisting that you and Loasby are wrong. At the same time, I can't rest easy until I have satisfied myself as to what Spanish Jack and Queenie Deane were up to that night."

"I can't say that I blame Blondy altogether," Sandra went on. "I'm going to do what I can for him. Through my attorneys I have engaged Samuel Goldstone to defend him. They tell me he's the best criminal lawyer in the City."

"Certainly the most expensive," said Lee dryly.

"I can't appear in it openly," Sandra said, "because that would make Sieg so angry. Sieg would like to see Blondy drawn and quartered. I suppose that is natural enough, but I must say I am a little weary of hearing him curse Blondy. If the girl was deceiving him, Sieg is much better off without her."

They went on to talk of other matters.

Two days passed before Lee received a report from the police on the old Buick car. He was then informed that Wayne Smither, a large dealer in repossessed cars on Webster Avenue, had been down to take a look at the car, and had positively identified it as one sold by him three weeks previously.

Three weeks! thought Lee. Not much help in that. Still, it might have been sold again.

He lost no time in visiting the Smither establishment across the Harlem River. Mr. Smither, a youngish and very smoothly turned-out gentlemen, was quite impressed by the call from the well-known Mr. Mappin.

"I remember the car well," he said, "because it had been on my hands a long time. I had it painted black, but it was a cheap job and only seemed to make the car look worse."

"To whom did you sell it?" asked Lee.

"A young woman. Gave the name of Jones, Miss Isabel Jones. I didn't have to investigate her credit because it was a cash transaction. By Golly, she was a good-looker, Mr. Mappin. And dressed up to the nines! The kind of girl you would expect to see driving a new Cadillac instead of an old jaloppy like I sold her."

Lee's heart sank. This was not what he wanted to hear. "Describe her," he said.

"A tall, slender, beautiful blonde. The real thing!" Lee took a photograph out of his pocket. "Have you ever seen this woman before?" he asked.

"That's her! That's her!" Smither said excitedly. "That's the very girl!"

"Hum!" said Lee. He took a pinch of snuff to compose himself. After a second look at the photograph, Smither's eyes widened. "Why, that's Letty Ammon, isn't it?" he said breathlessly. "Her picture has been in the paper every day. Her that was shot up in Westchester."

"The same," said Lee grimly. "I'd be obliged if you said nothing of my visit to you for the present."

"Sure, Mr. Mappin." A puzzled frown spread over Smither's face. "But the murder car in that case was described as a new Chevvy convertible, maroon color."

"That's right," said Lee, "but I've got to find out where the Buick car comes in, if she bought it."

"She bought it all right, Mr. Mappin."

"Please tell me the circumstances of the sale."

"Well, she came in here and said she wanted to buy a used car. Said she didn't know anything about the insides of cars and would trust me to give her a square deal. Of course, no man would want to deceive a beautiful woman like that; still, business is business. She said she didn't care what the car looked like, but it must be in good running order. That's different from most of my customers. I showed her the Buick. She had a typewritten list of questions that some man must have given her, and asked me them one by one and wrote down the answers. Brakes, clutch, differential, bushings, shock absorbers, and so on. I named her a price of four hundred dollars. She said she had to consult somebody and would be back in a few minutes. Maybe the man was waiting outside and had been looking at the Buick himself. I wouldn't know.

"She came back and made me a counter offer of three fifty cash down. I gave her a strong sales talk, but she stuck to her price and I accepted it. Then I took her for a trial ride. She drove; she could drive all right. Maybe the man followed us; maybe he was watching from the sidewalk. Anyhow, after we got back she said she was satisfied. She gave me the money and took title for the car and drove it away."

"What license tags had she?"

"I lent her my dealer's tags. She gave me the money and I made an application for the tags and sent it to Albany."

"What address did she give you?"

"A street and number in Scarsdale—wait a minute! She came in a few days later and got the tags. Afterward, the letter I sent her was returned with an endorsement reading: 'No such person known.' It was a false address!"

"Naturally," said Lee. "Can you give me the date of the sale?"

"Sure!" Smither looked it up in his ledger. "April 23rd; just three weeks ago, Mr. Mappin."

"Thank you very much," said Lee.

He drove downtown to consult with Sieg Ammon. "Sieg," he said, "did you know that Letty bought a car three weeks ago?"

Sieg's face was a study. "Letty buy a car? That's impossible, Mr. Mappin."

"It's a fact, though. An old Buick sedan. She had the assistance of a man, it seems."

"Was he seen?"

"No.

"What did she pay for it?"

"Three hundred and fifty cash."

Sieg laughed. "Utterly impossible, Mr. Mappin. Letty never had such a sum in cash. Nor the half of it."

"Then she got it from the man. She gave the name of Isabel Jones."

Sieg shook his head confidently. "There's a mistake somewhere. It just isn't possible."

Lee let it go at that for the time being.

From Hope House, he called up Inspector Loasby. "Inspector, will you please find out from the Warden of the City Prison on Welfare Island the date when John D'Acosta, alias Spanish Jack, was released."

In quarter of an hour, the answer came through. "April 28th, Mr. Mappin."

April 28th! Then on the day Letty bought the car Spanish was still locked up! Had there been another man in her life? Lee still found himself faced by a blank wall.

## CHAPTER TWELVE

BLONDY FARREN, as Westchester County's most important guest of
the moment, enjoyed the best accommodations the jail afforded.
His spacious cell contained a comfortable cot, a chair and a heavily
barred window through which he was able to look down on the
street. Lee Mappin, when he visited the jail, enjoyed such respect
from the local chief of police and the District Attorney that he was
given the privilege of consulting with Blondy privately in his cell.
True, the wicket in the door was left open and there was a keeper
stationed in the corridor, but if Lee and Blondy kept their voices
down he could not hear what they said.

Lee found Blondy much changed. Instead of the broken, apathetic figure he had seen the day of his arrest, Blondy's back had
stiffened, sanity and resolution had returned to his steady blue
eyes. He was agitatedly pacing his cell when Lee came. Lee got the
impression that he had been keeping it up for hours. Blondy, at
the sight of Lee, overflowed with gratitude.

"Gee! Mr. Mappin, it was kind of you to come! I never thought
you would. I had no right to expect it. But I had nobody else to go to."

"That's okay," said Lee. "If you had not sent for me I should
have come anyhow. There are several things I want to talk over
with you."

"It's so good to feel you have a friend!" said Blondy. "Of course,
I have a lawyer now, and he seems to be my friend, but how do I
know it's not just the big fee he's getting."

"Well," said Lee, "I'm not getting a fee from you . . . Let's sit down so we can talk without being overheard." Blondy sat on the bed, Lee on the chair, and their heads drew close together. "What did you want to see me about?" asked Lee.

"I need advice," said Blondy. "I can't make up my mind what's the best thing to do." He clapped his head between his hands. "I'm near crazy trying to decide."

Lee offered him a cigarette. "Light up," he said, "and spill it!"

"My lawyer tells me," Blondy began, "that with the evidence they have against me, any jury on earth would convict me of first degree murder and send me to the chair. He's Samuel Goldstone. I suppose you know him."

"Sure, everybody knows him."

"He's got a great reputation in the courts and I can see for myself what a clever guy he is, but how do I know if he's on the level with me? It's my life that's at stake, not his."

"Leaving that aside for the moment," said Lee, "let's look at it from a common-sense point of view. What does Goldstone want you to do?"

"He wants me to plead guilty to second degree murder. He says he can make a deal with the D.A. to accept such a plea. Then the trial will be just a formality and I'll get off with about fifteen years."

"From a practical standpoint I should say that Goldstone was right," said Lee. "Don't you want to take his advice?"

Blondy lowered his bright head. His two hands were clenched tight. "How can I say that I killed Letty?" he muttered.

"Have you got any family?" asked Lee.

Blondy shook his head impatiently. "No! Whatever happens there's nobody to be disgraced but me." He struck his chest violently. "How can I say that I killed her?"

"I'm not your lawyer," Lee said in a blunt, matter-of-fact voice. "Neither am I your prosecutor. I am not a public figure of any sort, and you can therefore be honest with me. *Did* you shoot Letty Ammon?"

Blondy jerked up his head. "No!" he cried, looking Lee in the eye. "How can I make you believe that? I would sooner have cut off my hand than hurt Letty! No! No! . . .." His voice faltered and a look of agony crossed his face. "Unless . . . unless . . .." he stammered.

"Unless what?"

"Unless it was possible for me to kill her when I was unconscious."

"What were your last conscious feelings?" asked Lee. "At the moment you passed out, were you full of rage and anger?"

"No. I only felt love for her."

"Did you pass out suddenly, like the blowing out of a light?"

"No. I drifted away like falling asleep."

Lee pondered on this.

"Don't you believe me, Mr. Mappin?" Blondy said imploringly.

Lee clapped him on the shoulder. "I am your friend, Blondy. I greatly wish to believe in your innocence. But I am an old hand. I have been fooled so often by the so-called accents of truth and the seemingly honest eye that now I must have corroboration from the outside."

"If you were on the jury, would you vote for my conviction?"

"I would not," said Lee heartily. "There is a big doubt in my mind."

"Well, that's something," said Blondy gratefully. "Thank you for that much, anyhow."

Said Lee: "This question of whether to take a fifteen year rap or risk the chair all depends on how much you value your life."

Blondy smiled hardily. "Not a hell of a lot," he said. ". . . But how do you mean?"

"Fifteen years in prison," murmured Lee, "or, a quick exit. Which?"

Blondy's eyes widened. "By God! you're right! I never thought of it that way! I . . .."

"Wait," said Lee. "Here's something else to consider. I'm working on this case. I can't say that I've made much progress, but I don't see to the end of it yet, by a long way. Now, supposing I am able to dig up evidence to corroborate your story, if you had pleaded guilty it would be very difficult to have the verdict set aside. But if you maintain your innocence, if any additional evidence was forthcoming, it would be easy to obtain a new trial."

Blondy sprang up in his eagerness. "That's right! That's right!" he cried. "You make everything clear. Now I see what I've got to do!" He broke off, glancing at Lee uneasily. "Mr. Goldstone will probably throw up the case unless I plead guilty. He said as much."

"Well, there are other lawyers," said Lee.

Blondy was blazing with eagerness now. "You're right! There are other lawyers. And then I wouldn't have to sit in a cell for fifteen years despising myself for caving in! Better a hundred times to burn than that! I'll plead not guilty. Nothing can change me now!"

"You have chosen rightly," said Lee.

Blondy had become quite cheerful. His lips were set in a firm line. "What did you want to see me about?" he asked.

"I have followed up several lines," said Lee, "only to find myself blocked in each case. Perhaps you can give me a new lead. First: Why was Queenie Deane following you and Letty that night?"

Blondy spread out his hands. "You can search me," he said. "Of course, Queenie had it in for Letty."

"How could Queenie have known that you and Letty had stopped at Schanze's?"

Blondy shook his head helplessly. "I didn't know myself that we were going there. Letty took me."

"It's hardly likely there could have been an understanding between Letty and Queenie."

"Likely?" said Blondy. "It's impossible! For what purpose?"

"I have reason to believe," Lee continued, "that Queenie followed you on to McGovern's and waited outside until you came out. And possibly she went on to the White Goose and at last to the burned house. I suppose you didn't see her again?"

"No," said Blondy. "I had it in mind that she might be following us, though I didn't know why. And I was watching out for her. But I never saw her again after Schanze's."

"Letty must have been shot a little after ten," Lee said, "and Queenie did not get back to town until an hour after that."

Blondy ran his hands through his hair. "If Queenie had it in for Letty, why should she choose that night? How would she know that Letty and I had planned to meet?"

"Let's leave it for a moment and take up the second line," said Lee. "That concerns Spanish Jack."

Blondy stared. "What the hell has Spanish got to do with it?"

"Ten days before Letty's death she came to my place in a terrible state of distress to say that Spanish was threatening her and to ask me to get him out of the house. That was all I could get out of her. She was so hysterical I didn't press her then. I sent Spanish on a fake errand to Boston, thinking I would learn the truth from her after she had quieted down. But she was killed before she told me."

Blondy listened to this with staring eyes. "I don't get it! I don't get it!" he murmured. "I could have sworn that Sieg filled Letty's whole life. You never know!"

"Well, let's go back to the time before you and Sieg went to Sing Sing. Did you ever have any reason to suspect that Spanish was bothering Letty?"

Blondy shook his head wonderingly. "None whatever! We all worked over at Sam Bartol's together . . . But Spanish might have been after her without our knowing it. Like all croupiers, he had an absolutely deadpan; he never let anything on. He didn't seem human to me. But I don't see how anything could have been going on; we three were so close."

"Possibly it happened after you and Sieg left Bartol's."

"That's more likely. Letty continued working there until Sam was killed and the place was closed for good."

"What did Letty do after that?"

"She told us she got a job as cashier in a steam laundry. Long hours and small pay. She was only living until Sieg got out, she said. . . . Maybe she was lying," Blondy added suddenly. "If she got into any trouble, she wouldn't want Sieg to know. Girls have to lie and I would be the last to blame them . . . Letty could have told *me* anything," he concluded in a lower tone. "I wouldn't have thought the less of her."

"Spanish came back from Boston secretly at noon on Wednesday," Lee continued. "On Wednesday afternoon he phoned for Letty to come to him at Fossberg's restaurant in Delancey Street. They talked and apparently he renewed his threats."

"What would that have to do with me?" asked Blondy, scowling.

"It seems to me that the state of distress Letty was in when she was with you Wednesday night had something to do with Spanish."

"Might be," said Blondy, "but it don't seem to hang together."

"Think back!" urged Lee. "Go over everything in your mind that Letty said to you that night."

Lee walked away to the window and looked out while Blondy pondered. The young man said at last: "It's no good, Mr. Mappin. The name of Spanish never came up between us. What I got from Letty was that it was something about Sieg that made her feel so bad, though she never said so right out."

"Well, there was the car," said Lee.

"What car?"

"There was another car went into that driveway in front of the burned house about the time you did. The rear tires had a tread that left a track of wavy lines."

"Well?"

"About a month ago Letty bought a secondhand car without Sieg's knowledge. That car was found abandoned in Varick Street on Thursday morning and towed away by the police. I have seen it and the rear wheels carry that kind of tires."

"God!" muttered Blondy. "What more?"

"Is it possible," suggested Lee, "that Spanish forced an admission from Letty that she was going to take you to the burned house that night. Could he have got there first in this other car and have been lying in wait for you?"

"Anything is possible," said Blondy, "but it don't seem to hang together."

Lee was forced to admit that he was right. "Letty had the assistance of a man in buying that car," he said, "but it could not have been Spanish. The car was bought on April 23rd and Spanish was not liberated from Welfare Island until the 28th."

"As far as that goes, it doesn't prove anything," said Blondy. "In spite of all the keepers can do, there's regular underground communication in and out of Welfare Island. Spanish could have sent out a letter to Letty, or have sent a man to help her get the car."

"I'll keep that in mind," said Lee. ". . . It was a Buick car of a five-year-old model," he went on. "It had received a rough coat of black paint. The upholstery was badly worn. One of the fenders had recently been bashed in . . ."

Blondy's eyes widened. "Which fender?"

"Right front fender."

"Old black sedan," cried Blondy excitedly. "Right front fender bashed in? By God! I can tell you something about that, if it's the same car!"

"Well?"

"I did it myself! Leaving Schanze's. The old sedan was parked next to my car, heading outward. When I backed out I was all excited, I didn't turn short enough, and I caught its fender with my left front fender."

"That's right," said Lee. "When I examined your car I saw the damage."

"Later, when we came out of McGovern's," Blondy continued, "the same car was there, parked among the others and heading outward as if for a quick getaway. There was nobody around that seemed to belong to it. It came to me that it might be following us; I thought maybe it was Queenie Deane's car."

"No! It appears that she was driving her own car, a smart green coupé."

"When we left the White Goose," said Blondy, "you can be sure I looked for the old sedan in the yard. But it was not parked among the cars there. As we drove away I kept looking back to see if we were followed. I didn't see any other car. Then I passed out."

"Well, we've made a step forward," said Lee. "It is safe to assume that the old sedan was at the scene of the murder . . . But unless Letty was in cahoots with the driver, *how did it get there before you?*"

Blondy changed color. "You're sure of that?"

"Certain. The track of your car passed *over* its track."

The two men stared at each other in silence.

"Apparently you had been drugged," Lee went on. "It must have happened in the White Goose because your head was perfectly clear up to that time. While you were in that place, did anybody approach your table?"

"Nobody except the waiter."

"Did you leave Letty at any time?"

"No."

Lee's face turned grim. "Well, you can see where this is leading us. Letty changed glasses with you three times in that place."

"I can't believe it!" cried Blondy. "I would have trusted her with my life!"

"Sure," said Lee. "If she had been left to herself. But we know she was under heavy pressure from the outside. In every one of us there is a breaking point. Perhaps Letty had passed it. It was Letty who drove you into the driveway in front of the burned house."

Blondy's head went down. "Oh God! I can't bear that!" he groaned.

"The truth must be faced out wherever we meet it," said Lee.

Blondy jerked up his head. "But if Letty had it in for me, as you say, how come it was Letty who was killed and not me?"

"There you have me," said Lee. "I've got to find out who was driving the old sedan."

After leaving Blondy, Lee stopped in the yard of the police station to re-examine the damage that the fender of Blondy's car had received in side-swiping the sedan at Schanze's. Clear to the eye were the flecks of black paint scraped off the other car, and also fainter streaks of gray enamel. Thus there could be no further doubt that the old sedan which had visited the scene of the murder was the same car purchased by Letty three weeks earlier.

## CHAPTER THIRTEEN

AT THIS TIME Westchester County possessed in Francis Enslin an ambitious young District Attorney, who was determined to make a name for himself. The Letty Ammon murder case which attracted nationwide attention, because of its romantic implications, provided him with a God-sent opportunity which he was not slow to take advantage of. With the object of putting to shame the near-by New York City authorities, who were notorious for their delays, he had Blondy Farren indicted almost overnight, and announced that he would be ready to proceed to trial inside of two weeks.

The celebrated Mr. Solomon Goldstone had retired as Blondy's counsel, and that did not help the prisoner any. Mrs. Cassells, under the circumstances, refused further aid to the prisoner and Lee took upon himself the responsibility of engaging young Walter Paget to defend Blondy. Lee had had his eye on Paget for some time. He thought he saw in the young man the makings of a great lawyer, but as yet Paget had no public reputation.

At the opening of the trial the prisoner's prospects looked dark indeed. The press generally was holding him up as a young monster in human form. Lee and Pager, after consulting together, had agreed that it would be unwise to call either Queenie Deane or Jack D'Acosta.

These would be hostile witnesses, and at the best there was no hope connecting either of them directly with the crime. Lee himself was to go on the stand to testify as to the letter from Blondy found in Letty's pocketbook, and also as to Letty's visit when she had told Lee that she went in terror of her life from Spanish Jack. The only real defense lay in Blondy's own story. Incredible though the story sounded, Paget had the hope that Blondy's steady gaze and clear, unshakable detail might at least arouse a doubt of his guilt in the minds of the jury.

The courtroom was crowded to the doors. Column upon column in the newspapers had been devoted to this case. For an added attraction, there was the famous Mrs. Nick Cassells in person. Sandra attracted more attention than the prisoner. She sat in the front row of court, exquisitely dressed and bejeweled, surveying the proceedings through a lorgnette. Beside her sat Agnes Delaplaine to keep her in countenance and in her free hand she held a bottle of smelling salts. Lee sat down beside her as a matter of course, and Sandra immediately whispered:

"Better sit on the other side of the room."

Lee, accustomed as he was to her caprices, ran up his eyebrows. "Why?"

"Because I'm against the prisoner and you're for him. You will be helping him more if you disassociate yourself from me."

Lee, smiling, immediately moved to the other side of the room. Presently Sieg Ammon took the place beside Sandra that he had vacated. Sieg looked handsome and beautifully turned out. His face bore a grim expression, as befitted a bereaved husband.

Lee measured the opposing lawyers. Both were young, personable and keen. They looked well matched. Enslin was a blond Apollo; he had a cocky air and loved applause; Paget was dark, small and quiet; and affected a modest air to impress the jury. Lee had already had proof that Enslin, the District Attorney, was fair and open-minded. He had no desire to triumph at the expense of the prisoner, but was disposed to give him every opportunity. Paget, who felt in his heart that his case was lost before it began, concealed his feelings behind a quiet, confident smile.

When Blondy was brought in, Sieg Ammon sprang up with clenched fists, and blazing eyes. A court attendant started for him. Meanwhile, Sandra agitatedly plucked at his sleeve and he dropped back in his seat and covered his face for a moment. Lee thought

that Blondy, neatly dressed and barbered, had never looked come-
lier. He was very pale but his glance was steady, his lips firm. Lee
could feel antagonism like a baleful current striking out of the spectators when they saw the prisoner. In their minds he was already
convicted. Blondy's seat at the counsel table brought him in profile to the courtroom. He bore the gaping stares of the spectators
with composure.

The judge at this session, by name McLanahan, was not known
to Lee. When he entered, Lee studied his face in no little anxiety.
From previous experience, Lee knew that the average jury pays
more attention to what the judge says than to the opposing attorneys, because they regard the judge as a disinterested referee.
Judge McLanahan was a man in his middle forties with rosy cheeks
and calm blue eyes. He looked merciful. Lee felt that they could
scarcely have done better.

The business of choosing a jury began. Enslin took them pretty
much as they came. Paget, who wished to recommend himself to
the court, was just as anxious to expedite matters, but he had to
watch out for prejudice and he used up his challenges one by one.
While this tedious business was in progress, an officer brought Lee
a note scribbled in pencil on a torn scrap of paper and folded over.

> Dear Mr. Mappin:
> You don't know me, but would you please out of
> kindness see me for one moment. I assure you it is
> terribly important. I have come three hundred miles
> to see you.
>
> Ann Brooke

That plain name pleased Lee; Ann Brooke. "Where is she?" he
asked.

"In the corridor," said the officer.

Lee followed him out. In the corridor he found a pretty young
woman with soft dark hair and brown eyes bearing an expression
of terrible anxiety. She was well dressed in a quiet style. At sight
of Lee, her eyes filled.

"How kind of you to come," she murmured. "I wrote to you because I read in the papers that you were a friend of Dick's."

"Dick?" said Lee. Then he remembered the language of the indictment. "Of course! I'm accustomed to think of him as Blondy."

"I went to school with him," she went on breathlessly. "I haven't seen him in ten years. I've come from Maryland. His parents are dead. He has no folks of his own. I . . . I felt I had to come, the newspapers are so down on him. I don't believe he's guilty. Even if he *is* guilty, he needs somebody to stand by him now . . ."

"That was a kindly impulse," said Lee.

"Would it be possible to get me into the courtroom where he could see that I was there?"

"You shall sit beside me," said Lee, more moved than he cared to show.

They returned to the front row. Blondy was immediately aware of the girl's entrance, and Lee saw her smile at him as a woman smiles at the man she loves when the world is against him. It made Lee feel almost tearful. Blondy blushed to his hair, then frowned a little and looked away.

"Oh!" whispered Ann in distress, "he isn't glad to see me here!"

"You shall see him when court adjourns," said Lee. "Then you can explain why you came."

"How kind you are!" she whispered. "To a stranger!"

Lee took a pinch of snuff to cover his feelings. "Well, I know a nice person when I see one," he said gruffly.

The jury box was filled by half past twelve and court then adjourned for an hour. Lee took Ann around to the jail. They were admitted to Blondy's cell together; "just for two minutes," the warden warned them. Blondy was eating his dinner.

The meeting was stiff and embarrassed, but not unfriendly. "You shouldn't have come!" said Blondy. "The trip is so expensive."

"I can spare the money," said Ann. "I just wanted you to know that you were not forgotten in Chestertown. We believe in you down there."

Blondy blushed all over again. It made him look wonderfully attractive. "Please tell everybody that I'm grateful," he said. "Thank them all for me."

A few minutes later, while Ann and Lee were eating in a restaurant, a hastily scribbled note from Blondy was brought to Lee.

> Please get her to go back home. Makes me feel ter-
> rible to see her sitting in the courtroom.

Lee shoved it in his pocket and considered the situation. Blondy
thinks she's in love with him, and so she is, but he doesn't have to
know that. He feels bad because he has nothing for her in return.
I'm not going to urge her to go home. The psychological effect of
her presence at the trial is good.

Lee left Ann long enough to scribble a couple of lines to Blondy:

> I'm not going to persuade her to go home. I suppose
> you think she's in love with you, but you're wrong.
> Her coming here was no more than a kindly human
> impulse. It's good for anybody to follow such an im-
> pulse.

When the court sat again, Enslin addressed the jury briefly.
Without attempting to indulge in any oratorical flourishes, he drew
attention to the inexorable facts of the case and left it to the jury.
In concluding, he said: "You will be told, and rightly told, that circumstantial evidence should be received with caution. But justice
very often has to depend on circumstantial evidence because men
customarily do not choose to commit crimes before witnesses,
especially premeditated crimes. The circumstantial evidence we
will place before you is supported and corroborated from several
sources. It cannot be controverted and, if true, there is only one
verdict that you can honestly find: murder in the first degree."

The taking of testimony began. Various police officers, medical examiners, photographers, fingerprint experts, etc. took the
stand to prove the finding and the identification of the body, the
nature of the fatal wound, the condition of the murder car and so
on. Paget, anxious above all to ingratiate himself with the jury,
declined to cross-examine any of these witnesses. He said: "These

men are all public servants; they have no axes to grind; the defense concedes that they are telling the simple truth."

The prosecution finished its case by the middle of the afternoon and Paget opened for the defense. Like Enslin, he belonged to the younger school of criminal lawyers; he made no assault upon the emotions of the jury, but set out to win them by a sweet reasonableness. He admitted that appearances bore hard against the defendant, but warned the jury of the danger of convicting a man on circumstantial evidence alone. Nobody saw the fatal shot fired.

"The defense will rest mainly on the story of the defendant himself," said Paget. "Every adult person has an instinct that warns him when another is lying. I ask you to observe the defendant with the closest attention while he is testifying; his bearing, his expression, his choice of words. And above all, I ask you to study how he conducts himself under the cross-examination of my distinguished friend, the District Attorney. Mr. Enslin is a highly expert examiner; he is famous for it, as you all know. The defendant is not obliged to take the stand; he cannot be forced to testify. Of his own free will he chooses to submit himself to the most merciless cross-examination that can be evolved, and he is content to stand or fall by the result."

Paget called Lee Mappin for his first witness. Enslin, dreading the effect of this name so renowned in criminology on the jury, interrupted his testimony with a barrage of objections. It was only hearsay evidence; it was immaterial; it had nothing whatever to do with the defendant on trial, and so on. Paget patiently argued the points:

"If it please the court, I suggest that it is highly material to the case, that Letty Ammon shortly before her murder came to this witness and confessed that she went in fear of her life from a source other than this defendant."

Lee was permitted to answer most of Paget's questions. He testified as to finding the letter from Blondy to Letty, but the copy he offered was not admitted as evidence.

Enslin savagely attacked him in cross-examination. This was a mistake in tactics, for Lee, more experienced than the youthful

District Attorney, was generally able to give a little better than he got. When he wished to gain time for an answer, Lee would take a pinch of snuff. This seemed to infuriate Enslin. He muttered loud enough for the jury to hear:

"A bit of old-fashioned stage business!"

"Oh," said Lee good-humoredly, "it's a gentle and harmless form of stimulant." He extended the snuff box. "Will you join me?"

"No, thank you," said Enslin stiffly.

The jury snickered.

"Mr. Mappin," asked Enslin. "What were your sentiments toward the unfortunate young victim of this crime?"

"Entirely affectionate," said Lee. "She was a lovely girl. I was sorry for her, too, because she had had a hard life."

"If you were so strongly attached to her, do you not wish to see her murderer brought to justice?"

"I certainly do," said Lee quickly, "when he is found!"

This brought a furious objection from Enslin. The latter part of Lee's answer was struck out. However, the jury had heard it. Paget, noting the effect, waited until Enslin had finished, and asked and obtained permission from the court to ask his witness one more question.

"Mr. Mappin, your qualifications in the matter of criminal psychology are known to all. You have been engaged in this case from the beginning, and all the persons concerned are well known to you."

"This is not a question," interpolated Enslin. "Counsel is favoring the court with an address."

The judge overruled him with a gesture. "Proceed, Mr. Paget."

"Is it your reasoned opinion," asked Paget, "that the defendant is guilty of the murder of Letty Ammon as charged?"

This brought an instant objection from the District Attorney and a long argument resulted. In the end Lee was forbidden to answer the question, but the jury had plenty of opportunity to see what his answer would have been.

Richard Farren was then called to the stand and sworn, and a ripple of excitement passed through the courtroom. This was what they had come to hear. Blondy clasped his hands loosely on his knee and waited for the first question with a composed air. He was *too* composed, Lee thought, with his long experience of the psychology of juries. If Blondy could have exhibited more feeling it would have recommended him to his fellow men.

Shepherded by his counsel, Blondy proceeded to tell the story of the events leading up to the death of Letty. In effect, it was the same story that he had told Lee and Inspector Loasby on the following day. If it had been told in the same words it would have sounded like something learned by rote, and Lee would have doubted, but there were human differences. Blondy overlooked certain details and included some new details.

"Did you wake up suddenly?" asked Paget.

Blondy considered before answering. "Not suddenly," he said. "It was like waking in a strange bed. For a moment, I wondered where I was. I had a feeling that something was wrong. It was so quiet; it was too quiet. Then I realized I had been sleeping out of doors; I was chilled. My hand fell against the leather upholstery and I knew I was in the car, but I couldn't remember how I got there. Then I saw Letty leaning over on the wheel and I thought she was sleeping. I put my arm around her shoulders. She didn't feel right, somehow. I put my hand over hers; it was cold, dead cold . . . I drew her to an upright position and I saw the wound in her head, I saw the blood. Then I knew . . ."

Blondy's head dropped. His hands were clenched on the arms of the witness chair. Lee glanced quickly at the jury. Their wooden faces gave nothing away.

Paget gave him a moment to get a grip on himself. "Was the blood still flowing?"

"No," answered Blondy very low.

"Had it dried?"

"Apparently not. Because when I took her in my arms it stained my hands and my clothes. But I wasn't aware of that."

"When did you become aware of it?"

"Not until the cops pointed it out to me after daylight."

Lee, hearing Blondy's story for the second time, after having had an interval to reflect on it, was convinced. If I have learned anything about human psychology in twenty years, he thought, he is telling the truth. Lee glanced at Ann Brooke and was surprised to see that her brown eyes were shining.

"Now I *know* that he is innocent!" she murmured.

Lee pressed her hand.

Paget turned over his witness to Enslin. Blondy awaited the District Attorney's onslaught calmly.

Enslin, leaving the counsel table, moved back and forth in front of the jury box. Blond, handsome and self-confident, he had recovered his good humor. He was presenting an attractive and convincing figure, and he knew it. He said:

"I am not going to take up a great deal of the court's time in a lengthy cross-examination. I am prepared to concede that the story told by the defendant is true—*with some very important omissions.*"

After giving this time to sink in, Enslin turned to the witness. "What were your sensations when you, as you say, passed out?"

Blondy hesitated.

"Why don't you answer the question?" demanded Enslin sharply.

"I don't quite know how to answer it," said Blondy. "I didn't have any sensations. It was like falling asleep."

"Did you suddenly become unconscious?"

Blondy considered before answering. "Not to say suddenly. I was conscious of a kind of creeping paralysis. Then I knew nothing more."

"A creeping paralysis?" echoed Enslin with a scornful smile. He glanced in the direction of the jury to invite them to smile with him.

"Call it what you like," said Blondy. "Everybody knows what it feels like to get sleepy all at once."

"I'm asking *you!*" said Enslin sharply.

"I'm trying to tell you," said Blondy quietly.

"At that moment, weren't you at a pretty exciting crisis of your life?"

"I sure was," answered Blondy somberly.

Enslin's forefinger shot out. "Then why didn't you fight against this sleepiness?"

Blondy explained as one might to a child. "When you get sleepy like that, nothing seems to matter any more. It's a comfortable feeling. You don't fight it. Then you're gone."

"Are you often overcome in that manner?"

"Never just like that," said Blondy. "Never in my life before."

"Then how do you account for it on this particular night?"

"I believe I was drugged," said Blondy.

Enslin angrily objected to this answer.

Paget, smiling broadly—he had not been able to get the suggestion before the jury that Blondy was drugged—said: "May I point out to counsel that it was a prompt and direct answer to his question?"

Blondy's answer was allowed to stand.

For over an hour Enslin hammered at the question of Blondy's unconsciousness, approaching it now from this side, now from that; dropping it for a moment, only to swoop on it again with an unexpected question. He did not, however, succeed in confusing Blondy or in making him contradict himself. Blondy did not even appear to be on his guard, but answered Enslin's questions quickly and thoughtlessly. If we had a jury of trained psychologists, thought Lee, the boy would go free.

When Enslin finally relinquished the witness, of the two it was the District Attorney who appeared to be the most fatigued. It was now past five, and court rose for the day. When the reporters crowded around Lee to ask his views on the case, and in particular to find out who the pretty girl was who had been sitting beside him, Lee carelessly mentioned that it was Blondy's childhood sweetheart. When they read this, Lee knew that it would probably annoy both Blondy and Ann, but he hoped it might have its influence on the jury.

Before returning to New York, Lee obtained the privilege of another brief interview with the prisoner. Knowing how prone young people are to misunderstand and to torment each other in an emotional crisis, he undertook to coach Ann as to how she should bear herself. She scarcely needed it.

"I know how Dick feels about me," she said with a secret smile. "I'll put him to rights."

When they entered the cell, Lee walked away to the window and looked out, leaving the two together. He could not hear what they said, but it was successful, for when he presently turned around at the entrance of a keeper, Blondy's strained expression had eased, and he was smiling at Ann as at a sister.

As they left, Ann said: "I'll see you in the courtroom tomorrow."

Blondy's expression sobered. "You will hear bad news," he warned her.

"I can take it. Today I heard what I wanted to hear; your side of the story."

"You're a good friend," said Blondy.

Lee knew that Sandra Cassells would be curious about Ann, but as long as Sandra chose to maintain her present attitude, he saw nothing to be gained by bringing them together. The newspapers would presently be in the hands of all with reports of the trial and photographs, and in order to save Ann from the stares of the curious, he took her to his own place for dinner. As the hours passed, he was more and more charmed with Ann's simplicity and candor; her good sense. Beauty *plus* character, he said to himself. Not very common.

"Chestertown is a very old place," she remarked during dinner, "with many beautiful old houses occupied by families equally old. As neither Dick nor I belonged to an old family, they never troubled us. Dick was the only boy that ever attracted me. I chose him while I was still in pigtails. . . . I don't mind telling you that," she explained with a smile, "because you've guessed it already, and I know you won't give me away."

"I will not," said Lee. "I am a general repository for indiscreet confessions."

"I don't think Dick is a hero or a superman," she went on. "I know he's just an average boy. I chose him because, well, because he was Dick! That's the only way I can explain it . . ."

"It is sufficient," said Lee.

"After his father and mother died, he ran away because he didn't want to be an object of charity. He never wrote to me, but I heard that he got into trouble. Somehow it got to be known around town that he was in prison in California. He had a boy's natural craving for excitement and adventure, and I suppose that's what led him into trouble. I never heard any more about him. I wouldn't be surprised to learn that he was often in trouble; bad trouble. Because he was a natural rebel and stubborn, too." Ann raised a pair of beseeching eyes to Lee's face. "But don't stubborn, rebellious boys sometimes turn out to be fine men?" she asked. "They have more in them than the tame ones."

"That is perfectly true," said Lee.

"I heard no more about him until I read that he had been arrested for murder. That was a terrible shock. There are certain kinds of murder that Dick might have committed, but not a woman, not a woman he was in love with. I *know* it could not be true. And so I came."

After dinner they read the late editions of the newspapers together. When it was announced that the taking of evidence was completed, great disappointment was expressed that the famous Mrs. Nick Cassells had not been called by either side. It was even hinted in certain quarters that the whole truth about this murder had not been brought out in court. Ann, after having sampled a couple of papers, threw the lot aside with scorn. She said:

"I used to respect the newspapers. But since I have read what they say about something that I know, I feel differently. This is just silly stuff."

Lee laughed.

Later he found Ann a room in a small and inconspicuous hotel where nobody would think of looking for her.

On the following morning, as soon as court opened, District Attorney Enslin started his address to the jury. It was a brilliant and forcible speech. Enslin seemed to tower over the jury box; he commanded the jury; he sought to bend them to his will. The inference was that any man who did not agree with him was obviously an idiot. Lee could not judge from a study of the double line of stolid faces how far Enslin was prevailing over them. The twelve represented an average selection of small merchants, clerks and workingmen.

"The prisoner made a very good showing on the stand," said Enslin sarcastically. "Why was he able to do so? Because he told the plain truth *up to a certain point*. Naturally he could not be shaken. I did not try to shake him *up to that point*. The most convincing of all liars is the liar who sticks to the truth *up to a point*. Then when he can no longer tell the truth in safety, does he lie? No! He says I can't remember. That's the oldest dodge known in a court of law. This defendant only improves on it a little, when he says: I was unconscious; I had passed out!"

Enslin paused and a small ripple of laughter passed through the courtroom. The judge whacked his gavel.

"The defendant suggests that he was drugged," Enslin went on. "Let us examine that possibility. According to his own story, nobody approached him all evening except three waiters, who could not have known in advance that he would sit down at their tables. Then, if he was drugged, he must have been drugged by his companion. And it was that companion, Letty Ammon, who was killed! Is it reasonable? . . ."

Later little Paget's turn came. Since he lacked Enslin's physical advantages and his powerful voice, instead of commanding the jury, he set out to persuade them. In his opening he subtly flattered them:

"As plain men of good sense and food feeling, husbands and fathers, most of you, I take it, you are not the sort of men to be swayed by oratory. I shall therefore speak to you very simply and plainly."

Later on Paget said: "In opening for the defense, I invited you to pay particular attention to the conduct of the defendant under cross-examination. It was an unequal contest; on the one hand, the brilliant District Attorney whose duty it is to cross-examine some defendant every day court is in session, and who is on to all their tricks; on the other hand, this defendant, not a highly educated man, and certainly never before on trial for his life. How did he emerge from the ordeal? My learned friend made much of the single point at which the defendant, he claims, ceased to tell the truth, but I call your attention to the fact that neither at that point nor at any other point did the skillful and experienced public prosecutor succeed in shaking the defendant's testimony.

"In the same connection, I want to point out something else. The People put a dozen witnesses on the stand, public servants of one kind or another, to testify as to what they found after the murder. The testimony of these witnesses does not conflict at any point whatsoever with the story told by the defendant. Surely, this would be impossible unless the defendant were telling the truth *at all points*. He first told his story, you remember, on the day following the tragedy. The statement he made then is in evidence, and if you wish to compare it with his story on the stand, you have only to ask for it.

"Both sides are agreed that Letty Ammon was at the wheel of the stopped car at the moment she was shot. The prosecution contends that after Letty had driven the car into the driveway in front of the deserted house, the defendant took his gun out of the glove compartment and shot her. Why? No motive has been adduced. There is no evidence that they were quarreling. Is it not more reasonable to suppose that Letty drove into that deserted drive and stopped to give her escort time to recover himself; that there was a marauder lurking behind the bushes; that when he saw a helpless man and an undefended woman, he undertook to rob them? He opened the glove compartment first; he found the gun, and when the woman resisted him he shot her. Her handbag, I would remind you, has never been found."

The two speeches occupied the whole morning session. During the recess, groups of people congregated on the principal corners of the town, discussing the case. There was not much difference of opinion among them; feeling ran high against the defendant. Lee took Ann Brooke out by a rear stairway to escape the gaping crowds. In Lee's car, parked in a side street, they ate the lunch that Jermyn had put up for them. Sandra Cassells took her party to Brookwood, which was not far away.

When all were again in their places, Judge McLanahan began his address to the jury. Lee judged from a slight alteration in the faces of some of the jury that they looked more to the bench for guidance than to the opposing counsel. The judge, in going over the circumstances of the crime, said: "At that point, the defendant says that he became unconscious." He paused for a second and went on: "It is for the jury to decide whether or not he is speaking the truth." Lee's heart sank. That unconscious pause, he thought, is likely to send Blondy to the chair. He could find no fault with the judge's charge, which was fair and dispassionate.

The jury went out at half past two and the judge retired to his chambers. Before half an hour was up, the jury sent the bailiff to notify his honor that they were ready to render a verdict and he returned to the bench. When he saw that, Lee gave up hope. The best he had hoped for was a disagreement.

Led by the bailiff, the jury paraded solemnly into the court-room. A hush fell on all. Their responsibility lay heavy upon the jurymen. It seemed to take them an interminable time to find their places in the box. The judge felt the strain; his rosy cheeks paled a little; both the lawyers were on tenterhooks; the spectators leaned forward in their seats breathlessly. Of all present, only the defen-dant showed an unchanged composure. He had steeled himself to hear the worst.

"The jury will rise; the prisoner will rise and face the jury."

"Gentlemen of the jury, have you agreed upon a verdict?"

"We have, your honor."

"How do you find the prisoner?"

"Guilty of murder in the first degree."

A sigh escaped from the spectators. Satisfaction! thought Lee. This was what they wanted to hear. Not for the first time in his life, Lee marveled at the cruelty of men in the mass. Individuals were merciful enough. Like wildfire, the verdict was communicated to those in the corridor and to the crowd outside the building. Their handclapping and cries of approval could be heard. Lee felt merely numb. He glanced anxiously at Ann. Her head was lowered, her little hands clenched. He heard her murmuring:

"Why are they *glad?* . . . It's unjust! It's unjust! . . . They're all blind!"

The prisoner betrayed no emotion. His eyes sought Ann's face and she raised her head with a radiant smile of affection and en-couragement. Lee thought: It would be almost worth it to win that!

The judge set a day for sentence, thanked the jury and, after discharging them, retired. The jury began to descend from their box. Sieg Ammon, his dark face alight with satisfaction, hastened across the room to thank each man effusively and shake his hand. Natural enough, Lee thought, but hardly in the best of taste. Sieg then, while Lee looked on grimly, led the jury back to where Sandra Cassells was sitting. The great lady extended her hand graciously to each man and commended him for doing his duty.

## CHAPTER FOURTEEN

LEE'S OWN INVESTIGATION of the murder was not terminated by the trial of Blondy, but only interrupted for a couple of days. Luckily, in our country men are not taken directly from the court to the place of execution, and he still had some weeks to turn around in. He was pursuing three lines of inquiry: Queenie Deane, Spanish Jack, and the old sedan. So far, no two of them had shown any disposition to converge. Lee wondered a little that Queenie had not attended the trial; this could be accounted for in two ways; either she was not sufficiently concerned to make the trip to White Plains, or she was *too deeply concerned.*

Since the death of Letty Ammon, Tappan reported that Queenie had formed a habit of dropping in at Hope House to see Sieg. Lee smiled grimly at the news. She's taking my hint that Sieg needs a woman's sympathy, he thought. Queenie usually came at eleven o'clock in the morning, which was about the hour that Sieg got out of bed. Thus she was sure of finding him at home; it was also an hour when she could be certain of not finding Mrs. Cassells in the house. The fact that Queenie herself was impelled to get up so early gave Lee a measure of the passion with which she was pursuing the handsome Sieg.

Lee, after calling at Hope House once or twice at this hour, was rewarded one morning by finding Queenie in the game room. Sieg had not come downstairs. Queenie was none too pleased to see Lee there. Lee was all affability. Talking about this and that, he asked carelessly:

"What do you think about the result of Blondy's trial?"

"What do I think?" she asked sharply. "What would anybody think? Blondy only got what was coming to him. . . . Though I feel sorry for him at that," she added as an afterthought. "Letty drove him to it."

"Then you're satisfied that Blondy did it?"

"Aren't you?" she parried.

"Not quite," said Lee, affecting to frown in perplexity. "There are so many little circumstances that have not been explained."

"You can make your mind easy," said Queenie. "I know that Blondy shot her."

"If you have any special information you ought to have taken it to the District Attorney," said Lee.

"He didn't need my evidence," said Queenie with a hard smile. "He had plenty without it."

"Tell me," said Lee, "in order to set my doubts at rest."

Queenie shrugged. "You know more about it than I do."

"Strange, isn't it," said Lee, "that you should be the last person who knew Letty to see her alive."

Queenie showed her teeth. "What do you think you're getting at?"

"Am I getting at something?" said Lee with an innocent air. "You did see her at McGovern's, didn't you?"

"I never went to McGovern's! I told you that before!"

"Sorry! I understood that you waited outside in your car until Blondy and Letty appeared."

"That's a lie and I have already nailed it! I only went as far as Schanze's."

"My mistake," said Lee.

Queenie gave him a long look of suspicion. Lee took a pinch of snuff.

Lee tried a shot in the dark. "When you were at Schanze's," he said, watching her without appearing to, "did you happen to see an old black Buick sedan waiting among the other cars?"

Queenie's face gave nothing away. "How should I notice what cars were there?"

"But did you see such a car?"

"I did not."

"When Blondy backed out and turned, he bumped into this car."

"I didn't see Blondy when he left."

Lee applied a little heat. "Are you sure," he asked sternly, "that you did not leave Schanze's in the old black sedan and pick up your car again on the way back?"

"I don't know what you're talking about!" said Queenie shrilly. "Sounds like nonsense to me. You and your black sedan!"

She was angry but the question had not frightened her. Lee could not feel that he had gained anything. The two lines refused to converge.

He tried another approach. "You said you left Schanze's about half past eight. You did not return your car to the garage that night until eleven-fifteen. What were you doing between those hours?"

Queenie's eyes betrayed a flicker of fright at this question, but she answered readily: "It's none of your damned business, but I have no objection to telling you. I was back at the hotel before nine-thirty. I left the car parked in the street." It must have occurred to her at this moment that if Lee had been asking questions at her garage, he could also ask at the hotel. "Perhaps you have forgotten," she added sarcastically, "that the Amsterdam has entrances on two streets. I can go in the back door and go up in the elevator without being seen from the desk."

Lee, smiling, had to confess himself checked.

He suspended further questioning for, at that moment, Sieg Ammon entered. Sieg, freshly scrubbed, ruddy and handsome as a young Arab chieftain, was himself again. He greeted Lee and kissed Queenie carelessly.

"Had your breakfast?" he asked her.

"No."

"Come on downstairs and let's see what there is."

Lee went on.

He made an arrangement with the manager of the Amsterdam to look over Queenie's mail before it was sent up to her. For several days his reports were negative, then Lee got this from him:

Today a business letter came for Q.D. which had in the corner of the envelope: 'If not delivered in 10 days return to P.O. Box 579a, New York City.' This looked a little mysterious so I thought you would want to know about it.

Lee immediately put through an inquiry to the post office and was informed that box 579a was rented by the Willis Detective Agency, West 56th Street. Lee lost no time in visiting the Agency. He knew Willis, the proprietor, and of course Willis knew him; he showed every disposition to treat Lee as a confrere.

"Are you willing to tell me what you know about Queenie Deane?" asked Lee.

"Sure, Mr. Mappin, if you will guarantee to protect me."

"I will protect you."

"Then I'm glad to tell you. I have information about Queenie and Letty Ammon that has troubled my mind. But if I had been questioned by the authorities I would have had to plead professional privilege."

"Well, go ahead."

"Queenie owes me a bill at this moment. On May 5th she engaged me to trail Mrs. Letty Ammon and report to her. Expense no object. I put two men on the case. They engaged a front room on Henry Street where they could watch Hope House at all hours, and they had a car handy so they could follow Letty if she took a taxi. Letty rarely left the house and there was nothing in the reports of any interest up to the day of her murder. On that day it was reported that she proceeded to Fossberg's restaurant on Delancey Street about three in the afternoon, had a talk there with a foreign-looking man about fifteen minutes, and then returned home. My operatives could not identify the fellow.

"At seven-thirty P.M. the same day, she came out of the house again. One of my men followed her down the street on foot while the other kept within hailing distance in the car. At the corner of Henry and Scammell Streets, Letty got into a maroon-colored convertible coupé and drove away with a man. My men did not get a good look at him but, as you know, this was Blondy Farren in his car. My men followed them up to Schanze's roadhouse in the Bronx. They settled down there drinking and seemed likely to stay a good while. Now Queenie had instructed us that if we ever found Letty with another man she was to be notified immediately. So one of my men went to call her while the other watched the couple. Queenie herself got up to Schanze's in a little over half an hour. Must have driven like hell. The couple was still sitting there. Queenie told my men that she would take over herself for the rest of the night and sent them home. That's all."

Lee thought this over. "You have answered one question that has puzzled my mind," he said. "Further than that what you have told me only confirms what I knew already. . . . If I could only take Queenie beyond Schanze's! . . . Are you willing to let me read the reports of your two men?"

"Sure, Mr. Mappin!"

A study of the reports gave Lee nothing further to go on. During all the days that Letty had been under surveillance, she had never gone out in the old sedan, nor was there the slightest clue as to where she kept the car.

Lee called at the Amsterdam and sent up his name to Queenie. The answer came back that Miss Deane was sick and begged to be excused. Lee then wrote a little note as follows:

> If you refuse to see me I shall ask for a new trial for Blondy Farren and you will be subpoenaed as a witness. It will not make a pretty story.

Queenie presently phoned to the desk that Mr. Mappin was to come up.

He found her pacing her room clad in a black negligee that made her look taller than ever. Her hair was standing out, her face was streaked. She burst out at Lee before he got the door well closed:

"How long have I got to put up with your nosing and snooping and persecuting? You've got no legal right to hound a person and

I'm damn sick of it! If you don't leave me alone I know what to do to protect myself!"

Lee was not disposed to be patient with her today.

"Cut out the tirade!" he said bluntly. "I'm a busy man and you've caused me to waste too much time already!"

"Me waste your time!" she gasped. "I like that!"

"Exactly," said Lee. "With all the lies you've told me that I have to patiently nail, one by one!"

"You're a liar!"

"Be quiet! And listen to me. I've learned a good deal more about your activities on the night Letty Ammon was killed since I talked to you."

"What do you think you've learned?"

"You had been having Letty followed for a week. Your men followed her up to Schanze's. They telephoned you. You went up there and took over. Those were the words you used when you sent the men back to town: 'I will take over.' I want to know what happened then?"

"Nothing," said Queenie sullenly.

"You can either tell me or tell the District Attorney."

"All right, I'll tell you!" she suddenly burst out. "And much good may it do you! I never lied to you. I told you my evidence would only clinch the verdict against Blondy. I didn't see him shoot her but I heard the shot!"

"All right. Tell me the whole circumstances."

"I followed them in my car from Schanze's to McGovern's," she said sullenly. "I had to be careful because Blondy had spotted me in Schanze's. At McGovern's I didn't go in. I walked around outside. I watched them through a window. When they came out I followed them to the White Goose."

"Was anybody following *you?*"

"How do I know? I never looked around me. At the White Goose I never went in, either. I watched them through the window."

"What was the purpose of all this?" asked Lee.

"I wanted to get something on Letty. I knew she was no better than any other woman and I wanted to show Sieg. I was waiting for them to go upstairs in one of those roadhouses; then I'd have her!"

"But they didn't."

"No, they didn't. When they left the White Goose I almost lost them. Blondy was suspicious and kept looking behind him. I had to give them a long start. I found them again in a straight piece of road. They turned out of the road. When I got to the place I saw it was a private entrance. I stopped my car. I meant to follow them in there, thinking I'd catch them. As I was getting out of my car, I heard Letty cry out 'Don't! Don't!' Then a scream and a shot. That scared me. I jumped back in my car and drove away from there."

"Could you see what happened in the driveway?"

"No. Nothing more than the flash of the gun."

"Did you hear any other voice?"

"No! I've told you every damn thing I know!"

"Why didn't you tell me all this in the beginning?"

"I didn't want to be called as a witness. What difference does it make anyhow?"

Queenie began to cry. Lee flung up his hands and let them drop. He made his way out.

## CHAPTER FIFTEEN

SPANISH JACK HAD ENGAGED a smart lawyer to defend him. A few days after his arrest, his lawyer had sued for a writ of *habeas corpus* and Spanish was brought before a magistrate. On that occasion, the District Attorney had succeeded in having him remanded; however, the case against Spanish was flimsy; he had a certain right to enter Hope House since he had recently been a boarder there, and if he had ransacked Letty's belongings it could not be proved that he had taken anything. Consequently, the next time he was brought up in court, Lee expected him to be discharged.

Lee went to see Spanish in the towering new jail that has taken the place of the old Tombs. Armed with credentials from the District Attorney's office, he was permitted to talk to the prisoner in one of the rooms allotted to counsel. A keeper waited outside the open door. Spanish, perfectly groomed even in jail, greeted Lee with a self-satisfied smirk. His well-cut suit of fine black broadcloth was like a badge of office. Spanish hesitated a little at every step like a tango dancer. The corner of a snowy handkerchief stuck out of his breast pocket.

"This is a great honor, Mr. Mappin!" Spanish liked to think that he was baiting Lee with his subtle impudence.

Lee didn't mind. "Well, we'll see," he said. "Let's sit down and talk."

"At your service," said Spanish, bowing.

Lee wasted no time in beating around the bush. "The last time I saw you," he began, "you asked me why I sent you on a wild goose chase to Boston. I didn't care to answer the question at that moment; since then you have read my testimony at Blondy Farren's trial and now you know the answer."

"That's right," said Spanish.

"Perhaps now you will be willing to answer my question. Why was Letty Ammon in such terror of you that your presence in the house made her hysterical?"

"I am not obliged to answer your questions, Mr. Mappin," said Spanish, "but I enjoy playing ball with you, and so I answer freely . . . Letty was afraid that I would tell Sieg Ammon that she and I had had an affair when we were both working at Bartol's."

"Was that after Sieg had left?"

"Yes. Sieg was in Sing Sing."

"What could Sieg expect?" said Lee. "A beautiful girl like Letty thrown on the world almost as a child, and forced to work in a place like Bartol's?"

"Sieg expected the impossible," said Spanish, smirking. "Letty, as you know, looked as pure as an angel and she had persuaded Sieg that she was so. That's why he married her. If he had discovered how he had been fooled, there would have been hell to pay. Sieg would have chucked her on the spot."

Lee pondered on this. It did not jibe with what Letty had told him and he preferred to believe Letty. "When you were released from Welfare Island," he asked, "why did you apply for a room at Hope House?"

"Need you ask?" drawled Spanish. "Letty was a very beautiful woman and I couldn't forget her. I was hoping that I might enjoy through fear what I had previously had through inclination. Fear, you know, would lend a certain zest . . ." He finished his sentence with a wave of the hand.

"By God!" said Lee grimly, "if you are telling me the truth you are the perfect blackguard!"

"You flatter me!" murmured Spanish, smirking. It gave him real pleasure to be held up as a monster of wickedness.

"That note from Letty to you that was found in your wallet," Lee pointed out, "that does not agree with what you have just told me. What was it that Letty was threatening to tell *me?*"

"The same that I have just told you. Letty was counting on your well-known moral views to have me put out of the house."

"You had already left the house."

"Oh, I had been carrying that note around for some days," said Spanish carelessly.

Lee did not believe this, but there was no date on Letty's note and he was unable to prove that Spanish was lying. "Her note was very strangely worded," he said. "What had she in mind when she wrote: 'If anything happens to me I have fixed it so that Mr. Mappin will be fully informed and you can't prevent it'?"

Spanish shrugged. "Don't ask me to explain what goes through a hysterical woman's mind. I doubt if she could have explained it herself."

"Something *did* happen to her," said Lee softly.

"Well, then," said Spanish impudently, "according to her you will be informed of all the circumstances."

There was something inhuman in Spanish's cool self-confidence. Clearly, he enjoyed matching wits with the celebrated Mr. Mappin; he believed himself the cleverer of the two. If I am patient, thought Lee, he may betray himself in the end through overconfidence. Lee therefore began to act as if he found Spanish too much for him. He took a new line.

"You arrived at Grand Central shortly after noon on that fatal Wednesday; that would be coincident with the arrival of the first fast train of the day from Boston."

"That's right," said Spanish.

"You taxied over to Mendes' flat in Brooklyn . ."

"Checked my suitcase first," put in Spanish, "because I didn't know if Piero would have room to put me up."

"Later," continued Lee, "you carried your friends over to Manhattan and treated them to a fine lunch at Fossberg's. You called up Letty Ammon and ordered her to come to you there . . ."

"Ordered her?" murmured Spanish, running up his brows. "I hope I was not so crude."

"Well, she came, and I find it difficult to believe that she came willingly . . . What did you want of her?"

Spanish answered readily: "I wanted to find out if it was she who had put you up to sending me to Boston."

"And you found out?"

"Sure! She couldn't hide it."

"And then?"

"I told her that I was back from Boston. And that she had better see to it that I got back my room at Hope House—or else!"

"How charming of you!" said Lee.

"Call it devilish if you like," said Spanish conceitedly, "but not crude. I always act with finesse."

"What did she say?"

"She said she'd try her best."

"When you left Fossberg's, where did you go?"

"I taxied up to a little club that I belong to on 47th Street. Show people belong to it. It is called the Ravens. I was there all afternoon. I see you've got a police report there. Notice that I brought forward, not one or two, but six members of the Ravens to testify that they had drunk with me in the clubhouse, or played billiards, or just talked. And I can get half a dozen more if you want."

"Six will be sufficient," said Lee dryly. "What time did you leave the Ravens and where did you go?"

"About six-thirty I went to Whitelock's restaurant for my dinner."

"Alone?"

"Sure! I enjoy my own company sometimes."

"So do I," said Lee. "You cannot therefore bring forward anybody who saw you at Whitelock's?"

"No. It's a very big place and at six-thirty it's crowded to the doors. Nobody would remember seeing me there."

"Then where did you go?"

"Bought a ticket and went to see *Hellzapoppin!*"

"See anybody you know there?"

"No. But luckily for me, I saved my seat check. Here it is."

Lee examined the check. "That's a proper check for that Wednesday night," he said, "but of course it's not proof that you occupied the seat."

"Have you seen the latest version of *Hellzapoppin?*" asked Spanish.

"I have."

"Well, does it go like this?" Spanish started to relate the scenes in their order.

Lee soon stopped him. "I am satisfied that you have seen the show, but still you have not proved that it was on that particular night."

"The seat check is pretty good proof," said Spanish.

"Where did you go after the show?"

"Back to the Ravens."

"You might have picked up the seat check in an ash tray there. Or in the street. People drop them everywhere after the show."

Spanish shook his head with affected regret. "Mr. Mappin, I wouldn't want to be you! You're a fine man; you've got a wonderful brain, but you're poisoned with suspicion!"

Lee enjoyed the comedy. "Well, Spanish, I'll tell you something since we're being frank with each other. You smell of wickedness and that's what makes my suspicions stand on end like quills upon the fretful porcupine."

Spanish did not much care for this figure of speech. He shrugged elaborately. "I can bring forward a dozen men to swear that I was at the Ravens at midnight."

"I am not interested in you at that hour," said Lee.

"What do you want?" said Spanish, spreading out his hands. "Blondy Farren has been convicted of the murder of Letty. The evidence was overwhelming. How many men do you want to send to the chair?"

"Only one," said Lee. "But the right one."

"Why should I want to rub out Letty?"

"I don't know. But I know she was deathly afraid of you."

"I enjoy scaring people," said Spanish smirking. "It don't mean nothing. It's just my fun."

"Pleasant fun," said Lee.

"I've done all I can to help you," said Spanish. "You're only butting your head against a wall now."

Lee thought: The evidence against him is destroyed and he feels safe. He said: "Well, let's get on with the story. After leaving the Ravens you went back to Brooklyn to spend the night."

"That's right. Called for my bag at Grand Central first. Didn't take it over with me first off because I didn't know if Piero had room. But he and the girl insisted on my coming back."

"Then in the morning—let me see, the first papers announcing Letty's murder were on the street about nine o'clock. I suppose you read of it."

"I did," said Spanish gravely. "And I may say I was shocked!"

"I'm sure you were. What did you do?"

Spanish looked at him sharply. "Mr. Mappin, I have a right to refuse to answer that question. I have still to be tried on the charge of unlawful entry."

"I am not a police officer," said Lee. "I assure you that whatever you tell me now will not be used against you at that trial."

"Okay! Your word is good enough for me. I had written Letty some letters. Pretty warm, you understand. I told her to destroy them, but you never can be sure about a woman. So I went over to Hope House. I let myself in with my key. There wasn't anybody in the front of the house. I took a chance and ran up to Letty's room and went through her things."

"Did you find your letters?"

"No, sir. Like a sensible girl she had destroyed them. So I got out."

"How come you had two keys to the house?"

"That's just a habit of mine. Whenever I have a latch key I have a duplicate made in case I lose one."

"Really! Why didn't you turn both keys in when you gave up your room?"

"Well, I was hoping to get back there, you know."

"Spanish," said Lee, "you put on an almost perfect show!"

Spanish smirked. "Why *almost* perfect, Mr. Mappin?"

"It's a little *too* good, Spanish. It sounds rehearsed."

Spanish raised his shoulders high in the Latin fashion.

"It's impossible to satisfy you!"

"I don't have to remind you," said Lee, "that there is one *very* suspicious incident that has not been explained. When we were driving back over Brooklyn Bridge in the police car, you drew a key out of your sock that had a tag attached, and tossed it into the river."

Spanish went into a silent fit of laughter. "That was for the handsome Inspector, Mr. Mappin. He was so damn conceited, he made me sore. I just wanted to take him down a peg."

"That tag had my name written on it. Looked like Letty's hand."

"But I tossed it right out of the window," said Spanish. "How could you read it? Could you swear on the Bible that that was Letty's handwriting?"

"No," said Lee. "I didn't have time enough."

"Could you swear that your name was on the tag?"

"That I could," said Lee coolly. "A man is so familiar with the shape of his own name, he can read it in a lightning glance."

"Mr. Mappin, in your experience haven't you known of men swearing falsely in perfectly good faith?"

"Certainly," said Lee.

"That's what you would be doing in this case, sir. That tag had nothing in the world to do with you."

"What was the key?"

"It was the key to my locker at the Sporting Club in Monte Carlo when I worked there. I carried it away with me by mistake. Always meant to return it. I stuck it in my sock just before we got into the police car, just so I could make that conceited cop look like a fool. And I did, too. Never thought it would take you in, Mr. Mappin."

"What was written on the tag?" asked Lee.

"My name, Jacques D'Acosta. That's the way I spelled it in France."

"There was writing on the other side of the tag, too. What was that?"

"That was my address in case I dropped the key and it was picked up. I had a room at Beausoleil, the French town above Monte. You know what those French addresses are; it's like writing your life story."

Lee looked at the man with a kind of admiration. "Spanish," he said, "you are one of the slickest articles I have ever met with!"

Spanish shook his head in pretended sorrow. "Ah, you don't believe what I'm telling you!"

"Not a word!" said Lee cheerfully.

"Well, in one way I'm glad if I haven't satisfied you," said Spanish, smirking. "Maybe you'll come to see me again. I've enjoyed our talk today."

"So have I," said Lee. He signaled to the keeper that the interview was over.

# CHAPTER SIXTEEN

WHEN THE USED-CAR DEALER, Smither, was brought down to view the old sedan in the police yard, he had immediately pointed out that the two rear tires were new. They were stamped with the name Schoenberg, one of the smaller manufacturers. They showed scarcely any wear. When Smither ran the engine, he said it was in better order than when it had left his hands; better compression, hence more power; new cylinder rings had been installed. Further examination disclosed that a new generator had been put in, and the brakes relined. "Quite an expensive job of repairs to put on an old shay like that," Smither had remarked.

The only clue that Lee possessed to the recent travels of the car—if it could be called a clue—was the card of matches he had found that had slipped back of the front seat. It bore the imprint of the Eureka Restaurant in Elizabeth, New Jersey. Lee borrowed the car from the police and had himself driven over there.

The restaurant was a new, popular-price establishment at the edge of the industrial district, shining with white tiles and porcelain table tops. It was midafternoon when Lee called and only a few tables were occupied. He judged from his long experience of restaurants, high and low, that good food was served in this place. A stout, placid woman at the cashier's desk helped carry out the suggestion of prosperity. Her name was Mrs. Lenassa and she owned the place.

"Excuse me for troubling you," said Lee. "Notice the car in front of the door. I want you to tell me if you have ever seen it before. I believe it belongs to a customer of yours."

She was astonished by the unusualness of the request. Upon adjusting herself, she assured Lee that she had never seen the car before. She brought up her daughter, who spelled her at certain hours at the cashier's desk, and two waitresses. All were positive that they had never seen the old sedan. Lee was obliged to charge off this visit to profit and loss.

At the Buick agency in Elizabeth, he was told that the car was unknown to them and that certainly the recent repairs on it had not been done in their shop. He inquired where Schoenberg tires were sold in that town and was directed to a service station. Here his luck changed, for the attendant recognized the car and remembered putting on the two tires. "Over a month ago," he said. Reference to his sales slips established the exact date: April 23rd. This was the same day that Letty had bought the car.

"Describe the driver," said Lee.

The attendant scratched his head. "I don't remember him very good, Mister."

"Are you sure it wasn't a woman?"

"It wasn't a woman. I would remember a woman."

"Was it a young man?"

"Not a young man. But you wouldn't call him an old man, neither."

"About how old?"

"I never could estimate a person's age, Mister."

"Was he a big man or a little man?"

"Medium size."

"What did he wear?"

"Nothing special."

"Well, was he well dressed or roughly dressed?"

"Neither the one nor the other. Just ordinary."

Patient questioning failed to produce anything further. However, just as Lee was ready to give up, the unobservant young man volunteered a piece of information that provided him with a fresh lead.

"I mind this fellow asking me where he could get some repairs done to his car. I directed him to the Buick Agency, but he says no, he wanted to take it to some jobbing garage where they'd do it cheaper, so I sent him to Baring Brothers."

At this place the job of work they had done on the old sedan was remembered. It was seldom that an owner was willing to spend so much on such an old car. He had given the name of John Adams; when his address was asked for, he replied that he had no address in Elizabeth as yet, that he had to find a room. There was considerable difference of opinion among the mechanics as to the customer's appearance; one estimated his age at forty, another said fifty, and a third insisted that he was an old man who was trying to conceal his age. This did not suggest any individual who had ever been mentioned in connection with the case, and Lee felt glum. His problem was complicated enough, without bringing in a new factor.

One mechanic remembered some details. "He come in for his car a week later and I noticed he hadn't shaved since. He was dressed like a workingman then. The first time he might have been a drummer in a small way, or a clerk." Another said: "Here's something, if it's any use to you. I remember when he brought the car here he stopped on the way out and copied down an address from our order board. He was carrying a little, worn old satchel, imitation alligator."

At the top of the board to which were pinned the orders in process of being filled, Lee found the card of a Mrs. Doughty, who advertised rooms to rent to single workingmen. Lee in his turn wrote down her address and set out in the old sedan to find it.

Mrs. Doughty's was more like a small hotel than a rooming house. It was a plain new building, especially designed for workingmen's lodgings at the edge of the great industrial district of Elizabeth. The proprietor was a grim woman who obviously would take no nonsense. At first, she was disinclined to furnish any information whatever, but, luckily for Lee, she had a younger sister full of curiosity.

"Ain't no man been living here lately by the name of Adams."

"Well, he might have given you another name. Adams wasn't his right name. He came on April 23rd. Middle-aged man, dressed like a traveler or a clerk at that time. Later he wore a workingman's clothes. He was careless about shaving. All the baggage he had was a small, badly worn satchel of imitation alligator. This was his car."

The sisters looked at each other. "Mr. Wilson!" said the younger. "Mr. Arthur Wilson. But that ain't his car. Mr. Wilson didn't have no car."

"Well, perhaps he didn't bring it home. All his doings were mysterious."

"Mysterious, that was Mr. Wilson," said the younger woman, nodding vigorously. "I always said so! Never talked about himself. Most men are always talking. You get to know all about them. Not Mr. Wilson!"

By this time, Lee had succeeded in gaining Mrs. Doughty's confidence. He was asked in, and the three of them sat down in the office.

"He didn't shave the first few days he was with you," prompted Lee.

"He never shaved the whole time he was here. Said he had an eczema and wanted to give it time to heal, but I couldn't see no eczema. His beard come in half white and he dyed it black. I saw the dye on his bureau. Dyed his hair, too. He was bald on top and let his hair grow long on one side so he could brush it all the way across. His black beard made him look pretty rough, but he was a quiet man, gave no trouble. Didn't make no friends with the other men."

"How long was he with you?"

"You say he come on April 23rd. Would be about three weeks."

"Three weeks less three days," said Mrs. Doughty. "He left on Wednesday, five o'clock, real sudden, though he was paid up to Saturday."

Letty Ammon had been killed about ten o'clock on Wednesday, May 11th.

"Said he had a call to a good job in Altoona," added the sister.

"Was he looking for a job while he was with you?" asked Lee.

"Not so's you could notice. He didn't worry none. Laid in bed half the day reading newspapers. Couldn't get enough newspapers.

Would go to the movies at night or drink in the bars. But always alone, the men say."

The older woman's eyes narrowed. "What's he wanted for?" she demanded.

"Suspicion of a crime," said Lee. "I can't tell you particulars."

Mrs. Doughty pursed up her lips. "He was too quiet by half. There was a kind of prison look about him Here's a funny thing. One day when I was cleaning his room I seen his specs on the bureau. He always wore dark-rimmed specs, but this day he forgot them when he went out. There was something in the paper I wanted to read and I put on his glasses. I couldn't see any different than I did before, and when I look at them close, I see there wasn't nothing in them but window glass. What do you make of that?"

"Part of a disguise. Along with the scrubby black beard."

The two women stared. "Well, you never can tell!"

"Did you ever have any talk with him?" asked Lee.

"Not to say talk," answered Mrs. Doughty. "Only to pass the time of day. He was polite enough."

"Did he have any visitors while he was with you?"

"No, sir."

"Receive any letters?"

"Nary a letter."

"Anything in his effects that caught your attention?"

"No, sir. He had nothing in his little bag but a couple shirts and the like. He bought himself a pair of rough working pants, corduroy, and a windbreaker and a cap, because he said they was more comfortable."

"Was that what he had on when he went away?"

"Yes, sir."

"What color were the new clothes?"

"The corduroy pants was ginger colored, the windbreaker was imitation leather, brown, the cap no color in particular, just dark, a cloth cap. . . . I can tell you something that caught my attention. One day when I was cleaning up, I seen he had cut a little piece out of the paper. It was the New York *Daily News*, the same paper we take, and I put ours and hisn together just for curiosity's sake to see what he had a mind to cut. I cut out the same piece myself and kep' it." She fetched a newspaper clipping from her desk. Lee read with inward amusement:

> Mrs. Nick Cassells' new hostel for released prison-
> ers at — Henry Street has been christened Hope
> House. It has been operating for a couple of weeks
> and new guests are constantly arriving. All Henry
> Street is interested in its new neighbors, but the
> management of Hope House continues to refuse to
> give out any particulars about the identity of the
> guests. Mr. Amos Lee Mappin, the famous author
> and criminologist, is associated with Mrs. Cassells
> in her latest benefaction. The house managers are
> Mr. and Mrs. Siegmund Ammon.

The clipping was accompanied by small candid shots of Sandra Cassells and of Lee himself. So candid were they that it didn't occur to either of the women that the subject of the second photograph was at that moment seated before their eyes. Lee handed the clipping back.

"Do you suppose he was planning to rob that house?" asked the sister with wide eyes.

"Well, I haven't heard that it has been robbed since," said Lee with a grave face. "One more question, ladies. After he had left, did you find anything in his rooms?"

"Not a scrap!" said Mrs. Doughty. "He was too smart for that." At the door she asked Lee with sharp curiosity, "What kind of police are you, Mister?"

"Federal," said Lee, running down the steps to avoid further explanations. He was satisfied that he had left them with plenty to talk about.

It was evident that Adams or Wilson, or whatever his name might be, had avoided letting them see his car at the lodging house for fear that he might be traced through it later. But he must have stored it some place near by. After an hour's search, Lee located the parking lot on Route 1, where it had been kept for two weeks. It had never been taken out during that time. It was then bearing the New York state license tags which had been issued in the name of Miss Jones of Scarsdale.

Before returning to New York, Lee paid a second visit to the Eureka Restaurant. He was now able to describe the man he was looking for to Mrs. Lenassa and her daughter; scrubby black beard, bald spot with hair imported from the other side to cover it, etc. They recognized him at once.

"Ate here regular for a short time," said Mrs. Lenassa. "Never told us his name. He looked rough, but he seemed to be well fixed for money. Ordered the best we had and plenty of it. Came at eleven o'clock for his lunch and five for his dinner, because he said he didn't like to eat in a crowd. That suited us all right."

The young woman put in: "He bought a packet of gum every morning when he left."

"So!" said Lee. "What kind?"

She pointed: "Triple X. Most everybody buys that kind."

"Well, it's a straw to show the way the wind was blowing," said Lee.

"The last night he come here, he had a pair of gloves. That struck me as funny. Warm weather it was and him dressed so rough and all. The gloves was stuck in the pocket of his windbreaker."

"Possibly the gloves were to avoid leaving fingerprints," suggested Lee.

Her eyes widened. "No! . . . Here's a thing I remember," she went on. "He carried a funny-looking coin for a pocket piece. I would see it when he drew his hand out with change. A piece of money with a square hole in the middle. Never saw that before. Once I asked him what it was. He said Chinese, and put it back in his pocket. Didn't let me look at it."

Lee made a note of the pocket piece. Further questioning elicited the fact that the bearded man had a favorite table in the Eureka and was usually served by the same waitress. This girl was brought into their conference. She remembered the man.

"Did you ever have any talk with him?" asked Lee.

"No, sir. He wasn't a talking man. Would just put away his food and get out. He was a big eater—excepting the last night he come."

"That would be May 11th."

"About that. There wasn't anything to fix the date in my mind. That night he ate a little and shoved his plate away. Wasn't hungry, he said. And that night, I mind, he had a pint in his pocket. Asked me for an extra glass so he could take a drink. I saw him take several."

"Was he drunk?"

"No, sir. Not so's you could notice. And that night, when he got up, he hands me a quarter. Never did that before. Sometimes he would leave a nickel on the table. Handed me a quarter with a smile and said: 'Wish me luck, sister!'" The girl shuddered. "I never liked that guy! He was ugly!"

# CHAPTER SEVENTEEN

OF ALL THE ELEMENTS of the problem that confronted Lee, the most baffling was that Letty appeared to have assisted in laying the train that led to her own murder. Every new fact that Lee dug up confirmed it. It was Letty who had purchased the old sedan; Letty had set the time and the place for her meeting with Blondy; it was Letty who had suggested driving up to the Bronx, who had insisted on stopping for drinks that she didn't want at Schanze's, at McGovern's and the White Goose; finally, it was Letty who had driven Blondy to the isolated spot where the man with the scrubby beard was waiting to kill her. In Lee's long experience of crime, this was something new. Alone at night, pacing his big living room, he brought up one hypothesis after another, only to reject it because it did not fit all the known facts.

The most plausible explanation was that the unknown man with the beard was Spanish Jack's creature, and had acted throughout under his direction. If this was so, the old sedan had no doubt picked up Spanish Jack by prearrangement on its way to the scene of the shooting, and either one man or the other had pulled the trigger. But this did not account for Letty's part in taking herself and Blondy to the spot.

Without appearing to make too much of it, Lee questioned each inmate of Hope House as opportunity offered. First, Soup Kennedy, the ex-safe cracker, because it was Soup who usually answered the doorbell and the telephone, and who took in the mail. He was a heavy-witted man who, under questioning, instinctively took cover

by making out to be even stupider than he was. Trying to get information out of him was like squeezing a dry lemon. Letty, he said,
had never received any letters that he could recall, only bills, nor
had she received any visitors. She was seldom called to the phone,
though she herself made many calls, generally to order supplies
for the house. She seldom went out unless it was with Sieg, or to
go to market. Soup often went to market with her to carry home
the basket.

All Lee got from him were two bits of information which might
prove to be of value later. On one occasion, Soup said, he had gone
to market with Letty, and when they got to Rivington Street she
had handed him money and a list of things he was to buy, and left
him on a certain corner with instructions to meet her at the same
spot an hour and a half later. She had not told him where she was
going, but had warned him not to tell anybody at home that she
had left him. At another time, he had seen her in her room writing
a letter that ran to a number of pages. She had continued this letter for several days, whenever Sieg went out. When it was finished,
Soup had had a glimpse of the fat envelope lying on her desk.

"To whom was it addressed?" Lee asked eagerly.

The answer was not what he expected. "To you, Mr. Mappin."

"To me? Are you sure?"

"Yes, sir. Written on the envelope was 'For Mr. Mappin.' Nothing else. No street or number. She put it in her handbag."

"I never got any such letter," said Lee.

The nearest that Soup could come to fixing the date of the letter was that it had been written after Spanish Jack came to live at
Hope House.

When Lee talked to Johnnie Stabler, the former Wall Street
clerk, Johnnie sought to make out that he had been especially close
to Letty because he was the only gentleman among the boarders,
but when Lee proceeded to pin him down, there turned out to be
nothing in it. Letty had scarcely ever spoken to Johnnie, and never
alone. Duke Engstrom, the brawny ex-train robber, could only re-
peat with emphasis that Letty was a fine girl, a fine girl! Further
than that he was dumb. Little Joe Spencer was becoming senile.

Letty had treated him like a child; the tears rolled down his wrinkled cheeks when he spoke of her. All he could remember were the puddings Letty made.

Hattie Oliver, Handbag Hattie, was old also, and a little windy in the wits. She described to Lee how she and Letty had spent hours together hemming table napkins and talking. This sounded promising until it turned out that Hattie had done all the talking. Hattie's eyes were turned inward; she was not aware of anything special about Letty.

Mary Kennedy, as cook, was closer to Letty, the housekeeper, than anybody in the house except her husband. Lee sought out Mary in the kitchen one afternoon when there was nobody else in that part of the house. At the mention of Letty, Mary shook her head heavily.

"Poor lamb! Poor lamb!"

"Is it her death you feel sorry for," asked Lee, "or her life?"

"Both," said Mary. "She wasn't happy in her life."

"Did she ever tell you why?"

"Not in so many words. Men was always after her. It sickened her."

"How do you know that?"

"One morning, when I went into her room, she was sitting in front of the dressing table brushing her hair. I never saw her look so pretty and I told her so. She stopped brushing and sat there with her chin in her hand, looking at herself as if it was somebody else she was looking at, and she didn't like her. And she said: 'It must be nice to be beautiful if you are born into a rich home. Otherwise it's a curse. Since I was fourteen years old, it's been a curse to me, Mary.' 'Why?' I says, and she says: 'I am always in trouble! It's just one thing after another.'"

"And then?" asked Lee.

"That's all, Mr. Mappin. She dry right up then and start talking about what to have for dinner."

"Did you get the idea that Sieg made her unhappy?"

"No, sir. Sieg treat her all right. They was the lovingest pair! Only he went out a good many nights."

"What did Letty do when Sieg left her?"

"Read to herself in bed."

"Had Letty always seemed so unhappy?"

"No, sir. When I first come and she and Mrs. Cassells was buying things for the house, Letty was as happy as any girl might be furnishing a house for herself without counting the cost. It was when the house opened that she changed."

"Was it when Spanish came?"

"No, sir, it was before that. It was when the house first opened."

This was not the answer Lee wanted, but Mary stuck to it, and he had to leave the question open. "Do you remember her last day?" he asked.

"Will I ever forget it?" said Mary. "The poor darlin'! When the boarders was around she could keep up pretty good, but when her and me was alone in the house the tears was running down her face. I was ready to cry myself. She said to me—she was smiling though her eyes was wet—she said: 'Mary, are you a good Catholic?' And I said: 'Not as good as I ought to be, Letty.' And she said: 'Pray for me, Mary! Because I can't pray!' Then she went out of the kitchen."

"Do you think she foresaw that she might die that night?"

Mary shook her head. "It was not fear of death that made her speak so, it was the fear of what she was going to do."

It was less easy for Lee to get Sieg Ammon by himself without appearing to contrive it. His opportunity came as they waited for Sandra one evening in the office at Hope House.

"Sieg," said Lee, "did you notice during Letty's last days that she appeared to have something on her mind?"

Sieg, who had ceased to grieve openly for Letty now, like the vigorous young animal he was, resented being reminded of his grief. His face flushed. "God! do we have to go into that again?" he burst out.

"You don't have to answer my question," said Lee mildly.

Sieg quieted down. "I'm sorry," he said. "Sure, I'll answer you. It's only because I hate to have my feelings stirred up. . . . Now that I look back at that time, I can see that Letty was worrying about something, but I can't honestly say I noticed it at the time. I am not a noticing kind of fellow. It was easy to jolly her out of it when we were together."

"Well, you must have thought about it since," said Lee. "What do you think was on her mind?"

"That's easy," said Sieg. "She was carrying on with Blondy behind my back. I suppose she had what they call a conscience, and that was troubling her."

"But if she had fallen for Blondy, why didn't she go away with him that night when he urged her?"

"She was afraid. That was Letty. She would and she wouldn't. And in the end Blondy got in a rage and shot her."

Lee had to admit to himself that this was a reasonable-sounding explanation—if it hadn't been for the old sedan and the scrubby-bearded man. He said: "But if she had intended even for a moment going away with Blondy, it seems as if she would have dressed more suitably."

"What good does this do?" cried Sieg. "Letty is gone and her murderer is convicted. Nothing we can do now will bring her back!"

"Of course not," said Lee. "But I can't let the matter drop because I cannot square Letty's actions with the known facts."

"Who ever could square a woman's actions?"

"That's too easy a way to pass it up. After all, women are human. . . . There's a new figure in the case," he added.

"Who's that?" asked Sieg quickly.

"Middle-aged man with a scrubby beard dyed black; hair also dyed and brushed across to hide his bald spot. Dressed in rough working pants and a windbreaker."

"Where does he come in?"

"He was almost certainly on the spot when the shot was fired. He drove the old sedan."

Sieg smiled. "You must excuse me, Mr. Mappin, but it seems to me you are imagining things."

"I've been in this business a good many years," Lee said with a shrug.

"Bearded men are not common nowadays," said Sieg, "but you see plenty of guys with their hair brushed over their bald spot. Know anything else about him?"

"Not much. On the night of the murder he was dressed in a pair of ginger-colored corduroy pants, a brown imitation leather windbreaker, and a cloth cap, all new. He had a small, badly worn satchel of imitation alligator. He was in the habit of carrying a Chinese or Japanese coin for a pocket piece. He chewed Triple X gum."

"Don't call up a picture of anybody I ever saw, Mr. Mappin."

"Possibly he was only hired for the occasion."

"By whom?"

"Well, say Spanish Jack."

"Spanish is capable of it."

"Sieg," said Lee, "there is one very personal question I would like to ask you."

"Shoot, Mr. Mappin!"

"Was Letty passionately in love with you at the time of her death? They say a man can always tell."

Sieg looked off into the distance. "A man may *know*, Mr. Mappin, but his self-conceit refuses to admit it. If you had asked me that question before Letty died, I would have said that I was everything in the world to her. Now that she is gone, I can see that she had changed. She was beginning to make excuses."

"Thanks, Sieg."

Sandra came in.

After dinner Sandra gave Lee a lift uptown. Lee judged that Sieg had been talking to her, for as soon as they started away, she opened up: "Lee, why on earth do you go on turning over the same dirt in the Letty Ammon case? I never knew you to be so obstinate. It's nothing but vanity. It's only because you will not admit that you were wrong in the beginning!"

"Maybe so," said Lee mildly. "But if it interests me, why not let me have my way? I'm not hurting anybody."

"You are! You're hurting us all! You're keeping everybody stirred up because you won't let the wound heal. You keep probing and probing and probing!"

"I haven't yet got to the bottom of the wound, my dear."

"Nonsense! That's only a clever answer! Doesn't mean a thing! Lee, darling, I'm thinking of you. I hate to see you becoming an object of ridicule!"

Lee took a pinch of snuff. "To whom, darling?"

"To everybody who knows the circumstances. To the police. Surely, with all their facilities, the police are in the best position to know there is nothing in this wild goose chase of yours."

"Ah, I see my friend Loasby has been airing his views!"

"Inspector Loasby is a very intelligent man!"

"Very!"

"It's especially hard on poor Sieg," Sandra went on. "Sieg has been trying so to get back to normal. His courage is wonderful!"

"There are others besides Sieg to be thought of, darling."

"Who?"

"Blondy for one."

"Blondy! That lout! You are simply fatuous on the subject of Blondy! . . . Seriously, Lee, I want you to give up this case. Surely there are plenty of other cases for you to work on."

"My dear, you might as well try to call off an old hound just when the scent is growing strong. That's what I am, an old hound. If I gave up this chase I would be false to my own nature, and that, I hold, is the unpardonable sin!"

"These are just words. I ask you for old friendship's sake, for *my* sake, to give up this ridiculous notion of yours, to act sensibly, and you put me off with empty words. I thought better of you, Lee!" Sandra touched her handkerchief to her eyes.

Lee was surprised by her vehemence. "Tell me, what is it to you?" he asked. "Why do you ask me to give up my work?"

"Can't you see?" she cried hysterically. "Murder has got on my nerves! For weeks I have had to live with this murder! I am steeped in murder! What I eat seems to taste of murder! I feel as if I must smell of murder! In the end I will begin to wonder if I didn't murder the girl myself! I can't stand it any longer. My nerves are in strings! Yet you won't let me forget it!"

"Why not go away for a while?" suggested Lee soothingly.

"Where could I go?"

"To Sea Isle; or to White Sulphur; an enchanting place at this season. Or, if you would like a little voyage, to Bermuda, or to California . . ."

"Wherever I went, I couldn't forget what was going on here."

"Look, if you will undertake to stay away from New York for a month, when you come back either Blondy will have been executed, or there will be another man in the death house in his place. I promise it!"

"You're only evading the question," said Sandra. "For the last time, I ask you: will you give up this foolish investigation?"

"No, my dear," said Lee quietly.

There was a long silence in the car. Finally Sandra said pettishly: "I'm going to close up Hope House."

"Hey?" said Lee. He knew this would come sooner or later, but the suddenness of the announcement took him aback.

"You heard what I said. The stigma of this murder has wrecked it. The press has taught the public to believe that the house is full of murderers. Every day people come and stand in the street and gape at it. We could never live that down. I'm going to deed it with all its contents to the Henry Street Settlement. They will find some use for it."

"What will become of the boarders?" asked Lee.

"I'll give them money. Anyhow, I didn't agree to support them for the rest of their lives. To come from Hope House is only an additional handicap upon them now!"

"What about Sieg?"

"Well, I feel I owe a little more to Sieg because of what he has been through. I'll see that he gets a position of some kind."

There was another silence in the car.

"Haven't you anything to say?" demanded Sandra sharply. "Don't you care? If you would co-operate with me, if you would allow this dreadful business to be forgotten, we could go on! But no! you have to keep it stirred up! You have to keep the people pointing and gaping at Hope House. So there's nothing for me to do but close it up!"

"My dear," said Lee, "you have forgotten that I opposed the idea from the beginning."

"Of course!" she said with extreme bitterness. "I might have expected you would say that!"

"It was a generous idea," he went on, "and worthy of your kind heart, but to my mind entirely impracticable. So you were mistaken, you see, if you expected me to urge you to keep it going. On the contrary, I say the sooner you close the house the better."

Sandra would not speak to him again during the balance of the drive.

## CHAPTER EIGHTEEN

It was Lee's habit when faced by an impasse, as in this case, to cast back farther and farther into the lives of the persons concerned. With the idea that the seeds of Letty's murder might have been sown during the previous year when she was working at El Mirador, he set about finding out what had happened over there. The career of El Mirador had ended with a murder, and there is nothing like murder to breed murder.

Spanish Jack undoubtedly knew as much about the last days of El Mirador as anybody living, or more, but Lee did not go to him again. Spanish enjoyed stringing him along too well. There were plenty of other sources of information about such a spectacular resort. The Hudson County police furnished Lee with the record of their investigation of the death of the proprietor.

Sam Bartol had maintained a luxurious suite for his own use in the tower of El Mirador. He kept a valet to wait upon him; no other servant. Such meals as he ate in his own rooms were supplied from the main kitchens of the establishment. On a night in April, he had dismissed his valet with instructions to report at noon next day. Later he had ordered an elaborate supper with wine and service for two to be sent up to his suite. It was assumed that he was entertaining a lady. The waiters who brought up the supper were not permitted to see her; they left everything and departed.

When Bentalou, the valet, came back next day he found his master lying dead on the floor of his living room, shot through the breast. The supper was eaten, the wine drunk, the lady gone. The gun was lying beside the dead man, and since the bosom of his dress shirt showed powder burns, it was possible that he had killed himself. But not likely, because Sam was riding high on the crest of success and prosperity. The gun was an old one that had undoubtedly passed through many hands, and the police were unable to trace its ownership. It might or might not have been Bartol's gun. A second gun was found on his person, and it seemed unlikely that he would carry two. Bartol was known to keep a considerable sum of money on his person. This was missing; but the showy and expensive jewelry he wore had not been taken. There was a private entrance to his suite with an automatic elevator. The whole staff was questioned; nobody had been seen to enter or leave. No clue to Bartol's guest was found. The investigation was dropped.

There was a mortgage on El Mirador which was foreclosed in due course. There were no bidders, and the real estate passed into the hands of the mortgagee, a respectable trust company. Naturally the place was a white elephant on their hands until another spectacular showman of the caliber of Sam Bartol should turn up. The fixtures were Sam's own property. He died intestate and there were several claimants to his estate. On account of these contests, nothing had been removed. The resort remained exactly as it was when the doors were closed for the last time. The Trust Company very willingly provided Lee with an order to view it.

El Mirador clung to the edge of the Palisades opposite upper New York. In the days of its glory, its glittering lights furnished a nightly temptation to the citizens of upper Manhattan. There was a bridge handy. The place was the last word in Babylonian luxury; it had everything from a private landing field to a huge conservatory-swimming pool which could be opened to the sky in fine weather or closed in during the winter. A wealth of tropical verdure had once surrounded the water, but that was gone now. The huge main dining room, circular in shape, was surmounted by a dome full of twinkling artificial stars. Half of it was filled with huge windows commanding a superb view across the river. In the front of the building was a bar five hundred feet long; the gaming rooms were upstairs.

Lee knew the place well. Shuttered now and under dust covers, it seemed to be full of ghosts. An abandoned pleasure resort in the cold light of day is the most melancholy place imaginable; haunted by the echoes of music and laughter, the popping of corks. On one side was a low stage which rolled out over the dancing floor for the performance. On this stage Letty had danced. Outside the windows lay the wide terrace where the guests had eaten on summer nights. The bar was closed off by steel gates which were politely unlocked for Lee. It was a fabulous place, two city blocks long from end to end. The bottles and glasses were still in place.

"There's a hundred thousand dollars' worth of liquor here, besides what's in the cellar," said Lee's conductor. "It's a big responsibility. We have a couple of watchmen at night."

"You could take a little nip whenever you felt inclined, without its being missed," suggested Lee.

"My wife and me don't touch it," said the man hastily. "That's why we got the job here."

He was a stout, intelligent Frenchman with beautiful manners, who had been a captain of waiters when El Mirador was operating. His wife, who shared in taking care of the closed resort, had been in charge of the linen. She was one of the neat, quiet, frugal housewives that only the French nation can produce. Together they showed Lee around. Lee hoped to get from them the gossip of the big establishment at the time the proprietor was shot, but he took care to make himself solid with the pair before he started asking leading questions. He encouraged them to talk about themselves.

They went up to the gaming rooms which were decorated in a rococo style, perhaps in imitation of Monte Carlo. There were the desks where Sieg Ammon and Blondy Farren had sold chips, had cashed them at the end of the evening, incidentally knocking down some dollars for their own pockets. The roulette tables, each with its wheel, were in place. Even the little ivory balls were there. Lee spun one of them around the wheel. Its clicking brought back strange memories. At one of these tables Spanish Jack's topaz eyes had kept watch with deceitful sleepiness. His rake had swept in the counters and pushed back the winnings to the fortunate ones. *"Rien ne va plus, Messieurs. . . ."*

To visit Sam Bartol's rooms it was necessary to descend to the ground and climb two flights again. Power for the electric elevator was turned off. The apartment occupied a two-story penthouse, or low tower arising from the front of El Mirador. Extensive terraces surrounded it, where shrubs and flowers had once been cultivated, but all that was gone. The first floor consisted of a foyer, an immense living room, dining room, pantry, and cloak rooms; upstairs there were bedrooms.

Sam Bartol's living room was kept as if its dead master was momentarily expected to return. Every object was in its place. The room had been famous among the initiates of café society. Lee found it, as might have been expected, rather theatrical. It carried out the last word in modern decoration. Floor, walls and ceiling were painted black. Against the blackness startling surrealist paintings stood out around the walls, while stands and tables bore a collection of weird sculpture, ranging from ancient Ming to modern Cambodian. Here and there on the floor stood immense roughly shaped wooden bowls heaped with colored glass balls. The deep-piled rugs were white.

"One of my biggest jobs is to keep everything dusted," remarked Mme Berthier.

By this time, Lee had succeeded in ingratiating himself with husband and wife, and he ventured to ask some questions.

"Whereabouts in the room was the body found?"

Berthier pointed to a spot near the entrance from the foyer. "Here! His head was pointing toward the foyer as if he was on his way out when he was struck. He was lying straight out with his arms stretched in front of him."

"There was an awful bloody spot in the rug," put in Mme Berthier. "We had it cleaned."

"Where was the gun?" asked Lee.

"Alongside the body, M'sieur."

"Not in front of his hands? Doesn't look then as if he had shot himself."

"Nobody believed that he shot himself," said Berthier. "The attitude of the body suggested that he was running, or at least that he was moving forward when he got it."

"About what time did it happen?"

"Supper was served at one o'clock. It had been eaten and the coffee was drunk. The two of them were sitting on that sofa at the far end of the room. The proof of that is, there were two partly drunk highballs on the little coffee table in front of the sofa. So the police figure it happened after two o'clock."

"I understand there never was any clue to the identity of Sam Bartol's supper guest that night."

"There was no clue, but there was plenty of gossip, M'sieur!"

"Pointing to whom?" asked Lee. "No harm in telling me if it was well talked over at the time."

"One of the girls in the floor show who was suspected of being the boss's favorite."

"Suspected!" put in Mme Berthier scornfully. "The fact was well known!"

"There was no proof of it," insisted Berthier. "The boss never singled her out for any favors—at least, not when anybody was looking. She was not known to visit his rooms. It was only because she was kept on for week after week that gave us the idea the boss had an interest in her. All the others were frequently changed because the customers liked to see new faces."

"What part did she take in the show?"

"In the ensemble, M'sieur."

"Was she beautiful?"

Berthier cast up his eyes. "Ah! *ravissante!* She was the most beautiful of them all!"

Mme Berthier's plain face was a study in scorn.

"She was not, however, one of the best performers,"
Berthier explained. "She was too quiet, too reserved."

"A great favorite with the male employees," said Mme
Berthier acidly. "As you will observe, M'sieur."

"And equally unpopular with the female employees," retorted Berthier, "for reasons that I will leave you to deduce . . . For myself, it was not her beauty which attracted me . . ."

Mme Berthier sniffed audibly.

"It was her good heart, her friendliness to all, so rare in a beautiful woman. Those others . . . !" He held up his hands.

"What was the name of this paragon?" asked Lee.

"Anita Western."

"But there was no proof that she was here."

Berthier shook his head.

"M. Berthier chooses to forget the proof," said his wife stiffly. *"Anita was out of the show that night.* She had reported sick."

"That is not proof, my dear," said Berthier. "It's only a suspicious circumstance . . . Even if Anita was here, nobody could make me believe that she shot Sam Bartol."

"That is obvious," said Mme Berthier sarcastically.

Lee guessed that Anita had long been a sore subject between the Berthiers.

"For why?" Berthier asked—and immediately answered himself. "Because she had everything to hope for from Sam living and nothing to gain by his death. Some woman was here, I grant, Anita or another; a man comes, perhaps a jealous lover. Observe! Sam springs to his feet and starts for him and is shot before he can pull his gun!"

"But," Lee objected, "if Sam was entertaining a lady, he wouldn't answer a summons to the door."

"Sam never got to the door. He was shot before reaching the foyer. The intruder had a key!"

"What about the valet, Bentalou?"

"He had what the police called an unshakable alibi."

"Did you know a croupier called Spanish Jack D'Acosta?"

"I know there was such a man employed here," said Berthier, "but I wasn't acquainted with him. Neither my work nor my wife's work ever took us to the gaming rooms."

"Was there any gossip around the place linking D'Acosta's name with the murder?"

"No, M'sieur. D'Acosta was questioned by the police like everybody else. They were satisfied with his story. He was not held."

"I will show you something that the police do not know about," said Mme Berthier unexpectedly. "I discovered it by accident a month ago. Too late, then, to go to the police."

Berthier laid a restraining hand on her arm. "Marie!"

She shook it off. "It can do no harm now," she said. "Observe, M'sieur!"

She was pointing to an ancient Russian icon which hung on the wall. It was a small, painted panel enclosed in a heavy gilded frame. "I found this while dusting." Her fingers moved along the edge of the frame until they struck a hidden spring. The wooden panel flew open, disclosing the photograph of a woman's face, wistful and lovely, a face that Lee knew only too well.

"*Voila!* Anita Western!" said Mme Berthier.

"And Letty Ammon!" murmured Lee.

"I always said she would come to a bad end!" said Mme Berthier virtuously.

Her husband turned on her. "Was it her fault if some bloody-minded villain took her life?"

"Undoubtedly she gave him cause!"

Berthier was gazing at the photograph. "Ah! La pauvre petite!" he murmured. "She was *too* beautiful!"

Madame slammed the panel shut.

Lee gave each of them a generous tip. "Say nothing about my visit," he said. "We will talk about this matter again . . . One more question: Was Spanish Jack D'Acosta known to be paying attention to Anita? Were their names ever connected in the gossip of the establishment?"

"Ask my wife," said Berthier.

"Never to my knowledge," said Madame.

"She would know," remarked her husband dryly.

UPON REREADING THE POLICE REPORT of the investigation following the death of Sam Bartol, Lee learned that a certain Mrs. Besson, of an address on West 72nd Street, had testified that Anita Western boarded with her. On the day preceding Sam Bartol's death, she said, Miss Western was indisposed, and at her request, she, Mrs. Besson, had telephoned to the management of El Mirador to report that Miss Western would not be able to show that night. Miss Western had remained in bed most of the day, but was able to come to the table for dinner. Immediately afterward she had returned to her room. Mrs. Besson had visited her during the evening and the night, and could swear that Miss Western had never left the house.

Lee went to call on Mrs. Besson. The boardinghouse was a superior establishment in a good neighborhood, catering principally to the theatrical profession. Mrs. Besson herself, with her hennaed hair, puffy cheeks and strongly girdled figure, looked like a former actress. She was a kindly soul, easily aroused to emotion. Lee's first question frightened her and brought tears to her eyes. She knew who Lee was.

"There is no occasion to be alarmed by my questions," he said. "The unfortunate girl is gone and there is no object to be gained by publishing the fact that Anita Western and Letty Ammon were one and the same. My aim is only to discover if there was anything in that unhappy business of last year which led to her murder."

He presently had Mrs. Besson talking freely. "It is true that I testified falsely before the New Jersey police last year. I wasn't sworn on the book. I *did* telephone to El Mirador to tell them Miss Western wouldn't be over, but it was not true that she stayed home all night. She didn't get home until near morning. She came to my room and wakened me. She was in a terrible state of nerves; shaking so she couldn't talk. I gave her a stiff drink and put her to bed.

"When she could talk, she told me that Sam Bartol had been shot and that she would certainly be suspected of it, because it was known that Sam was paying attention to her. She had been out with another man, she said, but as this man was married, it would ruin him to furnish her with an alibi, and so she begged me to swear that she had never gone out at all. Well, I didn't believe that she had been out with a married man. It wasn't like her. The state she was in made me think that she had seen Sam Bartol shot. How would she know he had been shot if she wasn't present? On the other hand, I didn't believe she had shot Sam—that gentle girl!— or if she had, it was in defending herself. So I lied for her. And now she's gone!" Mrs. Besson's tears overflowed altogether.

Lee patted her hand. "Don't worry, Mrs. Besson. Your lies did credit to your kindness of heart, but don't tell any more. It's always safer to be on the side of the police."

"I know! I know, Mr. Mappin! This will be a lesson to me!"

# CHAPTER NINETEEN

WHEN THE NEXT DAY came around upon which Blondy Farren was privileged to receive a visitor, Lee had himself driven up to Sing Sing Prison. It was his first visit to Blondy. On earlier occasions, Ann Brooke had gone. Ann had found herself a temporary job in New York in order to remain within traveling distance of the prison. Summer was in full tide now and Lee, on the way up, as the road gave him glimpses of the river, thought he had never seen such golden sunshine, sky and water so blue, nor such an unparalleled richness of verdure. The vigor and the beauty of earth oppressed his breast when he thought of Blondy in the summer of his life, shut away from it all.

Within the walls of the prison, a pall of horror seemed to hang over the little separate building where the men condemned to death were kept. Even so distinguished a visitor as Lee had to submit to be searched upon entering. When Blondy caught sight of Lee an agonized question leaped in the young man's eyes. Lee shook his head to cut short his suspense, saying:

"Not yet! But there is still room for hope."

Blondy immediately recovered his usual composure. It cut Lee to the heart to see his hollow cheeks and ashy skin. Only his eyes were as blue as ever—and as steady.

They sat down in a little room with an iron gate in the door frame. A warder waited outside the gate. Lee said:

"I have opened up several new lines, but I can't say I am in sight of the solution."

"It's wonderful to know that you are working for me on the outside," said Blondy. "That keeps me going."

"Skip the thanks!" said Lee. "This is my case now."

"God knows I've had plenty of time to think over what you already told me," said Blondy, "but I can't offer any help."

"Well, listen to the latest developments and put your wits to work. . . . I finally got Queenie Deane to confess that she followed you and Letty to Schanze's, then to McGovern's, then to the White Goose and at last to the place where Letty was shot. She says she had stopped her car outside that yard when she heard a cry and a shot. That frightened her so much that she drove away as fast as she could. She may or may not be lying about that last moment. I'm inclined to think she's telling the truth, because I have reason to believe there was a car lying in wait for you in the driveway of that deserted house."

"It's all as black as night to me," murmured Blondy.

"I have learned a lot more about that old sedan," Lee went on. "This is the car that Letty bought on April 23rd. At this point a new figure comes into the case. On the same day she turned the car over to a man unknown to me, who drove it to Elizabeth. He was such an ordinary-looking man that people find difficulty in describing him. One said he was forty years old, another fifty, and a third said he was a real old man trying to look younger than he was. He was partly bald and he allowed the hair on one side of his head to grow long so he could brush it over his bald spot.

"In Newark he bought two new tires of a little used make, and thank God for that! Otherwise I couldn't have traced the car. He also had some expensive repairs made and, when they were finished, he stored the car in a lot to be ready when he wanted it. He took a room in a workingman's lodging house and started to grow a beard. When the beard came in, he dyed that black, too, to match his hair."

"But a beard would only make him more conspicuous," objected Blondy.

"Quite! The beard suggests to me that this man was known to you or to others in the case, and that he grew it in order to avoid being recognized in case of a meeting. He wore spectacles for the same purpose."

"So far this suggests nothing to me," said Blondy.

"Wait! At six o'clock on May 11th, he drove away from Newark and at eight, as you have told me, the old car was parked outside Schanze's roadhouse in the Bronx. Later you saw it in the parking lot outside McGovern's. You did *not* see it at the White Goose. Why? Because he had driven on ahead to the yard of the burned house . . ."

"How could he have known?" groaned Blondy. "Letty must have told him!"

"That I cannot believe!"

"Letty had bought the car for him in the first place. You cannot escape the logic of the facts."

"But if the final meeting place had been agreed on," said Blondy, "why would he risk discovery by showing himself at Schanze's and McGovern's?"

"Here's how I dope that out: he wanted to make sure that Letty would carry out her part of the agreement."

"Why? Why? Why?"

Lee laid a hand on his shoulder. "Patience, Blondy! We *are* coming closer to the answer, though it is still hidden. . . . There is also Spanish to be considered. I have not been able to connect him with the bearded man, but God knows, his actions are suspicious. It is possible that his was the master mind back of the murder. The bearded fellow may have picked him up in New York on his way to the Bronx. Spanish claims that he attended the theater that night and offers me a seat check as proof. But a seat check is not conclusive."

"Why should Spanish Jack have it in for Letty?"

"That I don't know. She feared him, and to a certain extent he was able to make her obey him. That, I figure, goes back to the shooting of Sam Bartol last year."

"Hey?" exclaimed the startled Blondy.

"This will be another piece of bad news to you," said Lee reluctantly. "Letty was suspected of shooting Sam Bartol, though no proceedings were taken against her. I don't believe she did it, but there is a strong presumption that she was present when he was shot." He went on to tell Blondy what he had learned from Mrs. Besson.

"Oh, God!" groaned Blondy. "What next?"

"Can you throw any additional light on that time?" asked Lee.

Blondy shook his head. "This is all news to me. Sieg and I were locked up. All we knew was that after the killing of Sam Bartol, Letty went to work in the office of a laundry. The pay was small, she said, but in such a place she wasn't bothered by men."

"I am convinced that Spanish was mixed up in that affair," said Lee, "but I can't prove it."

"What were his suspicious actions that you just referred to?" Blondy asked.

"After he was arrested, as we were driving across Brooklyn Bridge, he took a key out of his sock that had a tag attached, and tossed it into the river. My name was written on that tag; I saw it distinctly. There was more writing on the other side which I could not read. But I saw my name." Lee struck his thigh. "Damn it to hell, Blondy! That is one of those absolutely cockeyed circumstances that makes the investigator tear his hair—if he has any! I never saw that key before! Key to what? And why my name on it? There is no key missing!"

Blondy grinned crookedly. "It's good to see you up against it," he said. "Makes the rest of us feel maybe we're not such complete boobs at that!"

"Here's another thing," said Lee. "After Spanish came to Hope House, Letty was seen to be writing a long letter. She went back to it several different days, but always when Sieg was out of the house. That letter was to me!"

"How do you know?"

"Because after it was finished and enclosed in an envelope, old Soup Kennedy had a glimpse of it and it was addressed to me! I am confident that Spanish had something to do with that. I never got the letter. It went into Letty's handbag!"

"If we could find that handbag," said Blondy.

"It has probably been destroyed," said Lee grimly.

"That's what happens to vital evidence! . . . Did you get a good look at it that last night?" he asked.

"Sure!" said Blondy. "It was a pretty thing. Very smart looking, like everything Letty had. Made of heavy corded black silk and perfectly plain except it had a gold clasp shaped like a scallop shell."

"The murderer must have taken it," said Lee, "or it would have been found. He took it for the evidence, not for the trifle of money it contained."

They thought this over in silence.

Lee said at last: "Let's get back to the bearded man. It sticks in my mind that he was somebody who is known to you. That's the particular thing that brought me up here today . . . Think back! . . . A man of fifty, say, of medium height, not yet showing any middle-aged spread. Partly bald. Dressed in an ordinary way when he came to Newark. Bought himself a pair of ginger-colored corduroy working pants and a brown imitation leather windbreaker. That's what he was wearing on the night of the murder. Together with his original hat, a grayish Fedora, not badly worn but of cheap material. He carried a little satchel of imitation alligator, badly worn."

Blondy shook his head. "Might be anybody you would see in the subway."

"He had an ugly look," Lee went on; "a close-mouthed man, suspicious of everybody. Never made friends; nobody seems to have liked him. One woman said he had a prison look."

Blondy raised his head quickly. "A prison look?"

"He chewed Triple X gum; used a lot of it. He carried for a pocket piece a Chinese or Japanese coin with a square hole in the middle . . ."

Blondy's eyes fired up. "Coin with a hole in the middle! Wait a minute! That suggests something!" Blondy jumped up and began pacing the little room. "Brings up a picture of a hand pulling out of a pants pocket," he muttered, "and opening to show a coin with a square hole in the middle lying on the palm!"

". . . Must have been a long time ago. It's quite clear before my eyes but I can't place it!"

Lee gave him his own time.

"A ragged pair of pants," Blondy muttered, "and a dirty palm! I see it plainly, but I can't place it!"

"Well, forget about it," said Lee. "It will come to you when you're thinking of something else."

WHEN LEE PUT HIS TALE before Inspector Loasby, the latter smiled in an indulgent, not to say pitying, manner and shook his head. "Mr. Mappin," he said, "I'm sorry to see you so hipped on this case. It's not like you."

"I might answer," said Lee good-humoredly, "that it is yourself who is hipped on the case. I have put ample evidence before you; but there are none so blind as those who do not want to see!"

"Mrs. Cassells says . . ." Loasby began.

Lee interrupted him. "Since when has Mrs. Cassells qualified as an expert on crime?"

"Of course not! But she knew all the people. It took place almost in her house, you might say."

"Let's leave Mrs. Cassells out of it."

"Mr. Mappin, you ask me to send out a general alarm for a certain man just on the strength of your deductions . . ."

"How are crimes to be solved except by deduction?" demanded Lee.

"You ask me to find a partly bald man with a scrubby black beard wearing a pair of ginger-colored pants. By this time he's had a shave and a haircut and has changed his pants. What chance is there of finding him when that is all I have to go on?"

"Practically none," said Lee. "But in this man lies the key to the murder of Letty Ammon. We've got to do something about it."

"I'll do my best," said Loasby.

## CHAPTER TWENTY

LEE'S THOUGHTS AFTER BREAKFAST, as he paced his big living room, clad in a dressing gown of blue brocade, ran thus:

When Letty wrote that long letter to me in Hope House, and put "For Mr. Mappin" on the envelope without any street address, it is clear she had no intention of sending it through the mail. It was to be handed to me personally. Well, she had plenty of opportunities to hand it to me, and since she did not do so, it is clear that it was to be given to me only in a certain contingency. This is borne out by the note from Letty that was found in Spanish's wallet. In it Letty said: "If anything happens to me I have fixed it so that Mr. Mappin will be informed of what took place, and you can't prevent it."

This suggests, thought Lee, that I was not to have Letty's letter until after her death. But I did not get it in spite of her careful plans. On the envelope containing the letter she wrote: "For Mr. Mappin." On the tag attached to the key the same words appeared in Letty's hand: "For Mr. Mappin." The inference is clear that key and letter were connected. Letty must have deposited her letter in a safe place and left the key to that place marked with my name. The writing on the other side of the tag would be directions to find the place.

At this point, Lee trotted into his study and pulled out a drawer of his desk. From among a number of others, he picked a thin, flat key two inches long, with the cuts to fit the lock at the end. Attached to it was a little tag bearing the number of his safe deposit box. His eye brightened. Same kind of key! he thought; all safe deposit keys are like that. The boxes are fitted with double locks, and the keys have to be long enough to reach the inner lock. The attendant at the bank has first to unlock your box with his pass-key, then you insert your key. Letty hired a safe deposit box for her dangerous letter. The clever Spanish, suspecting something of the sort, was the first to go through her effects; he found the key marked with my name and threw it in the river!

Lee, making a quick trip to Headquarters, persuaded Inspector Loasby to send a circular letter to all safe deposit companies on lower Manhattan describing Letty and asking them to report if any such person had hired a box from between April 28th and May 4th. (After May 4th, all Letty's movements had been shadowed.) Various names that Letty might have given were listed. "She probably gave her right name," Lee pointed out. "There is no reason why she shouldn't."

On the following day the Central Cortlandt Bank and Trust Company on lower Broadway notified the Inspector that on May 1st Mrs. Siegmund Ammon, of — Henry Street, had rented a box from them.

Lee and Inspector Loasby went around to the bank. Lee said to the President: "You must know, of course, that Mrs. Ammon is dead under tragic circumstances. Didn't that fact strike any of your employees?"

"No, Mr. Mappin. The name, you see, would be entered among our thousands of customers and forgotten. It is not a particularly striking name. Possibly when it came time to send out bills for the boxes somebody might notice it, but it is not likely."

"There may be valuables in the box," said Lee, "but I don't expect to find any. What I am after is evidence that will throw light on Mrs. Ammon's death. The key to the box is lost. How must we proceed in order to have it opened?"

"An order from the police will be sufficient."

Loasby wrote such an order on the spot, and a mechanic was sent for. The three men went down to the vaults to wait for him. The box rented by Letty was of the smallest size, a mere slit in the wall, scarcely more than an inch thick, among thousands of others. The mechanic arrived with his tools.

"What I expect to find," said Lee, while the three men watched the operation, "is a plain white envelope subscribed 'For Mr. Mappin' and containing a bulky letter."

The door to the tiny safe was forced, and a long, thin, japanned box drawn out. When the cover was lifted, there lay the bulky envelope endorsed: "For Mr. Mappin." Nothing else.

The bank president and the police inspector stared. "Why," said the former, "this is almost magical!"

Lee took a pinch of snuff. "Magic is hardly in my line, sir; say logic!"

BACK AT HEADQUARTERS, Lee read Letty's letter aloud to the Inspector. It was a pitiful document, written under great stress of emotion, repetitious in places, and sometimes scarcely coherent. Much of it dealt with matter already familiar to Lee. The most significant part had to do with what had happened at El Mirador.

> Sam Bartol was in love with me. He was a kind man and I wasn't afraid of him. He said we had to keep our friendship a secret for my sake, because if it got known around the place that I was the boss's girl, it would hurt my reputation. Sam was married and had a family. Then Sieg Ammon came to work at El Mirador. Sieg was the only man I ever loved or ever will. He was everything to me. Sieg never knew about Sam and me. I persuaded Sieg that we must never notice each other around El Mirador so people wouldn't talk about us. So Sieg and I only saw each other daytimes. Above all, I had to keep Sam from finding out about Sieg. Sam was a good fellow but he was only human and he would have fired us both. Nobody around El Mirador knew about Sieg and me except Spanish Jack, the croupier. He was after me, too. He was always watching me with his ugly yellow eyes.

So my life was just one lie after another. I lied to Sam and I lied to Sieg. *Please*, Mr. Mappin, don't ever let Sieg see this. I could stand it all right as long as I had Sieg, but after Sieg was fired from El Mirador, often I wished I was dead. Sam had Sieg framed and sent to Sing Sing. I hated him then for what he did to Sieg, but I couldn't let on. I had to make believe to be friends with him just the same as before. I was well paid at El Mirador, much more than I could earn anywhere else. I wasn't a good dancer. I needed the extra money so I could send some to Sieg every week to buy him little comforts in prison.

After Sieg had gone, Spanish pestered me the whole time. I suspected it was Spanish who told Sam that Sieg was cheating at the cash desk, but I hadn't any proof of it. Maybe Spanish told him, too, that Sieg and I were crazy about each other. Sam never let anything on after Sieg had gone. That's the way he was, a kind man, but cagey. It got worse all the time. Spanish found out where I boarded and used to come there in the daytime. When I moved he found me again. I hated him and his slinky ways like a cat. When he caught me alone, he'd go crazy. He showed me a gun and swore that if he couldn't have me, no other man should. It would make the cold shivers run down my back the way his eyes changed when he looked at you. Hypnotic eyes. I told Spanish if he didn't let me alone I'd tell Sam, and Spanish said if he was fired from El Mirador he'd kill me. And I believed him. I was afraid to tell Sam about him.

Then came the awful night when Sam was killed. When Sam asked me to have supper at his place, I would telephone over to the stage manager during the day and say I was sick. The door to Sam's apartment was masked by shrubbery and I could go in and come out without being seen. I went over to Jersey by taxi. It was one o'clock. Maybe Spanish was spying on me and saw me come. Sam made me stay upstairs when the waiters brought the supper. Sam would have everything just so for supper; champagne and everything. It was no pleasure to me. I didn't want to be there. I wanted to be with Sieg. I was only living for Sieg's release. Sam gave me an emerald ring that night. I sold it afterwards and sent the money to Sieg, week by week.

It was some time after supper, I couldn't tell you exactly, maybe two, maybe nearer three o'clock. Sam and I were sitting on the sofa with a couple of highballs when the door into the foyer opened quietly and Spanish slipped in. He had got hold of a key to the door. He was holding one hand behind him. I near died with fright. I still see him like that in my dreams and wake up screaming. Sliding his feet along the floor and showing his yellow teeth. Sam didn't know what fear was. He jumped up and started for Spanish. I screamed out that Spanish had a gun but Sam never stopped. When they came together, Spanish whipped his hand around and fired. I saw Sam drop to the floor and then I fainted.

When I came to, Spanish was hugging and kissing me. And Sam lying dead on the floor not ten yards away! If I had had a gun, I would have killed Spanish. I managed to get away from him and started screaming. He caught me and stopped my screaming with his hand. He gagged me with his handkerchief and tied my hands behind me so I couldn't pull the gag off. I struggled until I was so weak that when he took the gag off I didn't have the strength to scream any more. Spanish kept telling me I was in just as bad as he was. If I told the police that he shot Sam Bartol, he'd tell them I did it. His word was as good as mine, he said, and we'd go to the chair together. I didn't know but what he was right. And anyhow, Spanish kept telling me, if this gets out, Sieg will throw you over. When I thought of Sieg I wanted to die.

Spanish got me out of the place. I hardly remember. It was near morning then. Everybody had gone home. Spanish had parked his car outside the grounds. I had to go back to New York with him. There wasn't any other way. He wouldn't take the bridge because he thought somebody might remember the car. We made a long detour by way of Hoboken and the Holland Tunnel. Spanish took me to his flat. He thought he had me then. There was no more fight in me. But I made believe to faint and when he went for water, I got out of the place, I got into the street, and he had to let me go then. So I got back to Mrs. Besson's more dead than alive.

El Mirador was closed by the authorities. It never opened again. I had to stick around because I knew if I ran away it would fix suspicion on me. Mrs. Besson, my landlady, stood by me like a trump. I never told her the truth. She went to the police hearings with me. She swore that I had been home all that night and that let me out. The police had nothing on Spanish. He wasn't even suspected. When the investigation was dropped, I did a disappearing act. I told everybody I had a job in Buffalo, but I never left town. I took a room on Washington Heights and got work in the office of a laundry. Spanish never found me. But I never had a moment's peace or a good night's sleep until I read in the paper that he had been sent up for gambling.

When Sieg was released and we were married, I was hoping my luck had changed. Mrs. Cassells furnished that lovely home for us and everything looked swell.

For a few days I was as happy as a queen, and then
Spanish was let out of prison. The newspapers, of
course, told him where to find us. He came right
there. He persuaded Sieg to give him a room in our
house. What could I say? And so it has all begun
again. Spanish says if I don't give in to him, he will
tell Sieg about Sam Bartol. But I won't give in to him.
I have told him if he doesn't leave me alone I will
tell the police the story of the killing of Sam Bartol.
Spanish says he will kill me before the police get him.
Maybe he will. So I am writing this letter. I will put
it in a safe deposit box and will mark the key for you
and put it where it will be found after I am gone. So
if Spanish gets me he won't go free.

I don't want to die. I mean I don't want to leave Sieg.
Sieg is my whole world and nothing else matters to
me. I've had a hard life, but anyhow I've had that.
It's more than most women get out of life. So far as
I have seen, only a few women ever learn to know
what love is.

When Lee finished reading, the two men were silent. Then
Loasby lifted his fist and brought it down on the desk. "The skunk!"
he muttered. "The damn skunk! By God! it will give me pleasure to
see him burn!"

"Me too!" said Lee. "But this letter won't send him to the chair.
It's not legal evidence!"

"Then, by God, I'll find legal evidence!"

"Okay," said Lee. "I must stick to the murder of Letty Ammon.
This letter throws no fresh light on that."

"By the way," said Loasby, reaching for the telephone, "we'd
better find out what disposition is going to be made of Spanish's case."

After a little talk, he slammed down the instrument. "He's to
be brought up this morning in the magistrate's court, Part 2. Come
on, we've got to get a hustle on!"

They tore through the downtown streets in the Inspector's big red car to the accompaniment of a shrieking siren. Obstructions melted out of their path. It was close on noon when they entered the magistrate's court. His honor interrupted the current case long enough to lend the Inspector his ear. At Loasby's first words he shook his head.

"Sorry, Inspector! D'Acosta was before me only a quarter of an hour ago. Owing to lack of evidence, the District Attorney withdrew the charge against him, and I had to let him go."

Lee and the Inspector looked at each other. Lee said:

"He has no reason to fear any immediate danger. Send a man to watch the Ravens' Club and let you and me try Brooklyn."

Pausing only long enough for Loasby to telephone his office, they climbed back into the red car and were hustled back downtown and across the Brooklyn Bridge. When they turned into Sands Street, Lee said:

"Tell the driver to shut off his siren. There's no use advertising our approach."

Thus they drew up quietly before the old building on Sands Street. A taxicab was waiting there. This building had a hardware store at street level, with a door to one side giving entrance to the rooms above. As Loasby and Lee got out of the police car, this door opened and Spanish appeared, carrying a suitcase.

Seeing the police car, his waxen mask broke up and for a second a blazing hell of rage and fear showed in the yellow eyes. He dropped the suitcase and his eyes darted right and left like those of a trapped animal. Lee and the Inspector were both beyond the age of putting up a chase on foot, but the Inspector had two agile young officers with him. Spanish gave up. He picked up his suitcase, saying with his inimitable insolence:

"This is an unexpected pleasure, gentlemen."

Loasby matched him. Indicating the waiting taxi, he said: "We appear to have arrived at the psychological moment, Spanish. We'll give you a lift and you can save your taxi fare."

"What's it for?" asked Spanish.

"You'll learn soon enough."

"Have you got a warrant?"

"I have not," said Loasby coolly. "These men," he waved a hand in the direction of the waiting officers, "will have to be my warrant."

Spanish, with a shrug, got into the police car. This time they put him on the back seat between the two officers, who were instructed not to take their eyes off him until they completed their journey. They sped over Brooklyn Bridge. When they crossed lower New York without stopping and entered the Holland Tunnel, Spanish's eyebrows went up, but he said nothing. When they drew up in front of the Hudson County jail he could no longer keep silent.

"Why New Jersey?" he asked.

"That is where the offense was committed," said Loasby pleasantly. "Dope it out for yourself."

Spanish was led away.

## CHAPTER TWENTY-ONE

SANDRA CASSELLS was always precipitate in her actions. Having made up her mind to close Hope House, she lost no time about it. When Lee and Inspector Loasby returned to Headquarters after having delivered Spanish Jack into custody, they found Loasby's man Boker (alias Tappan) waiting to report. He said:

"Mrs. Cassells sent her attorney down to Hope House this morning to close up the place."

"What!" exclaimed Loasby.

"That's right, Inspector. Like a bolt from the blue! The lawyer said he had been instructed to hand each of us a hundred dollars and tell us to be out in a couple of hours. Apparently he was told to stick around until we got out."

"Well, I'll be damned!"

Lee said nothing.

Boker took a roll of bills out of his pocket. "Didn't seem quite right for me to take the hundred," he went on, "but I couldn't refuse it, either, without giving the whole snap away. What should I do with it?"

"Oh, give it to charity," said Lee. "Eh, Inspector?"

"Sure!"

Boker thrust the money back in his pocket with a grin. "Well, charity begins at home, they say."

"Was there much fuss in the house?" asked Lee.

"The hundred smackers helped to ease the blow, Mr. Mappin. Handbag Hattie and Mary Kennedy, they carried on some, and

Johnnie Stabler, he said it was an outrage to treat a gentleman like that, but they all started packing. I guess they're out by now."

"What about Sieg Ammon?"

"He didn't get no hundred, so I reckon he expects the Madame to do something better by him. He's still there."

"I'll run up to Henry Street," said Lee. "I want to have a talk with Sieg."

Hope House from the outside looked just the same as ever to Lee when he drove up before it; there was a sober dignity in the plain red brick façade with its neatly curtained windows, the blue door, the scrubbed steps. How incongruous with the passions it concealed! Lee paid off his driver and mounted. He had a latch key and used it as a matter of course. When the door swung in, he heard loud passionate voices inside. Instantly on the qui vive, he closed the door with care to make no sound, and listened. What a chance to hear the truth!

The voices came from the game room in the rear. It was Sieg Ammon and Queenie Deane. Queenie was yelling recklessly, Sieg trying to quiet her. It was difficult to hear what the man said. Pressing himself against the stair trunk, Lee stole back as far as he could without showing himself in the open doorway of the game room.

"You're a liar! a liar! a liar!" Queenie was yelling. "Don't you boast of lying to everybody else? Why should I believe what you tell me?"

"For God's sake, keep your voice down," begged Sieg. "You'll rouse the whole neighborhood!"

"I don't care! Let everybody know! You can't get away with anything like that!"

"I'm not trying to get away with anything."

"You're a liar! Why do you say I can't see you any more?"

"It's just for a little while, I told you. I've got to stay under cover for a bit. I mustn't be seen around."

"Why not?"

"Well, I've got a job on hand, if you must know. If I pull it off I'll be able to give you a handsome present. But I've got to disappear for a while."

"You're lying! You're going to that woman! Mrs. rich bitch! I know! Old enough to be your mother! You have no shame! You're nothing but a gigolo! A kept man!"

"Goddamn it, Queenie, there's nothing in that!" Sieg was losing his temper now. "Don't push me too far or you'll be sorry!"

"Hit me! Hit me! Hit me!" screamed Queenie. "I dare you to!"

"For God's sake, shut up!" shouted Sieg. His voice died away in a growl.

Queenie was noisily sobbing now. "Tell me you love me, Sieg," she begged. "Don't turn from me!"

"If that isn't like a woman!" muttered the exasperated Sieg with an oath. "To make a man mad and then expect him to love her!"

"You said you loved me! Over and over you told me you loved me!"

"Well, what of it? So I did at the time. You and I have had wonderful times together and we could have more if you wouldn't insist on being a damn fool. You know the kind of man I am. You've always known it. No woman owns me or ever will. To have a woman come crying after me just makes me sore!"

"Don't be so cruel to me!" wailed Queenie. "I love you so! You are everything in the world to me! If you leave me I'll kill myself!"

"That's the best way to drive a man from you. All this crying and carrying on! A woman could keep a man forever by making herself attractive to him. At present you're enough to turn a man's stomach!"

"You made me love you! Now you're trying to cast me off!"

"Okay! Okay! Have it your own way!"

"Just tell me where you're going to be and I'll be satisfied."

"Now you're starting all over!"

"You're going to live up at Mrs. Cassells' place."

"I am not!"

"Now you're free, maybe you're thinking of marrying Mrs. Cassells."

"There's nothing to it! How many times must I tell you that?"

"You're lying! I've seen the way you look at her!"

"My God! Jealous of a woman near sixty years old!"

"Oh, you're not in love with her! It's her money you're after. You're only fooling her like you fool all women! And I'm going to tell her! I swear I'm going to tell her!"

"Go ahead!" said Sieg coolly. "Do you think I couldn't talk her around?"

"Then it's true! It's true! You have admitted it!"

"I admit nothing. If I *did* marry Mrs. Cassells, what need you care? It wouldn't change anything between you and me. You would share in the profits."

"She'd take you away from me. I'd never see you again!"

A cajoling note came into Sieg's voice. "Aw, come on, Queenie! We're wasting time quarreling."

"Don't touch me!" cried Queenie sharply.

"Well, what the hell *do* you want?" growled Sieg.

"I want you to stay away from that woman!"

"Nobody is going to tell me what I can do!"

"If you don't stay away from her," said Queenie hysterically, "I'll go to her! I'll warn her! I'll tell her what you are! . . ."

"Listen, girl," said Sieg ominously, "if you ever try to interfere in my affairs, you'll regret the day you were born! . . . You're always calling me cruel. I've never been anything but kind to you, but I can be cruel! You don't know the half of it! I'll make you wish a thousand times over that you were dead . . ."

There was a yelp of pain from Queenie. "Sieg! Don't hurt me . . . !"

Lee could bear no more. Returning to the front door, he opened it and let it slam shut. Instant silence from the back room. As Lee made his way back, the frightened face of Sieg appeared in the open doorway. Seeing Lee, his features relaxed in a grin.

"Oh!" he said. "We collected all the boarders' keys. I thought . . ."

"You thought it must be Mrs. Cassells," said Lee briskly.

Sieg gave him a long look of suspicion, but Lee's innocent face deceived him. He stood, barring the way into the game room, but Lee coolly walked past him. Queenie was at the far side of the room, with her back turned, hurriedly repairing the damage to her make-up.

"Oh!" said Lee, emphasizing the innocence. "I'm sorry to butt in."

Queenie turned around with an overfriendly smile. Lee was no favorite of hers. "What an idea, Mr. Mappin! You're not butting in. I just came."

Lee noted the telltale red spot on her wrist. She concealed it under her other hand.

Sieg said: "Queenie didn't know that we were closing up here. It was a big surprise to her."

"To me, also," said Lee.

"How did you hear of it?" asked Sieg.

"Over the telephone," said Lee blandly.

An awkward silence fell on the three. Sieg's attitude was: What the hell do you want? Lee's only desire now was to get out of the house. He said:

"Is Mrs. Cassells' attorney here?"

"He's gone."

"Then I'll go on to his office," said Lee with his bland air. "See you later, you two."

He taxied up to his own place, where he had a hasty lunch. Afterward he set off for Brookwood in his own car. He would not warn Sandra of his coming, knowing that if he was still in her black books, he would not be allowed to see her. He was much troubled by what he had heard at Hope House. He had known Sandra to do many foolish things in her time, but surely, surely she could not so entirely have taken leave of her senses as to look on Sieg Ammon as a possible husband.

In the hall at Brookwood, old Dunstan, Sandra's butler, welcomed Lee with a benignant smile. He knew Lee as one of his mistress' most prized friends, and was not aware of strained relations.

"Madam has not come downstairs today," he said. "I will see if she can receive you."

He was gone a long time. Possibly Sandra was giving him the devil for betraying to Lee that she was in the house. When he returned, his serene old face gave nothing away.

"Will you please come up to the boudoir, Mr. Mappin?"

Lee followed him up the broad shallow stairway. After opening the door of Sandra's boudoir, Dunstan melted away. Sandra was wearing a white lawn negligee, one of those marvelous productions of the art of a French needlewoman, perfected by a French laundress; the delicate flutings and ruffles were as crisp and fresh as flower petals. Must have taken a woman a whole day to iron it, Lee thought prosaically. Sandra could wear such a garment, too, without looking anywhere near her age. Her skin was soft and pink, her enormous vague, blue eyes wistful and childlike. Lee always took warning when he found her looking childlike.

"Do sit down," she drawled. "How are you?"

"Never better," said Lee. He kissed her hand. "And you?"

Sandra threw herself back in a chaise longue. "Horribly out of sorts, darling. You've come at a bad time. If you're wise, you'll take yourself away again as soon as you can, for something tells me I'm going to disappoint you!"

"I'll take my chance of it," said Lee. He saw that her instinct told her he had come on a disagreeable errand, and she was resolved to stall it off. "What has upset you?" he asked.

"It's that horrible business of Hope House. I hate to fail in anything I undertake. And through no fault of my own."

"The best antidote is to start something else immediately."

Sandra turned a bracelet on her wrist. "Are you by any chance looking for an angel?" she asked with delicate insolence.

"No, my love," said Lee.

"Perhaps in the fall I may take up something else," said Sandra languidly. "I'm going away first."

This sounded ominous. It was only a few days since Sandra had violently repudiated the idea of travel. Lee did not remind her of that. "Where?" he asked.

"Oh, I don't know. I've never been North. I thought of Gaspé, the island of Anticosti, perhaps as far as Newfoundland."

"How would you get to those out-of-the-way spots?"

"I suppose one could charter a comfortable yacht in Montreal, couldn't one?"

"I suppose one could," said Lee dryly. He looked around for inspiration. Sandra at heart had simple tastes, which were reflected in the arrangement of her own room. It showed nothing of the oppressive magnificence of downstairs; but white paint, chintz-covered furniture, plenty of space to move around in. Awnings outside mitigated the heat of the sun, the windows were wide open, the light sash curtains blowing.

"It's perfect," said Lee. "I wonder how you can bring yourself to leave it."

"I go away for the pleasure of coming back again," she said. She yawned delicately. "Would you like a drink, darling?"

"No thanks. Too soon after lunch."

"You're not very entertaining this afternoon." She started telling Lee about a moving picture she had seen the night before.

Lee could have nailed her attention by telling her what he had overheard at Hope House, but he rejected it. Experience had taught him that the direct method was seldom the right method to use with the circuitous Sandra. If he did tell her, she would certainly blurt it out to Sieg the moment she saw him. Lee didn't want Sieg to be warned so soon.

"Whom will you be taking North with you?" he asked.

"That's the rub," said Sandra. "It will be safer to go alone."

"My darling, you would bore yourself to extinction in a week! Rather than that, you had better invite even me!"

"Not this time, darling," said Sandra with a secret smile.

Before the eye of Lee's mind rolled the black-faced headlines:

HUSBAND OF MURDERED GIRL MARRIES
LADY OF MILLIONS

And so on and so on. How to deal with an infatuated woman, that was his problem. He decided to administer a minor shock.

"Do you know, I learned today that the police have had a man planted in Hope House for weeks past. It was Tappan. He came in to Headquarters to announce the closing of the house when I happened to be with Loasby."

Sandra hoisted herself quickly from the chaise longue. Her eyes sparkled with anger. "Inspector Loasby did that to me!" she cried. "What a mean, underhand trick! After I have gone out of my way to be nice to the man! After I have entertained him here! I'll never speak to him again!"

Lee let her rail on. "I expect Tappan's reports would make interesting reading," he said carelessly.

Sandra whirled on him. "What do you suppose he has said about us? Horrible man! Lee, you're close to Loasby. Can you get me a look at those reports? If you have to bribe people, I'll put up for it. We'd be perfectly justified in getting back at Loasby that way. It would be tit for tat!"

"Well, I'll see what I can do," said Lee. There might be something in Tappan's reports, he thought, that would help to open Sandra's eyes.

"What a thing for Loasby to do!" she muttered, pacing the floor. "Serves me right for trying to make friends with such a creature!"

Having diverted Sandra into this side issue, Lee carelessly introduced his main theme. "What's to become of Sieg Ammon now? Do you want me to find him a job?"

"Thanks, no, it won't be necessary," said Sandra.

"What have you in mind for him?"

"I'm going to bring him up to this place as a superintendent," said Sandra very offhandedly. "The gatekeeper's cottage is empty. He can have that. The people here just lie around and collect their wages, and I'm tired of it!"

"I agree," said Lee, just as offhanded, "but do you think Sieg is the right one to make them work? I can't see it. Sieg will sack the men and chuck the girls under their chins . . ."

Sandra lowered her eyes. Lee saw that she was so angry she couldn't trust herself to speak for the moment. "Not that I blame him," Lee went on with a cheerful air. "He's at the proper age for chucking chins. All the girls fall for him. I can only look on and wonder!"

"What girls?" asked Sandra in a strangled voice. "Well, there was Letty. And Queenie Deane. And I'm thinking of what Blondy told me. Sieg was Blondy's hero. All the girls fell for Sieg, Blondy said."

Sandra began pacing again. "Letty's death has changed him."

"Naturally," said Lee with a reasonable air. "But how long will it last?"

Sandra could bear no more. She whirled on Lee with her face working like a small child's. "What are you trying to do?" she cried. "Bait me? Trying to see how far you can go?"

"My dear!" said Lee, looking very astonished.

"Drop it! Drop it!" she cried. "You're not so innocent as you're making out! You can see how it is with me. You can see that I'm mad about Sieg!" She began to sob tempestuously. It was dreadful to see the exquisite Sandra brought so low.

"My dear, I'm so sorry!" murmured Lee. He meant it then.

"I know I'm no longer young," she wailed. "I've never had anything in my life. Nothing but money and show; superficial things. Before I die I must have something real . . . something real . . ."

"Sieg will never give you anything real," said Lee gravely.

"You don't know!"

"Are you going to take him North with you?"

"Yes, I am! So make the most of it!"

"You are not by chance thinking of *marrying* him?"

Sandra struggled to recover her composure. "Of course not!" she said scornfully. "How can you be so silly? Why, Sieg's a mere boy. He's ten years younger than me."

Lee thought: More like twenty!

Sandra attempted to laugh it off. "What could have put such an idea into your head?"

"The logic of circumstances, my dear. Sieg is a levelheaded fellow. He would naturally insist on marriage."

By Sandra's glance of pure terror, Lee knew he had hit upon the truth. The only way she could refute it was by losing her temper again. "Everybody's against Sieg!" she cried passionately. "You too! Other men hate him because he's so virile! He's never had a chance. Nobody knows him but me!"

Lee thought: Night-club singer and great lady, sisters under the skin!

Sandra stormed on: "What if I should marry him? It's nobody's business but mine! I'm free and independent. I can do what I like. I don't give a damn for what anybody says about me. I never did!"

"The newspapers," Lee pointed out, "so soon after Letty's death!"

"I shan't tell them. I shan't tell anybody."

"This is what I was afraid of!" murmured Lee. "Why marry him, Sandra?"

She turned pitiful again. "I've got to marry him," she cried, beating her breast. "I've *got* to! It's the only way I can have him for my own!"

"He wasn't faithful to Letty," said Lee. "What reason have you to suppose he would be faithful to you?"

"How do you know he wasn't faithful to Letty?"

"The police investigation showed that."

"Who was the other woman?"

"The Deane girl . . . You are preparing a hell on earth for yourself, Sandra!"

Sandra flung up her arms. "I don't care!" she said desperately. "I'm bound to be unhappy anyhow. But at least I'll have my moment of joy!" She turned her big, tear-filled eyes on Lee. "Don't you understand?"

Lee sprang up and opened his arms. She came and, laying her head on his shoulder, wept unrestrainedly. "Of course I understand, my dear. I feel for you from the bottom of my heart. I haven't the slightest feeling of blame for you, but only grief."

"Grief?" she questioned.

"Because of the inevitable degradation that awaits you."

Sandra wept afresh.

After a while, Lee said: "Will you do one thing for me?"

"Anything—but give up Sieg," she said.

"Don't rush into marriage. Wait a little. Wait a month."

"What good will that do?"

"Well, who knows? Common sense may intervene."

"I'll wait two weeks. Not a day longer!"

## CHAPTER TWENTY-TWO

MEANWHILE THE DAYS were passing and the police search for the bearded man brought no results. A man was found who had seen such a man hanging about Schanze's on the night of the murder. This did not advance the case, because Lee already knew the man had been there. In Varick Street the night watchman of a big wholesale establishment testified that he had seen the old sedan drive up and stop across the road about midnight, and remain there. At that time the car had license plates. The watchman was too far away to read the numbers. The driver of the car must have removed the plates while the watchman was making his rounds; when he got back he failed to notice that they were missing. However, he had seen the driver crossing the road, heading east. He was not carrying anything in his hands at the time, so he had rid himself of the little satchel. His elbow was pressed against his side as if he might be concealing something under his coat. From that moment the bearded man in the corduroy pants and the windbreaker was lost.

Reports from out of town of the arrest of suspicious characters took Loasby's men in various directions, only to meet with disappointment. For his own part, Lee felt confident that the man had never left New York. If he had meant to conceal himself out of town, he would naturally have made the first stage of the journey in his own car. Somebody in New York was providing him with a hideout. Lee already knew that somebody had been supplying him with money. There was nothing to indicate that the man had had a companion in his car at any time on the night of the murder.

In the hope of providing the police with something more to go on, Lee made a second visit to Elizabeth. On account of the generous tips he had distributed, he was well received by Mrs. Doughty, the lodging-house keeper, and her sister. They submitted amiably to a lengthy cross-examination. It brought out little that was new. "Wilson" certainly had been in communication with his principal during the days he was living at Mrs. Doughty's, yet both women were sure that he had never received a visitor, nor a letter, nor a call to the telephone. Neither had he ever been seen to use the telephone. From what the women told him, Lee compiled a little list of the saloons in the neighborhood that the lodgers frequented.

In two of these places, Lee's inquiries were received with shakes of the head. The third place, Murphy's, was a cheerful, shabby, old-fashioned saloon of the sort beloved by workingmen; Murphy himself was serving behind the bar. The bearded man was remembered here as a solitary guy who used to stand at the far end of the bar, drinking one whisky after another. He was a surly fellow who discouraged anybody who tried to engage him in talk. He never got drunk; he never made any trouble; he just wanted to be left alone. In talking about him, Murphy referred to him as "Wilson."

"How did you learn his name?" asked Lee.

"He was called to the phone a couple of times." Murphy indicated the booth against the wall.

Lee's spirits rose.

"So!" he said. "Did you answer the phone?"

"I did, sir."

"Was it a man or a woman calling?"

"A man both times."

"Would you know the voice if you heard it?"

"How would I?" said Murphy. "Just a man's voice over the wire."

"It wasn't by chance a drawling voice with a foreign accent?" Lee imitated Spanish's voice.

"No, sir. An American voice. I could swear to that."

"I suppose you couldn't hear anything that was said?"

"No, sir. Wilson was always careful to close the door of the booth when he went in."

"Did he ever make any calls himself?"

"Yes, sir, I have seen him go in and drop his nickel. Wait a minute," Murphy volunteered; "here's something I remember. Once after he was called to the phone, when he come out he asked me for pencil and paper to write down an address before he forgot it. I didn't have a pencil but I shove my fountain pen across the bar. Couldn't find no paper. While I was looking, he wrote the address on the sweat band of his hat. 'I'll copy it off when I get home,' he said."

"You didn't see what he wrote?"

"No, sir, I was behind the bar."

"What kind of hat was it?"

"Gray Fedora."

"Then this happened before he bought his workman's clothes."

"Must be."

Lee toddled back to Mrs. Doughty's.

"Can you tell me," he asked her, "about when Wilson bought his new pants and his windbreaker and cap?"

She shook her head. "How would I remember a thing like that?"

"Well, was it when he first came?" persisted Lee.

"No. He had been in the house some days, maybe as much as a week when he come out in his new clothes."

"Did he bring his old clothes home with him?"

"No. I never see them again. I took it he traded them in."

"In that case, he got them in a store where they dealt in secondhand clothes as well as new."

"I reckon so."

"Did he tell anybody where he bought his things?"

"No, sir."

"Did he ask anybody where to buy such things?"

"Not as far as I know."

This was as far as Lee could get with the two women. Feeling somewhat discouraged, he started for the Eureka Restaurant. It was two blocks south from Mrs. Doughty's to the main street where the trolley cars ran and the stores were, then three blocks west to the Eureka. This was the route that the bearded man must have followed four times a day, and Lee as he walked along tried to put himself in the man's place. Suppose I was looking for a place where I might provide myself with a disguise? he said to himself.

Nearing the restaurant, he saw across the street, a cheap-John clothing store with a row of suits on hangers swinging in the breeze. He crossed over. The proprietor was out in front of his store on the look-out for customers; when Lee paused he sized him up with no welcome in his eye. Natty little Lee, dressed with the care of a slightly old-fashioned tailor's engraving, was certainly not his kind of customer.

Lee greeted him politely. "Would you mind stepping into the store?" he said. "I'd like to have a little talk with you."

"What about?" grumbled the man. "Want to buy something?"

"Not today," said Lee. "I want a little information about a customer of yours."

"I don't give out no information to strangers."

"At what rate do you value your time?" asked Lee.

"What's that to you, Mister? Dollar and a half an hour."

"Cheap at half the price," murmured Lee. He glanced at his watch. "Very well," he said aloud, "I will pay you for the time I cause you to waste."

The dealer relaxed and led Lee into his dark and stuffy shop. Lee described the man he was trying to trace, the clothes he had bought and the clothes he had turned in.

"Yeah, he was my customer," said the dealer. "I remember him because of his scrubby beard. When he said he wanted a workingman's clothes, I thinks to myself: If it's a job you're looking for, you'd better spend a dime for a shave, Mister." He showed Lee a windbreaker and a pair of pants like the ones he had sold the bearded man. The corduroy pants were a light brown or ginger color.

Concealing his eagerness, Lee asked casually: "What became of the clothes he turned in?"

"I sold the suit, Mister. Wasn't worth much; shoddy stuff, prison made."

"That's my man . . . And the hat?"

"Gee! How do you expect me to remember an old hat? What kind of hat?"

"A gray Fedora with a narrow brim; black band. It was fairly clean but of cheap material; the felt was roughed up."

"I know," said the dealer. "Such hats are hardly worth a dime a dozen. How would I know what became of any one of them? I have a closet full of old hats in the back of the shop."

"Let's look them over," said Lee.

When the old clothes dealer opened the door of the closet, the hats poured out, dusty, stained and battered. Lee sat down to examine them.

"Two dollars for a gray hat that has an address inked in on the sweat band," he said.

Brown hats, black hats, green hats were tossed to one side. They eagerly looked inside each gray one. "Would this be it?" asked the dealer.

Lee looked and was filled with a pleasant sense of satisfaction. On the band was written in ink: 1004 Madison St. "That is it," he said.

Back to New York he carried his prize.

After the briefest of pauses for lunch, he hailed a taxi and gave the driver the address in the hat. He knew that Madison Street was on the lower east side of New York, and somewhere in the neighborhood of Henry Street. Of what he was going to find at this number he had not the remotest idea.

Number 1004 proved to be a shabby tenement house of the "dumb-bell" type, which under the law may no longer be built. Though it was a dreary abode and far from clean, it was not one of the worst specimens; it seemed to be inhabited by foreign workingmen and their families. It was six stories high and had four families to a floor; there were two small stores at street level, an Italian pizzeria, and a shop where plaster images were made. The entrance door to a house of this sort is never locked.

A preliminary survey of the premises suggested no possible connection with the Letty Ammon case. Yet it seemed certain to Lee that her murderer had made an appointment to meet somebody at this address. He started with the two stores. It was somewhat difficult to make himself understood to the Italian proprietors. No luck here. Beginning then at the top of the house, he made his way from door to door asking questions. A slow and discouraging business; infinite patience was required to lull the suspicions of the foreigners and convince them of his good will. It was a veritable house of all nations. All the flats were rented. When there was no answer to his knock, Lee made a note to return to that door later.

Six o'clock had come when he finished the rounds of the house. He stood in the lower entry, tired out and disheartened; he had turned up not a single clue. After all, he was on a wild goose chase, it seemed. Noticing that light was coming in at the rear of the long narrow hall where he stood, with the instinct of leaving nothing unexamined, he went back to investigate its source. He found an open door leading to the narrow, stone-paved yard of the tenement house, an untidy spot covered with litter.

How astonished was Lee to find himself looking at the back windows of Hope House. There was no mistaking the freshly painted blue window sashes and the neat curtains hanging within. All the windows were closed. Sandra was in process of deeding the house to the Henry Street Settlement, but the Settlement had not yet taken possession. What an extraordinary coincidence—then instantly Lee realized that there was more than coincidence in this.

A seven-foot matchboard fence separated the two back yards. An agile man could have hauled himself up and dropped on the other side, but not one of Lee's figure. In the yard of the tenement house, a ragged boy was preparing to break up a big packing case for firewood. Lee offered him a dime to push the case against the back fence so he could stand on it and look over. The boy lost no time in accepting.

To explain his presence, Lee said: "I'm thinking of buying that house."

"Gee! That's where the convicts used to live," volunteered the boy. "Little Sing Sing, we call it. They was a guyl muyded in there last month, so they close the place up."

"No kidding!" said Lee.

"Well, it was up in Westchester where she was muyded, but she come from in there."

Lee climbed on the case and looked over the fence. The yard of Hope House was a model of neatness. Still standing around were the evergreens in tubs that Sandra had had placed there. A strange thought was taking shape in Lee's mind. Could the bearded man have found a refuge in Hope House following the murder? He searched along the top of the fence. To a protruding nail clung a scrap of tan colored thread. Lee examined it under his pocket magnifying glass. The crinkly, furry thread had been torn from a piece of corduroy. There could be no doubt of it, the man in the ginger pants had gone over this fence in the dark and had hooked himself on a nail.

The boy in the yard below, looking up at Lee with mixed respect and derision, said: "Okay, Shuylock Holmes! I'm wise to you!"

"Keep it dark!" said Lee, climbing down and handing him another dime.

Lee was obliged to lean against the box for a moment. His head was whirling. All his patiently built-up theories were demolished at a stroke. After killing Letty Ammon, the bearded man had come directly to Hope House. Lee had to start all over with that as a beginning.

He hastened around the block into Henry Street. He still had a key to Hope House and he let himself in. The windows had been closed for days; the air was close and still. He ran downstairs to the kitchen. This room had a door opening on the yard with glass panes in the top. There was no key in the lock; it was fastened with a strong bolt. Somebody had let the bearded man through this door on the night of the murder. Where had he been hidden then? Weeks had passed since that night, and Lee feared that he could scarcely hope to find traces of the man's passage now.

# CHAPTER TWENTY-THREE

LEE MAPPIN, hot with the excitement of discovering a new trail, called up Police Headquarters. It was not Inspector Loasby he wanted this time, but Detective Boker. Boker was off duty for the night, he was told. Obtaining his telephone number, Lee found him at home, and at seven o'clock Lee and Boker were sitting down to dinner in Lee's apartment. Lee had confidence in Boker's keen, intelligent, humorous eye. In the meantime, having learned where the Kennedys were living, Lee had sent a message to ask the couple to come to his apartment later.

Lee had changed to the sort of clothes he liked to wear at home; a crimson brocade dressing gown and a smoking cap that resembled a turban to cover the bald pate.

Boker was doing full justice to the tasty food Jermyn had put before them, and to Lee's good wine. Looking around him, he said: "You got a mighty nice place here, Mr. Mappin. It's exactly what every man would have for himself if he had his own way." Boker heaved a sigh. "But of course, for a married man it wouldn't be possible, even if he had the price. Woman runs the home!"

"Well, of course, I can have everything the way I want it," said Lee. "Just the same, I don't recommend bachelorhood for a man. I would trade all this for a bustling wife and a couple of noisy kids, and think myself the gainer. Just consider what an old stick-in-the-mud this has made me!"

"I wouldn't call you that," said Boker. "What was it you wanted to talk to me about, Mr. Mappin?"

"Let's take the edge off our appetites first," said Lee. "This *poulet à la bonne femme* of Jermyn's is worthy of our full attention. The wine is beside you, Boker."

"Thank you, sir. What did you say it was that we're eating? I would have called it chicken."

"Chicken under any other name tastes just as good, Boker."

Later Lee said, lighting a cigarette: "Boker, I've turned up some important new evidence in the Letty Ammon case, but I want you to answer a few questions before I tell you what it is, because I don't want your answers to be influenced in the slightest degree by what I have learned today."

Jermyn was in and out of the dining room. "Is it all right to speak before him?" asked Boker.

"Just the same as if we were alone."

"Okay! Fire away, Mr. Mappin."

"First, I want you to tell me, as well as you can remember, everything that happened at Hope House the night Letty was killed. The slightest detail may turn out to be important. Begin with after supper."

"Well," said Boker, "you and Mrs. Cassells and Sieg Ammon was in the office talking business and Letty had gone out—to the movies, as we thought. The rest of the boarders was in the game room; Hattie Oliver, Joe Spencer, Johnnie Stabler and Duke Engstrom. Spanish, as you know, had left us."

"Let me interrupt you for a moment," said Lee. "I want to get the layout of the house fixed in my mind. The three of us were in the office at the front of the first floor. Was anybody in the back room?"

"No, sir. That room had been furnished as a parlor, but nobody ever went in there and Mrs. Cassells said she was going to make another bedroom out of it."

"Had it been closed up?"

"No, sir, the door to that room was always open."

"Go ahead."

"On the second floor, Sieg and Letty had the two connecting rooms in front, and Hattie had the back room."

"Who was in the extension?"

"That had been Spanish's room. It was unoccupied. On the top floor Joe Spencer and Duke Engstrom had the two small rooms in front; Johnnie Stabler and me the two in the rear. My door was opposite the head of the stairs."

"I've got it straight."

"I was reading a book," Boker continued, "and the other four was playing cards. It was a game called Michigan, pretty noisy. The fellows said that Hattie cheated. I heard the front door open and close. I didn't see who it was; later you told me you had gone out. After a while you came in again. Later I heard the door again. I thought at the time that this was Letty coming home from the movies; now I know it was Sieg, the first time he went out. I changed my seat to across the room where I could see the front door, and I saw Sieg come in after fifteen minutes or so. He ran out again almost immediately."

Boker stroked his face in the effort to remember. "The next thing I mind was hearing angry voices from the basement. Soup Kennedy quarreling with Mary. They was always quarreling. This time it lasted so long I went out and opened the door to the basement stairs to listen. The cardplayers couldn't see me. The voices were so loud I didn't have to go downstairs to hear. Soup and Mary were in their room in front. Mary accused him of having left the door into the yard open. Soup swore he had bolted it. Mary said he was a liar. She had been back and found it unbolted. And so on. This didn't seem important, so I went back to the game room and left them to fight it out."

"Maybe it is important," said Lee. "Go on."

"The card game broke up about ten-thirty. Hattie went up to bed, Joe and Duke went out to get a drink; Johnnie Stabler talked to me—you know, about what a smart guy he was. He never tired of the subject. I was wondering where Sieg had gone and why you and Mrs. Cassells stayed in the office. I had guessed from the look in Sieg's face that something was wrong. But I didn't know then that Letty had not come home. Joe and Duke came in and they all went to bed. Sieg came in and he looked worse than before. So I just stayed there with my book in case I might be wanted."

"Could anybody have come up from the basement without your being aware of it?" asked Lee.

"No, sir! The door to the basement stairs is just outside the game room door, not ten feet from where I was sitting."

"Go on."

"You and Mrs. Cassells left the house. That was about midnight. You both looked bad. Sieg came back to the game room. 'Why the hell don't you go to bed?' he said. 'Oh, I got a good book,' I said; 'I ain't sleepy.' 'Get the hell to bed,' he said; 'we can't let the lights stay on all night.' And he started to turn out the lights. 'Anything the matter?' I asked. He didn't answer me. So I started upstairs. I went up one flight only and stood there by the rail listening. I couldn't hear nothing from below. In a couple of minutes Sieg went into the office again. Pretty soon you came back. That surprised me. You went into the office. I stayed up there in the hall near a couple of hours, I guess, listening and watching."

"Did you see or hear anything?"

"Not a thing, Mr. Mappin. Except sometimes I heard Sieg cursing in the office. Sounded like he was walking up and down the room. Once I heard him cry out: 'I'll kill him! I'll kill him!' You were trying to quiet him. Finally I heard the telephone ring and I judged from the sound of your voices that meant more bad news. Then you came out and started upstairs and I skipped up ahead of you to my room, where you found me reading. You told me what had happened. You asked me to look after Sieg."

Said Lee: "You've got a good memory, Boker."

"Thank you, sir. It's part of my business."

"What happened after I left the house?"

"Not much, sir. I suggested Sieg ought to have a drink and, Gee! he drunk off near a tumblerful of Scotch. Said he'd go to bed then and I took him upstairs. I offered to stay with him, but he said the hell with it. I left him lying on his bed. I went up to my room and sat there in the dark with the door open. I felt bad on account of Letty. After a while I heard Sieg's door open . . ."

"Quietly?"

"No. He wasn't taking any care to be quiet. He walked along to the stairs. I went down the upper flight as quick and soft as I could and I was in time to see him jam his hat on and go out the front door. It seemed natural the poor fellow would have the impulse to walk the streets and I let him go."

"Did you hear him come in again?"

"Yes, sir. It was near morning then. I heard the front door open and close. I heard Sieg stumbling up the first flight. And when I looked down the second flight I saw Sieg come along the hall and go into his room. He was good and drunk then. I couldn't blame him."

Lee thought over all he had heard. Afterward he told Boker what he had learned that afternoon.

"Good God!" ejaculated the detective. "Then the killer came to Hope House! He was hidden there that night! Must have been Soup Kennedy left the yard door unbolted for him."

"So it might appear at first glance," said Lee, "but upon thinking it over, if Soup had left the door open for this purpose, it doesn't seem likely he would carry on a noisy quarrel with his wife on the subject for an hour afterward."

"That's right!" said Boker. "But who else could have done it?"

"I have felt from the beginning that Spanish Jack was behind this murder," said Lee. "It would be like Spanish to choose this house as a hide-out for his man, because this is the last place anybody would look for him."

"Spanish was in Boston!"

"He came back at noon on the day Letty was killed."

"But he certainly wasn't in this house that day or night."

"Apparently not. But Spanish's arm is long. He's accustomed to bending other men to his will. He might have worked on one of the men in the house while he was living here. Did you notice him chumming up with anybody?"

"There was Johnnie Stabler. They was pretty thick. Johnnie, he admired Spanish's elegant foreign manners. Us other men wasn't gentlemanly enough for Johnnie. And Spanish would string Johnnie along to make him feel good."

"Could Johnnie have unbolted the yard door that night?"

"Don't see how, Mr. Mappin. Earlier he could, but after Mary Kennedy bolted it again, I don't see how. Johnnie was under my eye all evening. I saw him go upstairs. Until I went to bed myself the basement door was right in line with my eye every minute. After I went upstairs, Johnnie's room is next to mine; my door was never closed; I did not sleep until morning. How could Johnnie have got in or out?"

"In that case," said Lee, "we must keep Soup open as a possibility, though I hate to think of the old man in connection with murder."

The Kennedys presently came. Very much impressed by the honor of being received in Mr. Mappin's home as guests, they could hardly stop bowing and curtsying to Jermyn in the hall. Seated in the dining room, they refused food, but their old eyes glistened at the sight of tall highballs. Lee put them in a place where a strong light fell in their faces. A well-meaning but somewhat thick-witted old pair, he felt confident they could not fool him. Lee said at once:

"It was not Blondy Farren who killed Letty Ammon!"

Their eyes widened. "Who was it, sir?"

"A rough-looking man with a three weeks' growth of beard. Dressed like a workingman. After killing her, he returned to New York, parked his car in Varick Street, crossed town on foot and passed through the tenement house on Madison Street that backs up to Hope House. He climbed the fence between and entered Hope House. Somebody had unbolted the door for him."

The old couple stared; their mouths dropped open; Soup scratched his head. Both were speechless. Lee, watching them, felt sure that the finest actors in the world could not have given so good a performance, if it was not real.

"You and Mary were overheard quarreling about the unbolted door that night," Lee said accusingly.

They looked at each other in terror, speechless still. Finally Soup stammered: "I bolt that door! I swear it, Mr. Mappin! Mary said I leave it open but she was wrong. I remember bolting it. I see myself shooting the bolt acrost!"

"Afterward, Mary bolted it again," suggested Lee.

"I sure did, Mr. Mappin!" asserted Mary.

"What time would this be?"

"About ten o'clock," said Mary. "We was already in bed, and I got up and went out in the kitchen to get a cracker to nibble on, and I seen the yard door was unbolted, and I bolted it."

"Somebody unbolted it after that," said Lee. "The man didn't get to the house until half past twelve."

"When I got back to bed me and Soup lay there fussing for a while," Mary went on.

"Mary made me mad," put in Soup, "and I got up and made believe to read the paper, but I never left the room, did I, Mary?"

"That's right, Mr. Mappin. He was never out of my sight."

"And when Mary quiet down, I got back in bed."

"Did you leave your bed after Mary was asleep?" Lee demanded sternly.

Mary answered for him. "He couldn't do that without waking me, Mr. Mappin. 'Cause he slep' on the inside."

"Maybe he climbed over the foot of the bed," suggested Lee with a twinkle.

"No, sir! No, sir! No, sir!" asserted Soup in distress. "I never knew nothing after that until morning."

"You heard no suspicious sounds?"

"No sir!" they answered together.

"The stairway from above comes down outside your bedroom door. Do you keep that door closed at night?"

"Yes, sir, and Mary she made me lock it, too. Plumb foolishness, I said at the time."

Lee dropped the subject, picked it up again, approaching from various angles, but without ever tripping up the old pair. Finally, after refilling their glasses, he let them go.

# CHAPTER TWENTY-FOUR

Lee and Boker adjourned to the living room, where they lit fresh cigars.

"Leaving aside for the moment, who let the man into Hope House," said Lee, "the question is, what became of him after he got in? It doesn't seem likely, in a house so full of people, that he would venture upstairs. In the basement there are only three rooms, the Kennedys' bedroom in front, kitchen in the rear, and dining room in the extension."

"There's the cellar," Boker pointed out.

"Ah!" said Lee. "I've never been down cellar in that house."

"The entrance is from the kitchen," said Boker. "The stairs are under the main stairs."

"What sort of place is it?"

"Pretty grim for a lengthy stay," said Boker, "but, as the old saying goes, any port in a storm. It was cleaned up when the house was renovated for Mrs. Cassells. It's paved with brick."

"Tomorrow we'll look it over to see if the visitor left any evidence of his stay there."

"Okay, Mr. Mappin. As far as that goes, it's as black as your hat night or day. You could look it over just as well tonight. It's only half past eight."

"Boker, you're a man after my own heart!" said Lee.

"We'll drive down there. I have a key to the house and we'll take a battery of flashlights. Let us take Jermyn, too. He's a good man to have along."

The tall, angular, leathery Jermyn, who cherished the secret dream of becoming a detective, was delighted to be taken along. When Lee changed the flamboyant dressing gown and turban for sober jacket and hat, they were ready to start.

"We'll go in my car," said Lee. "When you get out, keep your flashlights out of sight."

Arriving before the Henry Street house, they entered without attracting any particular attention from the street. The car was instructed to wait a few doors off. The electric current had been turned off in the house, and they proceeded through the hall by the eerie radiance of their flashlights. Nothing had been changed inside, for Sandra, with one of her queenly gestures, had presented the outfit to the Settlement intact.

"I suppose we could be arrested for trespassing," said Lee. "Let us hope for the best."

Down to the basement they went, around through the kitchen and on down the cellar stairs. The three flashlights cast patches of phosphorescence on brick floor, stone walls and low wooden sleepers overhead. Tall Jermyn and Boker had to duck; Lee's head just missed the floor beams. Apart from the cleaning it had received, no changes had been made in the ancient cellar. The original brick floor remained as it had been laid. The bricks were not cemented, but merely laid on the earth in a herringbone pattern. So well had the job been done that the floor was still level as a board. Around the sides, where it had never been trodden on, a faint, greenish scum covered the dark bricks. The whole place smelled faintly like an open grave.

Even during the few weeks the house had been running, a certain amount of litter had accumulated in the cellar; crates, boxes, baskets and other miscellany. In the middle, an old-fashioned coal-burning furnace rose out of a shallow pit. In the front of the cellar coalbins, still partly full, extended out under the street. They could be filled from a manhole in the sidewalk. At the other end, a wooden partition had been built across from wall to wall with a door in it having a hasp and staple.

"There were some empty trunks belonging to the boarders kept in here," said Boker. "Maybe four or five trunks. It was padlocked then. Now it's open and empty."

Lee was looking at the furnace. "I suppose there was a fire here at first?"

"Sure! To take the chill off the house and dry out the new plaster. It was allowed to go out about the first of May."

"It had turned very warm by the 11th," said Lee. "There was no fire then."

He opened the door of the furnace and cast his light inside the firebox. It revealed a bed of ashes and partly burned coal—also a small, clean piece of paper. He drew it out.

"What's that?" asked Boker.

"Wrapper from a stick of Triple X gum."

"Not very conclusive evidence."

"Every little bit helps," said Lee. "We may accept it as a fact that the bearded man rested himself down here on the night of May 11th."

Lee picked up a carpenter's spirit level which appeared brand new. "Now how in hell did that get down here?" he asked at large.

"Perhaps one of the workmen left it behind him."

"Spirit levels are expensive," said Lee. "No workman is going to abandon one that he has only lately bought. Besides, no carpenter work was done down here so far as we can see."

"What about the partition at the end?"

"That was put up for a previous tenant. It's been here a long time."

Lee laid the spirit level aside. "I wish you fellows would stay in one place," he said. "You're getting in my way."

Boker and Jermyn seated themselves against the wall, one on a crate, one on an upturned basket. Lee, almost bent double, moved swiftly back and forth, pausing, poking, peering, like an old sleuth hound happy in following a fresh scent. One could almost imagine one heard him sniff, but it was his eyes he was using, not his nose. He dug patiently in the coal pile and collected some infinitesimal lumps of clay that he stowed in an envelope. He set aside various objects that interested him; a dustpan and broom—he gave a long scrutiny to the broom straw and set it down with the greatest care; two old coal shovels, likewise examined closely, and finally the heavy iron bar used for shaking down the furnace. When he examined the business end of the bar under his magnifying glass, an exclamation broke from him.

"Can either of you fellows supply me with another envelope?"

Boker produced an old envelope. "What have you found?" he asked.

"A couple of long black hairs," said Lee, carefully stowing them away. "The microscope, I believe, will reveal that they are dyed."

"Oh, my God!" murmured Jermyn.

After some further searching, Lee straightened up. "The visitor never left the cellar," he said. "He—or rather, what remains of him—is still here."

Jermyn with an exclamation of horror cast his light wildly back and forth.

"Oh, he's not in sight," said Lee dryly. ". . . He was hit over the head with the shaker. One blow seems to have done the trick, because there's no blood on the iron, but only a couple of hairs. His grave was undoubtedly prepared beforehand. That seems to have been a one-man job, because only one of the two shovels was used for the purpose. Afterward it was washed. The gravedigger committed a serious error in not rubbing coal dust on it afterward. I can now figure a purpose for the spirit level. That was to make certain that the bricks were laid true after the grave was filled in. The broom, of course, was for sweeping up the last particles of dirt. Bits of dirt are still clinging to the straw. The rest of the dirt was thrown on the coal pile and some coal raked over it."

"Nice work, Mr. Mappin," said Boker.

"The only thing that remains for us to do is to uncover the spot he chose for the grave," Lee went on. "That ought not to be difficult. Let us first look at the floor of the closet that was always kept locked. . . . By the way," Lee asked suddenly, "who had the key?"

"It hung in the kitchen where all could see it," said Boker.

"Ha!" said Lee. "You will be familiar with it, then. You appear to have cleared everybody else in the house. Perhaps you're the man we want."

Jermyn looked at the detective officer in fright.

Boker wiped his face agitatedly. "That's a grim jest, Mr. Mappin! It was Soup Kennedy who had free access to the cellar at all times."

Lee said nothing. They proceeded to the back of the cellar. The wooden partition had been erected directly on the brick floor. Within, there was a space about twelve feet by twenty-three.

"Plenty of room for him to work in," remarked Lee, "even with a few trunks."

Boker and Jermyn cast down their lights while Lee, on his knees, went over the floor foot by foot with his glass. Presently he put the glass in his pocket.

"Don't need it. With all his care, the marks of the broom are visible. And here's a brick with the edges a little chipped. Must be the first one he pried up . . . What have we got to pry up the bricks with?"

"There are some ordinary tools in the kitchen," said Boker.

"Go fetch them, please."

As Boker started up the stairs, Jermyn said nervously, "Hadn't I better go with him? He might run away."

Lee laughed shortly and gave him a little clap on the shoulder. "It's not as simple as that, my Jermyn!"

Boker returned with a screw driver, a chisel, a hammer. It was a tedious job to pry up the first of the neatly-fitted bricks. Afterward they had merely to be lifted out. They exposed a considerable space of the packed clay beneath. Though it had been carefully stamped down, it was impossible to make it look the same as that which had lain undisturbed for a hundred years. The limits of the grave were plainly visible.

"He threw water on it to make it settle," muttered Boker. "He thought of everything!"

"*Almost* everything," said Lee. "If he felt safe down here, of course he took his time. This job wasn't completed in one night."

Boker and Jermyn started digging, one at each end, while Lee between them held the light. Sweat ran down their faces; Jermyn's face was greenish, and even Boker, whose business was crime, was far from comfortable. In Lee a situation like this always aroused a macabre humor that was disconcerting to his associates. He quoted the grave-digger's song from *Hamlet*:

> A pick-axe and a spade, a spade,
> For and a shrouding sheet:
> O, a pit of clay for to be made
> For such a guest is meet!

As they went deeper and deeper, Lee said: "He did his job thoroughly!"

Finally Jermyn, with a little yelp of terror, stammered, "I . . . I . . . struck something soft, sir!" He was shaking as with an ague.

"Climb out and give me the shovel," said Lee. "Lay the flashlight on the edge of the hole and you can go upstairs."

Jermyn, however, doggedly refused to give up. They dug more carefully now, a few spoonfuls of earth at a time. Gradually a shrouded form began to take shape. The body was wrapped in a cloth.

"At least he provided him with a shroud," said Lee.

Abandoning the clumsy shovels, the two diggers scooped up the loose earth by handfuls. Finally they were able to work their hands under the body. Wrapped in its stained sheet, they lifted it out and laid it on the bricks alongside. Jermyn, shaking like a leaf, walked away and sat down on the bottom stair, burying his face in his arms.

"I can't look!" he muttered.

Lee unwound the sheet. The body was in only a fair state of preservation. Easy to recognize the rough, bearded chin and the partly bald head. There was an ugly abrasion on the bald spot now, and the thin hair was matted with blood. The face was blackish; it was difficult to picture what the man had looked like in life. The body was clad in the garments as described: the imitation leather windbreaker, the ginger-colored pants. The cheap cap was with it.

There was a loaded gun in the hip pocket; in the side pocket of his pants, a Japanese five-sen piece.

The license plates from the sedan lay in the bottom of the grave, and Letty's black handbag with the scallop-shell clasp had been rolled up with the body. A cursory examination of the contents revealed Letty's two letters to Blondy and Blondy's replies. The handwriting was still legible. There was also a small bottle containing a colorless and odorless liquid.

"The balance of the knockout drops," said Lee.

Boker was on his knees examining the abrasion on the man's head. "His skull has not been crushed," he said. "There appears to be no other wound. Perhaps he was only stunned by the blow . . ."

"In that case he was buried alive," said Lee.

"Oh, my God! how fiendish!"

"It wouldn't make any difference to this fellow," said Lee coolly. "If his wind was stopped he never regained consciousness."

"What I can't figure out," said Boker, "is what he did with the rest of the dirt. After he put the body in the grave there must have been a lot left over."

"I have a theory," said Lee. "We'll test it out directly."

In the cold white glare of the flashlights, Lee studied the ruined face of the dead man. "I never knew this fellow in life," he said slowly, "but sometime, somewhere, I have seen him once." He held a hand above the upper part of the face, then the lower. In the end, it was the lips twisted in a perpetual, ugly sneer which gave him the clue.

"I have it! It's Jimpson Souter!"

"Who's he?" asked Boker.

"He was a pal of Sieg Ammon's and Blondy Farren's some years ago. The three of them bummed across the continent together. Later Sieg and Blondy met up with Jimpson in Sing Sing. When Jimpson got out, he expected to get a room at Hope House, but Sieg wouldn't have him here. Jimpson came one night when I was in the house—this was before you came, Boker—and Sieg beat him up cruelly and threw him out."

"By God!" cried Boker. "Then he killed Letty to get square with Sieg!"

Lee gravely shook his head. "Let everything remain as it is," he said. "Our first duty is to notify Inspector Loasby and let him take charge. Come on!"

With what relief they breathed the pure air of above ground! There was a key in the door leading to the cellar. Lee turned it and took it with him as a precaution against possible prowlers. Water had not been turned off and they washed their hands at the kitchen sink.

"One feels as if the smell would cling forever," said Lee.

Driving uptown, Lee stopped at the first all-night drugstore to telephone Loasby. Since Loasby slept with a telephone beside his bed, Lee had no difficulty in getting him. He told him succinctly what they had laid bare in the cellar of Hope House.

"My God!" exclaimed Loasby. "Then you were right from the start!"

"Skip that," said Lee. "I'm not handing myself any bouquets. Where can I meet you and hand over the keys? I'm on my way to Brookwood."

"I'll meet you there," said Loasby. "The body can wait for an hour."

"If you get there first, meet me at the entrance gate. And cut out the siren."

"I get you, Mr. Mappin."

Lee, Boker and Jermyn, in Lee's car, sped uptown at high speed by the deserted East River Parkway, across the Harlem River, through the Bronx and into Westchester County by the Hutchinson Parkway. At this time of night, it was like driving in the open country. Inspector Loasby had not so far to go and the big red car was waiting for them inside the gates of Brookwood. A third car arrived presently with two of Loasby's men.

A neat cottage stood within the gates. "Let's try here first," said Lee.

They pressed the button alongside the front door and heard the bell sounding within. There was no answer. They knocked sharply and only silence answered. They went around to the back of the house and knocked again. The kitchen door was of flimsier construction, and after a brief consultation between Lee and Loasby, a husky plain-clothes man jimmied it open without risking too much noise.

The neatly furnished cottage contained three rooms; a kitchen with a breakfast nook, living room and bedroom. It was empty but in the bedroom there were plentiful signs of occupation; drawers full of costly shirts and underwear for a man; a whole row of fine suits hanging in the closet. Lee was first to mount the stairs to the attic. Three trunks stood under the eaves. At a sign from Lee, the plain-clothes man broke the locks with his jimmy.

The first trunk contained Letty Ammon's stage clothes; the second was empty; the third was half full of lumps of yellow clay.

"My theory was correct," said Lee.

Loasby exploded in wonder. "Sieg Ammon, by God! You knew this?"

"Well, I suspected it since I learned that Mrs. Cassells was going to marry him."

"Come on, let's get him," growled Loasby. "He isn't far."

The three cars moved silently along the drive and came to a stop in front of the great house with its endless ranks of dark windows like a palace of the dead. The plain-clothes men, the chauffeurs and Jermyn moved silently to surround the house while Lee and Loasby mounted the steps and pressed the bell. Without any great delay, an inner door was opened and a flashlight was thrown through the massive iron and plate-glass grille into their faces. Nothing further happened. Loasby was in plain clothes, and the servant hesitated about opening the door. Loasby exhibited his badge on the palm of his hand and the door was opened. A watchman faced them wonderingly, with his clock hanging from his shoulder by a strap.

"I am Lee Mappin," said Lee, "and this is Inspector Loasby. We must see Mrs. Cassells on a matter of urgent importance."

"I can't go to the Madam's room," stammered the watchman. "I'll wake Mr. Dunstan."

"All right," said Lee. "Please lose no time."

Soon old Dunstan came shuffling toward them in dressing gown and slippers, his kindly face furrowed with concern. He said at once:

"Mrs. Cassells has gone away, Mr. Mappin. She left by car after lunch today—or should I say yesterday, for Montreal."

Lee's face turned grim. "Who went with her?"

"Mr. Ammon, sir. He drove the car."

"Which car did they take?"

"The Packard convertible, sir."

"And Mrs. Delaplaine?"

"No, sir. Mrs. Delaplaine is no longer in Mrs. Cassells' employ."

"We'll follow," growled Loasby.

"I understood they were going to stop the first night, that is tonight, at Rouse's Point near the Canadian border," said Dunstan.

Lee looked at his watch. "Four o'clock. Rouse's Point is about two hundred and fifty miles. We should do it in six hours and a bit, and Mrs. Cassells is not an early riser. It will simplify matters if we can take him on American soil, Inspector."

"Let's go," said Loasby.

Dunstan clung agitatedly to Lee's sleeve. "Mr. Mappin, what is it? What is wrong?"

"It's Ammon that the police want, Dunstan. Nothing to do with Mrs. Cassells."

Dunstan scowled. "Well, I hope they get him in time," he said darkly.

Lee pressed the old man's hand.

Loasby gave one of his men the keys to Hope House and sent him down to Headquarters in the big car with instructions to start the machinery of the Homicide Bureau going. With his other officer and chauffeur, he rode in the less conspicuous police car. Lee took Boker and Jermyn in his car and his chauffeur to drive.

# CHAPTER TWENTY-FIVE

THE DAWN WAS BREAKING as they sped out between the Brookwood gateposts and headed north. The eastern sky crimsoned, the branches overhead were filled with the twittering of birds, but the weary faces of the men in the two cars were gray and grim. At seven o'clock they paused in Albany for a hasty breakfast, then on through Mechanicville, Schuylerville, Whitehall and the shore of Lake Champlain unrolling its beautiful panorama for mile after mile. Nobody looked at the scenery. Ticonderoga, Fort Henry, the city of Plattsburg. It was a little short of eleven when they rolled into the small town of Rouse's Point and drew up before the principal hotel. There was a green Packard convertible parked in the side yard of the hotel that Lee recognized.

"We are in time," he said.

Lee and Loasby entered the hotel. The clerk automatically pushed the register toward them and Lee glanced down the page. He saw "Mrs. Phillips of New York City; Mr. Charles Anderson" written there in Sandra's tall, angular hand.

"We're not stopping," said Lee. "We want to see Mrs. Phillips and Mr. Anderson."

The young clerk smiled sentimentally. "They've just stepped out," he said. "In fact, they've gone to get married. Perhaps you know that."

"We could guess it," said Lee with a grim smile. "I hope we're not too late for the ceremony. Where is it?"

"They already had their license and I directed them to the Reverend Mr. Seaton. It's just a step. Turn to the right when you go

217

out of the door, and to the right again at the first corner. You can't miss the parsonage because it's next door to the church."

Lee and Loasby ran out through the door, careless of their dignity. Climbing into their cars, they breathlessly pointed the way. It was no more than a couple of hundred yards around the corner to the parsonage. They tumbled out of the cars again and Loasby, with a significant jerk of the thumb, ordered his men to look to the rear of the house. Lee and Loasby ran up on the porch. Without waiting to ring, they threw open the door and entered. From the room on the left came the sound of a voice intoning a prayer. Lee banged the door open and they ran in.

The scene was self-explanatory; a pleasant-faced parson in a black coat standing book in hand with his back to the front window, and facing him Sieg and Sandra; the parson's two servants beyond them. Sieg, handsome, ruddy, virile, perfectly turned out; Sandra, slim, fragile, exquisitely dressed, with a whole cascade of orchids descending from her shoulder. Their faces, when the door banged open, presented a study. The wildest confusion succeeded.

"What does this mean?" asked the parson.

"Stop the ceremony!" shouted Lee.

Sandra's face was convulsed with passion. She looked her age then. "How dare you! How dare you!" To the parson she cried: "I know this man! He has no rights over me! Put him out of the house! I demand it."

Sieg said nothing. With a perfectly expressionless face, he looked from side to side for possible ways out.

All the others were talking at once. The minister, unable to make head or tail of it, was begging them to leave his house and settle their difficulties elsewhere. Finally, with a roar, Lee made his voice heard above the others.

"Are these two legally married?"

"No," said the minister.

"Thank God for that!" said Lee. He dropped into the nearest chair and wiped his face.

"What is the impediment to this marriage?" asked the confused minister.

"This is Inspector Loasby," said Lee. "The would-be bridegroom is wanted by the New York police."

"I don't care! I don't care!" screamed Sandra. "Marry us first. I demand it! Nobody has any right to stop us. Marry us and then let them take him!"

"Sandra!" protested Lee.

"What is the charge against him?" asked the minister.

"Murder," said Loasby bluntly.

The book dropped from the minister's nerveless hands.

"It's a foul lie!" screamed Sandra.

Sieg had his eye on an open window facing the rear. Reaching it in four long strides, he dived out headlong, carrying the screen with him. "You'll never put me behind the bars again!" he shouted.

Loasby made no move. His men were outside.

Sandra tottered toward the window crying pitifully: "Sieg! Don't leave me!"

Boker's face appeared outside the window. "Got him safe, Inspector."

"Handcuff him," said Loasby.

Loasby left the room, followed by the minister and the servants.

Sandra turned a bitter face toward Lee.

"How I will hate you for this!" she murmured.

"I know," said Lee soothingly. "It's natural . . . But this you must know, Sandra: Sieg made away with his wife so he could marry you. That's why I had to act the way I did."

"It's a lie! Sieg was with us at the time Letty was killed."

"Exactly. He hired a man to do it. Then he killed that man."

"I will never believe it!"

"The evidence is complete."

Sandra started for the door. Lee seized her wrist. She struggled, but he held her. "Listen, Sandra. We have to take Sieg back to New York. I beg you not to accompany us!"

"I won't leave him!"

"You will not be allowed to ride in the same car. When we get there you will not be allowed to see him."

"I don't care! I'll follow!"

"Think of the hideous story the newspapers will make of it!"

A gleam of common sense came into Sandra's eyes. She jerked her wrist out of Lee's grasp and sat down.

"All right," she said in a strangled voice. "But I hate you for shaming me! I will always hate you!"

"I'm sorry for that," said Lee. "If you had kept your word to me, I could have broken the news more gently. The two weeks aren't up yet."

She made no answer. Leaving her sitting there, Lee went out.

They were bundling the handcuffed Sieg into the police car. He was loudly demanding to be allowed to see "Mrs. Phillips."

"Take him away," said Lee. "She doesn't want to see him any more."

An hour later they were heading south again. Sieg's suitcase had been picked up at the hotel. Sieg was placed between Lee and Loasby on the back seat of the police car, and the detective officer rode beside the chauffeur. Boker and Jermyn were following in Lee's car. Sieg was allowed to smoke as many cigarettes as he wanted. At first he was inclined to be defiant.

"You men haven't got a thing on me! My hands are clean. I'll make you both look damn silly for this!"

After he had gone on in this strain for a while, Lee looked across at Loasby and the Inspector nodded. "Okay," he said, "tell him what we've got."

"We have dug up the body of Jimpson Souter in the cellar at Hope House," Lee said coolly. "The license plates of the murder car were in the grave, also Letty's pocketbook with its incriminating evidence. Later we found the trunk full of dirt in the gatehouse at Brookwood. There are various other bits of evidence to complete the case; but I reckon I have told you enough."

Sieg was silent. He dropped his cigarette out of the car window; his ruddy face paled; his head went down. Presently he muttered: "Can I have a drink?"

"Sure!" said Lee.

The following car was hailed and Lee procured his flask. Sieg let the raw liquor run down his throat. Soon he took another. Some color returned to his face; he lit a fresh cigarette.

"Well, I played for big stakes," he said with an ugly grin. "A million a year! It was worth it."

"Anything you say can be used against you, you know," the Inspector reminded him.

"The hell with it! I want to get my story before the public. You guys needn't think you can have all the publicity."

"Okay," said Loasby. He spoke to the detective on the front seat. "Take down what he says, Kramer." The officer produced notebook and pencil.

"It was a guy up in Sing Sing first told me about Mrs. Cassells," Sieg began. "She was interested in convicts, he said. I needn't mention his name. So I wrote to her when I got out and she told me to come and see her. She fell for me at sight. Meanwhile I had married Letty. I married her because I'd been thinking about her all the time I was locked up. In prison a man goes loco thinking about some particular woman, night after night. After the first few days I regretted it. Letty was too much in love with me. It was like having six lumps of sugar in your coffee; kind of sickening.

"Well, after I had met Mrs. Cassells a couple of times, I began to see that I could make her dance, too, to any tune I wanted to play. Rich and high-toned as she was, she was only a woman like any other. That's always been my trouble, women fall for me like duckpins in an alley. So I began to think things out. Boy! a million a year! It took a man's breath away. And right in my grasp! The woman was crazy about me; could refuse me nothing. And naturally, she couldn't expect to live forever. . . ."

"Not as your wife, she wouldn't," muttered Loasby.

Sieg grinned widely. "Well, I made up my mind not to have any slip-up," he went on. "I took things slow and thought everything out. I persuaded her to take the house on Henry Street and open it up as a boardinghouse for ex-convicts. Boy! when I saw that brick-paved cellar, it was just what I wanted! The house provided me with the right kind of base, and besides, it brought me in contact with Mrs. Cassells every day. I played her to the limit, and she was getting crazier and crazier about me. It was almost too easy!

"When Jimpson was released from prison, he was just the kind of tool I required. Too old and too broken by prison life to operate on his own, but he could carry out orders and was ready for anything. I promised him twenty-five thousand a year for life from the day I married Mrs. Cassells. Easy to promise. I never intended to pay him a cent. Of course, I couldn't let Jimpson live with a handle like that to use against me. He would have bled me white. But the fool never suspected what was in my mind. Our first move was to stage that fight at Hope House before you all. Naturally, after seeing me beat Jimpson up like that, nobody would ever suspect he was my confederate. I gave him fifty smackers for taking that beating. He stayed drunk for a week on it. Afterward I sent him over to Elizabeth to lie low until I had everything ready. We had a car waiting till we needed it."

"Letty bought that car," put in Lee.

"That's right, Letty bought it. I forget what story I told her. I could always make Letty do anything I wanted. . . . The next step was to work on Letty, see? I told her I had killed a man before I came to New York, and Blondy saw me do it, and now Blondy had fallen for her and was threatening to inform against me unless I handed her over to him. She already knew that Blondy was crazy about her, so the story sounded plausible. I took my time working it up until she was near crazy worrying about Blondy. And when she was ripe for it, I told her the only way we would ever know an hour's peace was by having Blondy put out of the way."

"Why did you pick on Blondy?" asked Lee.

"Because he *was* crazy about Letty. And it would seem perfectly natural for him to shoot her in a passion when she turned him down. That's exactly the way it turned out, didn't it? It's only by an accident that Blondy escapes the chair."

"Blondy had been your partner for ten years. Didn't that count with you?"

Sieg smiled. "Nothing counts with me but big Sieg!" he boasted.

"Go on with your story."

"When I told Letty what she had to do, she cried and carried on all night, but I saw I could make her do it. She couldn't stand out against me. I never told her she had to smoke Blondy herself, you understand. She couldn't have faced that. I told her she just had to lead him into a trap, and I would have him taken care of. I told her when she drove into the yard of the burned house, Blondy would be passed out and she could leave the car so she wouldn't have to see him shot, and I'd have her picked up in the road outside and brought home. Then next morning Blondy would be found shot in his car with his own gun and everybody would think it was suicide because of disappointed love. And nothing more would be heard of it. That's what I told Letty.

"I dictated the letters that Letty wrote Blondy. Blondy didn't fall as easy as I expected, and she wrote him twice before he came on. I made Letty leave one of Blondy's letters lying half out of her handbag where Mrs. Cassells would be sure to see it and read it. That planted the explanation of the shooting beforehand, see?"

"Where did Spanish Jack come into all this?" asked Lee.

"He didn't come into it. That was a mare's nest you discovered for yourself. Whatever happened between Spanish and Letty when I was in Sing Sing had nothing to do with me."

"Poor Letty!" murmured Lee. "The victim of *two* scoundrels! . . . Go on!"

"Meanwhile, I kept Jimpson posted on everything he had to do," said Sieg. "I furnished him with a gun in case Blondy didn't bring his, but he did. When the night came, Jimpson took a gander at Letty and Blondy through the windows of the different road-houses where they stopped. That was to make sure Letty was going through with it. When Jimpson saw her switch glasses with Blondy in the White Goose, he knew it was all right, and he drove on to the burned house to wait for them."

"Did you know that Queenie Deane was following them too?" asked Lee.

Sieg looked at him sharply. "The hell you say! No, I didn't know it! Did she see anything?"

"She didn't see the shot fired. She heard Letty cry out, then the sound of the shot. . . . Go on!"

"When Letty drove into the yard," Sieg continued, "Blondy was dead to the world. Jimpson seized Letty and held her in her seat while he reached for the gun. I had warned him to wear gloves,

and to shoot her on the side where Blondy sat. Afterward he laid
her forward on the wheel in a natural position, and then he beat it
for New York in his car. It was as simple as that. He parked the car
in Varick Street, as I had told him. The license plates were tied on
with string, so he could pull them off easy. He walked across town,
passed through the tenement house fronting on Madison Street
and came over the back fence into the yard of Hope House.

"Meanwhile, I was taking care to let you and Mrs. Cassells see
me all evening. Boy! did I put on a good show! You've got to give
me that! Getting more and more anxious when Letty failed to come
home, and flying off the handle altogether when I thought she had
gone away with a man!"

"Yes, I'll give you that," said Lee grimly. "You put on a good show!"

"Mary Kennedy gummed up my plans a little," Sieg went on,
"by bolting the yard door after I had unbolted it. I didn't have a
chance to get downstairs and unbolt it again until I sent that guy
Tappan or Boker to bed. I suspected that guy was too nosey. When
I unbolted the door Jimpson was waiting in the yard. I let him in
and went back upstairs. You stayed with me until two o'clock and
maybe I wasn't cursing you, but I didn't see any way of getting you
out of the house without arousing suspicion.

"When you went I made out to go to bed. Then I got up and left
the house by the front door. I was suspicious of that guy Tappan. I
walked around the block, skinned over the back fence of the tenement
house, and entered by the yard door. I had left it unbolted on purpose.
Jimpson was waiting for me in the cellar. I had planned out every move.
The iron shaker was lying by the bottom step, ready to my hand. I
said to Jimpson: 'Come on, I made a bed for you in the trunk closet.'
He stooped over to pick up the license plates and Letty's bag and I
let him have it. One crack was enough. Hardly made any sound.
Then I dragged him back, wrapped him in a sheet I had ready, and
laid him in the bed I had made for him!" Sieg laughed, and glanced
from Lee to Loasby to see if they appreciated his crack.

"I shoveled in the earth as well as I could in a hurry," he continued, "because I didn't want to be caught by daylight. Then I
locked the closet, put the key in my pocket and left the house by

the yard door the way I came. Came in by the front door, making out I was drunk, and staggered into my own room so anybody would hear me if they were awake. Later I sneaked down to the basement and bolted the yard door so Mary Kennedy wouldn't raise a squawk in the morning. During the next few days I took my time making everything neat and shipshape in the cellar. . . . That's the story," Sieg concluded, "so what do you think of it?"

Lee said: "It is the most fiendish and cold-blooded pair of murders I ever encountered."

Sieg laughed out of bravado. "Well, that's something coming from you!" He swallowed the rest of the liquor in Lee's flask.

Sieg insisted on having his confession read over to him. He made several alterations as the officer read from his notes. "I don't want a single word changed," he said, with the vanity of an author. "Never mind if the grammar isn't okay. I want it to sound like me."

"When it's typed it will be handed back to you to read over and sign," said Loasby stiffly.

Afterward Lee remembered how Sieg smiled.

SOME TIME LATER, having left the shore of Lake Champlain, they started across a high viaduct over one of the tributaries of the Hudson River. A fine view of distant mountains opened to the east.

"Boy! what mountains!" said Sieg. "Would you mind stopping a minute, Inspector? Reckon it's the last honest-to-God mountains I'll see."

Loasby good-naturedly told the chauffeur to pause. Lee was dozing in his corner. Sieg leaned forward to see better. With lightning swiftness, his manacled hands struck down the handle of the door on Lee's side. The door swung open and he was out. Loasby clutched at him, but Sieg tore free, pulling the Inspector half out of the car. All the men shouted at once and piled out. Sieg tore across the road, placed his bound hands on the parapet of the bridge and vaulted clean over. Several hands clutched at him, but his body was wrenched from their grasp. It went hurtling down. Lee turned away.

They found his dead, broken body in the shallow stream.

# CHAPTER TWENTY-SIX

LEE MAPPIN AND INSPECTOR LOASBY immediately returned to New York, leaving Loasby's officers to settle the formalities necessitated by Sieg Ammon's suicide with the Washington County authorities. Once more, during the succeeding days, the case of Letty Ammon was blazoned forth in the nation's press. Sieg was buried quietly in a village near the spot where he had died; thus depriving the populace of New York of the opportunity to make a holiday of his funeral.

Three days later Lee and Ann Brooke took the Empire State Express for Albany. They went by train because it was quicker. With them they carried a copy of the statement made by Sieg Ammon. It was not signed, of course, but the four men who had heard him make it had attested to its accuracy.

The Governor was expecting them. He signed a pardon for Richard Farren and handed it to Ann. "I do not often have a duty to perform which gives me so much pleasure," he said smiling.

He made Lee a complimentary little speech. "I have read of your work in the past, Mr. Mappin, and I have read some of your books. In this case you appear to have performed a great public service in preventing what would otherwise have been a shocking miscarriage of justice. I congratulate you, sir."

Lee, out of sheer pleasure, took a pinch of snuff. "Thank you, Governor. I am inclined to congratulate myself a little. It is usually my fate to send men to prison. It's a pleasant change to be able to get one out."

They took the first train back to Sing Sing, where Lee's car was waiting for them. They carried a suitcase into the prison. Both were shaking with excitement. When Blondy was brought to them, his face was likewise pale and moist, his eyes a little wild. He had read the newspapers, but he knew nothing as yet of a pardon.

"It's not a visiting day," he stammered, "and two of you together. . . . What does it mean?"

Lee shoved the suitcase toward him. "Here, go put on these clothes," he said gruffly. "I'm in a hurry to get back to the city."

Blondy, with a blank look, took the bag and let it fall. He dropped in a chair and wiped his face. Suddenly a look of joy broke there like the sun coming out. He sprang up, flung his arms around Ann, and kissed her roundly. Turning to Lee, he shook his hand as if he would shake it off the arm.

"I can't believe it! I can't believe it!" he said breathlessly.

Ann had taken the kiss with a matter-of-fact air. When Blondy ran away with the suitcase, she said quickly to Lee: "Of course, under those circumstances, a kiss doesn't mean a thing."

Lee shook his head. "You strange little being!" he said. In spite of her nonchalance, he could see that she was under a strain.

"Please, Mr. Mappin, do me one last favor," she said hurriedly.

"Surely, my dear!"

"When we get in the car, you sit in the middle."

"That wouldn't do at all!"

"*Please*, I ask it. I have a difficult part to play."

"Very well, my dear."

Blondy presently returned, wearing the clothes of a free man. His face still bore a wondering expression. After the good-bys and good wishes had been exchanged, when they stood outside the gates of the prison, he drew a long breath and lifted his face to the sky. Lee said afterward that he wouldn't have missed Blondy's look at that moment for a year's income. The young man was transfigured. He said not a word.

Ann climbed into the car first and instantly, as if she feared Lee might forget their bargain, reached back to him, saying: "You next, Mr. Mappin. So you can talk to both of us."

Lee thought Blondy looked the least bit disappointed at this arrangement. He hoped he was not mistaken.

During the long drive to New York, it was up to Lee and Ann to keep the conversational shuttlecock in the air. They talked about everything and nothing. Blondy looked out of the window like a man starving for the sight of green trees and bright water. At one point Ann said:

"I got a letter from the Kent County Commissioners yesterday."

Blondy looked around. "What did they have to say?"

Ann, affecting to be pleased to death with her letter, went on: "Well, you know I've been working for them as secretary for five years. I wrote the other day to ask if I could have my job back, and this letter was to say yes."

"Going back to Chestertown?" said Blondy.

"I've already given up my job in New York," said Ann brightly. "I'll be much happier in Chestertown. I know everybody and everybody knows me. Their ways are my ways. I'll be pulling out day after tomorrow."

"Oh!" said Blondy flatly. . . . "I'd like to see old Chestertown," he presently added.

"Well, why don't you? They read the newspapers. You'd get a big welcome."

"That's just it," said Blondy. "I couldn't stand it. They know too much about me. About my beginnings and all. I would feel as if I could never escape from their eyes."

"What are your plans?" said Ann in a casual voice.

"Reckon I'll go back to Cleveland. I can get my job back. Of course, the men in the mills, they read the papers, too, but they don't know me very well and they don't give a damn. They'd soon forget."

An unhappy silence followed. Ann looked very attentively out of her window, and Lee suspected that her eyes were full of tears. Just the same, he did not believe that she was playing a losing game. He said, to fill in the hiatus:

"We'll be in town by four. I have a little business to attend to. The car can put you down wherever you want to go. Or you can keep it for the rest of the afternoon. You're both dining with me at seven, and Blondy will sleep at my apartment. My servant, Jermyn, knows how to keep the reporters at bay."

"I have to go to my office," said Ann briskly. "I promised to come if we got back in time. I'm breaking in the girl who is to take my place."

"Oh!" said Blondy, with a falling inflection. "Then I'll be left alone!"

Ann looked out of her window again. This time Lee was sure it was to hide a smile, "Oh, well," she said carelessly, "I suppose I can go to the office tomorrow. I can say we didn't get back before closing time. We can go to a movie."

Blondy shook his head. "I like the smell of outdoors better."

"All right, we'll go to the Zoo. I'm told there's a very fine Zoo in the Bronx."


SHORTLY BEFORE SEVEN, the two presented themselves at Lee's apartment for dinner. Something had happened during the interim; he could not be sure what. Both were visibly charged with emotion. When Ann went away to tidy herself for dinner, Blondy said confusedly:

"Mr. Mappin, I want to talk to you for a moment. I'm . . . I'm afraid Ann may come back before I get it out."

Lee led him into his study and closed the door.

"Mr. Mappin," Blondy began, "I . . . I don't know what you'll say to this, after the way I carried on about Letty and all. Like a man out of his mind. That's right, too, I was out of my mind. I . . . I don't know how to tell you what has happened . . ."

"Do you mean that you and Ann have come to an understanding?"

"Why, yes," said Blondy, enormously relieved. "How did you guess it? Do you think it's all right, Mr. Mappin?"

"Well, for God's sake, why shouldn't it be?" cried Lee, clapping him on the back. "I was only afraid it wouldn't happen!"

"Well, that's a load off my mind," said Blondy. "I have told Ann the whole story and she said it was no surprise to her because she had guessed it already. It's not like it was with Letty. Letty was like a fever in my blood. I was mad about her. She would always drive a man out of his mind. Not her fault, of course. You could never have a peaceful life with Letty. I could never feel again like I did about Letty. Not twice in a lifetime. Ann is different. She's like a drink of cold water when a man is parched. I've told her everything and she says she's satisfied; she likes it better the way I feel about her. She thinks we can make something out of a life together. And she says she feels just the same way about me, sensible and affectionate without any of this crazy business . . ."

Lee rubbed his lip to conceal a smile. He knew this part wasn't true.

"So we've decided to get married and go out to Cleveland together," Blondy concluded.

Lee gravely shook his hand. "My boy, you don't know it yet, but you'll find it out. You have won one of the prizes."

"Well, that's the way I feel about it," said Blondy, grinning widely. "Not that I deserve it."

"The hell with your deserts," said Lee. "Make the most of it!"

To the great chagrin of Lee Mappin and Inspector Loasby, they were notified by the District Attorney of Hudson County that since Letty Ammon's statement was inadmissible, and there was no other evidence against Spanish Jack D'Acosta, he was forced to order his release.

Loasby banged his desk in anger. "There is something wrong with our code when a black scoundrel like that goes scot free! We all know that he killed Sam Bartol."

"One must be philosophic about it," said Lee, shrugging. "This rule of law which lets one guilty man go free, may save a dozen men who are innocent."

Lee laid the case before the Federal authorities. Spanish Jack was not a citizen. As a consequence, when he was released from the Hudson County jail he walked into the arms of Federal detectives, who whisked him over to Ellis Island. There was a hearing at which Letty's statement was read, and Lee gave evidence. Spanish

Jack, on the grounds of "moral turpitude," was ordered deported on the first ship to the country of his birth.

"I'll be back," he said to Lee with his inimitable insolence.

"Not while I am alive," said Lee.

A WEEK AFTER Mr. and Mrs. Blondy Farren had departed for Cleveland, Lee was called to the telephone. A well-known soprano voice, bored, sophisticated, casual, hailed him over the wire:

"Hello, darling! Will you come to dinner on Wednesday? Just a small party. Black tie. Emilion has promised something exceptional for your benefit."

"I would be charmed, darling," said Lee.

"Splendid! Seven-thirty as usual."

Lee hung up smiling. This was so like Sandra! She had come to her senses. She wanted to be friends again, but she was warning him that no reference must ever be made to what was past.

He went to Brookwood, had a marvelous dinner, and enjoyed himself to the full. He was relieved to discover that the other guests were just ordinary nice people; Sandra had not as yet discovered any more outlandish protégés to trot out. But she would! she would! Also he was glad to find that poor Agnes Delaplaine had been restored to her place at the foot of the table.

He got up to go when the other guests moved, but Sandra laid her graceful hand on his arm.

"Wait five minutes," she said. "I want to talk to you."

Over highballs in Sandra's boudoir, he made light conversation while he waited for Sandra to open what was in her mind. She twisted a bracelet round and round on her wrist.

"I hear that Blondy Farren has married his childhood sweetheart—what's her name?"

"Ann Brooke," said Lee. "It's a fact."

"Men have short memories," said Sandra with just a hint of bitterness. "However, I'd like to give them a present."

Lee, knowing Sandra, was surprised and genuinely moved. "Bless your heart!" he said. "That's a generous impulse!"

"It's nothing of the sort!" said Sandra pettishly. "For God's sake, don't turn on the sentimental tap or I'll be sorry I spoke of it."

"What do you propose?" said Lee calmly.

"Well, a young couple just starting like that, no money, I thought of giving them a little house in whatever town they are going to live."

Lee said with a grave face: "Too much! It would destroy their sense of independence. They have to have a house, of course. Give them something to put in it; something that young couples have to wait for. Give them an electric refrigerator."

Sandra moved her thin shoulders impatiently. "A refrigerator is so unromantic!"

"Unromantic!" cried Lee. "My dear lady! the best things in life come out of the refrigerator!"

Sandra smiled unwillingly. "You fool! . . . All right, you shall help me pick it out."

Peace was restored.

# COACHWHIP PUBLICATIONS

## ALSO AVAILABLE

1

HULBERT FOOTNER
THE ADVENTURES OF
MADAME STOREY

ISBN 978-1-61646-236-9

COACHWHIP PUBLICATIONS

COACHWHIPBOOKS.COM

THE
MYSTERY
OF THE
FOLDED
PAPER

HULBERT
FOOTNER

ISBN 978-1-61646-255-8

ORCHIDS
TO MURDER

HULBERT
FOOTNER

ISBN 978-1-61646-262-8

COACHWHIP PUBLICATIONS

COACHWHIPBOOKS.COM

WHO KILLED THE
HUSBAND?

HULBERT FOOTNER

ISBN 978-1-61646-256-6

COACHWHIP PUBLICATIONS

ALSO AVAILABLE

THE MURDER
THAT HAD
EVERYTHING!
HULBURT
FOOTNER

ISBN 978-1-61646-258-2

COACHWHIP PUBLICATIONS

COACHWHIPBOOKS.COM

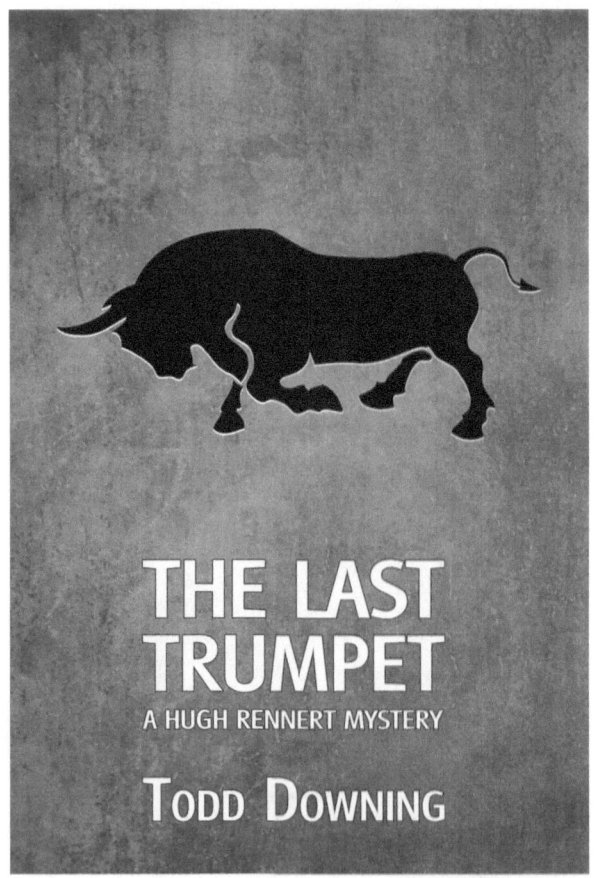

THE LAST
TRUMPET
A HUGH RENNERT MYSTERY

TODD DOWNING

ISBN 978-1-61646-152-2

COACHWHIP PUBLICATIONS

ALSO AVAILABLE

THE QUINNY HITE
MYSTERIES

CHINESE RED · HERE LIES THE BODY

RICHARD BURKE

ISBN 978-1-61646-247-5

# COACHWHIP PUBLICATIONS

## COACHWHIPBOOKS.COM

MURDER OF
THE HONEST BROKER

WILLOUGHBY SHARP

ISBN 978-1-61646-211-6